**All Jade could do was stand there
and gawk at the sum
of what she'd wrought . . .**

Pierce Brosnan's clone.

No, no, *no!*

He was perfect; over six feet, with steel-blue eyes, jet-black hair, the works.

He also had bloodshot eyes, a couple days' stubble on his face, and th   butter-fly ban   is left cheekl   ouble. The sc

As he   and great ha   candles burning in every window, he looked . . . *angry*, like a guy who wouldn't mind stuffing a body into a trunk right about now.

He also looked really, really good in candle-light.

Avon Contemporary Romances by
Jenna McKnight

WITCH IN THE HOUSE
LOVE IN THE FAST LANE
A DATE ON CLOUD NINE
A GREEK GOD AT THE LADIES' CLUB

WITCH
IN THE
HOUSE

Jenna McKnight

AVON

An Imprint of HarperCollinsPublishers

This is a work of fiction. Names, characters, places, and incidents are products of the author's imagination or are used fictitiously and are not to be construed as real. Any resemblance to actual events, locales, organizations, or persons, living or dead, is entirely coincidental.

AVON BOOKS
An Imprint of HarperCollins*Publishers*
10 East 53rd Street
New York, New York 10022-5299

Copyright 2007 by Ginny Schweiss
ISBN: 978-0-06-084369-4
ISBN-10: 0-06-084369-1
www.avonromance.com

First Avon Books paperback printing: October 2007

Avon Trademark Reg. U.S. Pat. Off. and in Other Countries, Marca Registrada, Hecho en U.S.A.
HarperCollins is a registered trademark of HarperCollins Publishers.

Printed in the U.S.A.

10 9 8 7 6 5 4 3 2 1

Acknowledgments

Thank you to the witches around me who generously shared their beliefs, their way of life. Among them, Jan O., my friend. If I took a few liberties with the Craft, it's because they all told me that each witch must do what feels right to *her*. And so I gave Jade, Annie, and Courtney free rein to do things their own way.

And where would I have been without all the great resources on Craft, the shop owners who like to share, the wonderful authors who live their lives in tune with the energy around them? May the Goddess and Spirits of your choice smile upon all of you.

Many thanks also to P.I. Dale A.F. Johnson, retired police officer, who generously allowed me to tap his knowledge of firearms and laws. Any incongruities herein are plot devices, not errors on his part.

Chapter 1

Like a lemon drop on speed, the maid of honor darted across the front of the church, her yellow toe-length dress rustling with every step. The guests' heads swiveled in unison as they tracked her agitated progress through the opposite archway, after which they turned to each other and resumed whispering. Not calm, smiling, happy-to-see-these-two-finally-going-to-tie-the-knot wedding speak, either.

Mason Kincaid, the groom, handled it like a pro; ten minutes earlier, he'd retreated to the choir loft in the back of the church. Only his best man knew where he was, and that was because he'd followed him. Something about doing his job.

Mason was standing shoulder to shoulder with

Anthony now, feet spread comfortably, hands in the trouser pockets of his tux, watching another lemon drop rustle across the nave below.

"There goes another one," he remarked.

Organ music played softly in the background, as if it were quite normal for bridesmaids and grooms-men to buzz back and forth across the church before the ceremony, half of them chattering on their cell phones, the other half comparing notes while franti-cally waiting for call backs.

"Yellow dresses, black tuxes," Anthony mused over the swarm of activity. "Looks like a hornet's nest, my friend."

"Please. Don't say that in front of Brenda." Mason raised his arm, absentmindedly lifting his sleeve and pronating in one smooth motion.

"I think you can get tennis elbow from that," Anthony said.

"From what?"

"Checking your watch every thirty seconds. What? Don't tell me you thought Miss Terminally Late would be on time once in her life."

"Yes," Mason said, nodding with absolute cer-tainty, turning the bezel on his watch, as if doing so would somehow make Brenda more aware of the time. "We discussed it at the rehearsal last night."

"Uh-huh."

"And in the car on the way to dinner." Mason felt the need to substantiate his statement because An-thony was shaking his head with a look that said,

You poor sap. "On the way home, too. She swore she wouldn't be late."

He never knew whether to worry about Brenda when she wasn't on time or wring her neck when she finally arrived, but constant repetition had dulled the tendency to worry. Except this time she'd promised. She'd never promised before.

All her friends were here. All she'd talked about for weeks was "her day." She loved fresh bouquets, candlelight, and ribbon. Her apartment had turned into a veritable testing lab for all three in her quest to mix the right sizes, right widths, right textures, blah blah blah. More than once, Mason jolted awake thinking he was the star attraction at a funeral.

It wouldn't have been so bad if Brenda had consoled him, but forty-two long, *lonnng* days ago she'd gotten the crazy idea that "waiting until our wedding night" would somehow make it more special. This, after five years together.

He had to hand it to her, though. Every female guest—and several of the men—stopped in surprise just this side of the door, oohing and ahhing at the end result. The small, intimate Pensacola church normally inspired hushed hellos and quiet whispers, but today it was transformed into a vibrant, living hothouse, plush with cascades of white and yellow roses, mile upon mile of white ribbon, and row upon row of white tapers.

And just think, after today, life would go back to

normal. After a week of sex, sun, and scuba diving, Brenda would move into his condo, not a candle, flower, or ribbon in sight.

Five forty-five. Fifteen minutes to go. She'd promised.

Candle flames flickered and fluttered along the center aisle as ushers escorted a few last-minute, wide-eyed guests to their seats.

Mason's four-year-old niece broke out of safekeeping and tore down the aisle, her new Mary Janes raising a clatter on the narrow wooden steps as she climbed to the loft. Mason turned toward the uncontrolled sobbing that punctuated each step before Lily launched herself into his arms and buried her head against his neck.

"Aw, did seeing all those people scare you, sweetheart?" Mason crooned. He cuddled Lily against his chest, patting her tiny back.

Hand him a Glock and point him in the right direction, and he was a fierce adversary, a warrior. Hand him Lily, though, all warm and trusting and smelling of baby shampoo, and paternal emotions arose out of nowhere to throw him a curve. Every time. When he looked at strangers' kids, he didn't feel warm and fuzzy and think about having his own. Not even when he had sex with Brenda.

Used to have sex, he amended.

"Tell you what," he said softly, aiming to console the little girl. "You don't have to walk up that big, long aisle if you don't want to."

Quietly, Anthony sang, "Brenda's gonna kill you."

"She's only four." Mason fell into a slow, automatic

sway, soothing his nap-deprived little niece. "You'd better let my sister know I have her."

Anthony handled that by cell phone, ending the conversation with, "He's right beside me. Really. He's fine."

"Don't tell me. She was afraid I took off."

"She says it's in my job description to make sure that doesn't happen."

Mason grinned, as if Anthony would even try. After all, they were guys. They had a bond, an obligation to respect each other's freedom. They left most of the this-is-for-your-own-good bullshit to parents and siblings.

"Hate to disillusion you," Mason said, "but I believe you're supposed to ensure a clean getaway if I change my mind."

"No way, man. Brenda'd hunt you down like last time."

"She didn't hunt me down. And what do you mean, like last time? We were on a break."

"She *did* hunt you down—you're just too stupid to know it. She found out where you'd be and paraded another man in front of you. I warned you; you told me to stuff it. You fell for it hook, line, and sinker. This ringing any bells?"

Mason tugged at his collar, thinking it was awfully tight and maybe he should have rented a larger size. No way Anthony was right.

"I'm guessing it'd be bad luck to throw my best man off the balcony minutes before the wedding, so I want you to know I'm resisting."

Anthony snickered.

"Aren't you supposed to be supportive today? It's, you know, *in the job description.*"

"Hey, I'm supportive," Anthony said. "I'm not telling the maid of honor where you're hiding. Geez, does Brenda know about her?"

Mason cast a nervous glance toward the steep, narrow stairs guarding him from his fiancée's girlfriend. Women threw themselves at him every day; he could handle that. But Brenda's best friend? That was murder waiting to happen. He just wasn't sure whose.

"Relax, she's up front with the others," Anthony said. "Oops, looking this way."

Mason stepped back from the rail, hoping he'd been quick enough to elude her sights. "Go tell her you couldn't find me."

"She *saw* you."

"She can't see fifty feet without her glasses."

"Is that in my job description? You have to let me know these things because if I'm supposed to be looking out for you, my friend—"

"Let's put it this way—if she comes after me, you have to throw yourself between us."

"Take the bullet, as it were?"

"Absolutely."

"Like when that moray eel came at us, and you ducked?"

"I was diverting its attention."

"From *you* maybe." Anthony raised his hand briefly to acknowledge someone below. "Relax. Ken just told her it's me up here."

At six o'clock, Lily got a second wind. She wiggled out of Mason's arms and scampered off to watch the organist.

At the same moment, in the nave below, a skinny, uniformed courier marched up the center aisle between the tall, beribboned candelabra. In a nasal, high-pitched voice, he called out, "Message for Mr. Kincaid. Is there a Mason Kincaid here?"

"Uh-oh," Anthony intoned. "Another eel."

Mason cocked his head, assessing the situation in about one second flat. "You don't suppose emergency rooms send couriers, do you?"

"Don't think so, buddy."

"Police departments?"

"There isn't a cop alive who'd be caught dead in that getup."

"Morgues? Why are you looking at me like that?"

"I'm waiting to see if you duck again or see what it says."

"Oh, I can guess what it says."

Mason stared at Anthony until he finally sighed and said, "You want me to get that for you?"

"If you wouldn't mind."

"Okay, but don't kill the messenger. Meaning me, not him."

Anthony thumped down the stairs, with purpose if not speed. As he entered the nave, a hush fell over the church. You could hear a boutonniere drop as everyone, guests and wedding party alike, held their breath and craned their necks for a better vantage point.

The hell with reflecting. Mason was on the move now, nervously pacing the limited space in front of the choir benches, watching everyone below like a condemned man contemplating the crowd circling his gallows. The wedding party grouped into a tight pack near the altar, a couple of whom whispered into their cell phones, though who was left to call was anyone's guess.

The guests scooted along the pews, sliding toward the center aisle in their Sunday best, cramming together so they'd miss nothing. And when Anthony accepted the envelope from the courier and glanced upward, all heads turned toward the rear of the church. All eyes raised to the loft. And just as quickly, upon seeing Mason, everyone turned back around, their whispers more urgent.

Mason no longer cared if they saw him. He'd done everything Brenda had asked. He'd committed to taking their relationship to the next level. He'd learned to navigate through the disarray in the apartment without complaint. He'd let her have her six weeks of chastity. He'd agreed to no more than four dives while they were on their honeymoon. After all that, he damn well didn't deserve getting stood up on his wedding day!

When Anthony stopped before him and proffered the envelope, Mason couldn't bring himself to touch it. "Read it," he said, already planning which bar he'd drink dry tonight.

"Could be personal."

"It sure as hell better be."

"All right, all right," Anthony said, feigning calmness that did nothing to reassure Mason. "Just remember what I said about killing the messenger. No throwing me over the rail or anything."

"Would you just get it over with?"

Anthony slipped his finger under the flap and pried it open. He pulled out several pages, looked them over, and said nothing.

"To me," Mason snapped.

"She's pregnant."

That knocked the wind out of Mason. He'd thought he'd known what was coming, in spite of all the time and expense and planning Brenda had put into the scene below, but *pregnant*? That sure as hell wasn't it.

He slumped onto the first choir bench. He had trouble catching his breath to speak.

"But we— We were careful, you know. We—"

They'd talked about kids. They hadn't agreed on how many; that was a topic for down the road. Neither of them had said, "But if we get pregnant soon, it's all off."

"She's feeling sick, is that it? Just can't make it today?" Mason hated the hopeful tremor in his voice, because he knew in his heart that a little nausea didn't justify a courier instead of a phone call.

Anthony shook his head. As the quiet stretched between them, he asked, somewhat hopefully, "You want me to go? You know, give you some space?"

If she didn't want him, fine. But she wasn't taking his child, maybe a little girl as sweet as Lily, and— "So why isn't she here then?"

Anthony sighed, guyspeak for "Don't make me tell you this."

"There's *more?*"

Anthony nodded, stepping away from the edge of the loft, strategically keeping the stairs at his back for a quick getaway. "Remember Lyle Thomas, the guy Brenda paraded around to make you jealous?"

"It's *his?*"

Mason accepted that with mixed feelings, a small part relief, a large part anger at Brenda for toying with him. One second he thought he was going to be a father, the next he wasn't. One minute he was about to be married, the next he wasn't. He eyed the rest of the pages in Anthony's hand, and when he spoke next, any hint of a tremor was long gone.

"I'm guessing that's not all. Hell if I can imagine what's left, though."

"His bill." Again, Anthony proffered the pages.

"He's billing me for knocking up my fiancée?" Mason bellowed, forgetting what great acoustics the church had. As his outrage permeated the far corners, it set off a riptide of two hundred guests snapping around in their seats.

"No, idiot. Well, I don't think so." Anthony shuffled through the pages quickly. "Flowers. Flower arranging. Candles—ooh, that could be code, you think? Ribbon. Labor, delivery—hmmm, the sign of things to come. Setup. Who knew he was the florist, huh?"

Mason snatched the bill out of Anthony's hand and quickly scanned to the last page, where Brenda's flowing script instructed him to pay the bill in full within thirty days. Underlined, for God's sake. And then circled in red.

"That's it. I'm outta here. See that Lily gets back to her mom, okay?"

"Sure, but, uh, I think— I mean, it's my job to remind you—"

"*What?*"

"Mason, you have to go downstairs and tell the guests."

"I think they heard." Mason ripped the bill down the middle and tossed it in the air. Torn pages floated over the wall to friends and family below. "You coming with me?"

"Where?" Anthony dialed Lily's mother.

Mason stripped off his tie. "The nearest bar. Better yet, I have two tickets to Aruba—you choose."

Late the next morning in northeastern Missouri, Lyle Thomas ran through the front door of Jade Delarue's historic home and made a beeline for the nearest fireplace.

"Brenda backed out!" he shouted with unrepressed glee, popping around the walnut-paneled study like a live wire, brushing snow off his butt and legs because he'd slipped and fallen on the way in. "Can you believe it? I can't believe it. I get another chance!"

"So, no wedding last night," Jade said, grinning at his exuberance.

Lyle's excitement was catching, even though she'd expected this very outcome. Unlike Harry Potter or

Samantha Stevens, Jade didn't wave a wand around or twitch her nose, set things on fire, or summon quirky physical manifestations that talked back, but she did know her stuff.

Lyle threw his arms around Jade and hugged her soundly. He lifted her off the carpet and swung her in a circle.

"She called last night and said she loves me and she was crazy to think she should go back to Mason. Thank you, thank you, thank you! I am so happy my sister dragged me here and made me tell you everything and made me let you help!"

When Lyle set Jade back on her feet, she ran her fingers through her hair, attempting to restore some kind of order to soft, dark spirals that seized any opportunity to go their own way.

"That's great news, Lyle. Now we should—"

"I didn't want to come, you know. I kicked and screamed all the way from Hannibal, but Mary kept saying that if I didn't want my one true love to slip away, then a road trip to see you was just the ticket. She said I had to be straight with you, or you wouldn't have anything to do with me, and I was."

There was no stopping him. It was as if he'd come to life overnight. He circled the room, pausing only as he noticed the decorations for the first time.

"You people celebrate Christmas?" he asked with surprise.

Jade wasn't offended; unlike many, Lyle didn't utter *you people* in a negative manner.

"We call it Yule," she explained.

"Oh. Don't worry, by the way. Mary told me most people think you're just an herbalist, and I can't ever tell anybody otherwise—you know, about what you do. Though why you do it here is beyond me. If my parents hadn't gotten married in January forty years ago this weekend, I sure as heck wouldn't be back here now. Not in Missouri in the middle of winter, no way. I would've begged off this trip."

"Come on," Jade urged. She turned toward the door in an attempt to move Lyle on to the next step, as there was still work to be done. "Let's go into the conservatory and—"

"But what was the point in staying in Pensacola if Brenda was marrying that lowlife, right?" Lyle motored on, then shot his arm in the air, and shouted, "Mason Kincaid, eat your heart out!"

Jade's lips twitched with amusement. "How many cups of coffee have you had this morning?"

"Five maybe six, I lost count," he said, running the words together.

"Lyle!"

He grinned. "Sorry. I'm just so happy."

"You have what you want."

"Yes!"

"Right. Then it's time to thank the spirits for acting so quickly. Let's go into the—"

"Can't. I'm on my way to the airport now."

"Oh," Jade said, taken aback. Generally clients were awed by her skills and followed directions without question. Some out of gratitude; some a little bit afraid of her, though no one ever said so. "But we're not finished."

Regular clients—ones not shoved through the front door by well-meaning sisters—never left early. More work needed to be done to ensure Lyle's success in the relationship department. It was precisely why Jade preferred working with fully committed guests, the ones who made their own reservations and arrived on their own.

"It already worked," Lyle said with finality, clearly meaning *case closed*.

"Yes, and now you have to—"

"I have to get to the airport."

Jade blew out a breath, hoping he'd notice her exasperation and come around. Seconds passed. She couldn't very well hog-tie him to the hearth.

"Let me give you something before you go, then," she acquiesced. "It's important. It'll take just a second."

She left the study immediately, leaving no room for argument.

When the coffee wore off, Lyle would be afraid that Brenda would leave him again, just as before, so Jade had assembled a charm bag. The pouch contained elements chosen just for him. Its purpose wasn't to keep Brenda with Lyle against her will, that would be wrong, but it would remind him to nurture his second chance at love. Carrying it would lend some stick-to-itiveness.

Jade returned to the study, and as she placed the red flannel bag in Lyle's hand, she curled his fingers over it, and hers over his. She held his attention, demanding his focus as she instructed him with a sense of urgency.

"Keep this on you every day," she said. "It's small. It won't be noticeable in your pocket."

"What's in it?"

"A romantic charm."

Lyle danced from one foot to the other. He'd never stay long enough to learn about a postbreakup cleansing spell for Brenda.

He said, "I'll check it out later."

"You should. It's important you identify with it." He'd understand the birthstone beads she'd sewn to the drawstrings, and the engraved, entwined silver rings inside. Not so the rest of it.

Lyle turned the bag to and fro in his hand, testing its weight, the feel of the contents. With a sly grin, he said, "This won't get me arrested at the airport, will it?"

"Not unless there's a new ban on goat tail hair that I haven't heard about. Or spikenard root. Now this"—Jade handed him a small glass vial—"is oil infused from the root. Add a drop to the bag every Friday."

"You really think I'll need this? I mean, *she* called *me*. I think she's hooked," he said with a boyish grin.

"Every Friday," Jade reiterated. "Like clockwork."

"Okay." That settled, Lyle darted toward the front door like a kid who'd heard the recess bell. "Thanks again for everything, Jade. If there's ever anything I can do . . . I mean that."

Outside, he ran across the snow-covered garden rather than follow the meandering flagstone walk to the driveway. He managed to stay on his feet, but then nearly took out the curbside mailbox with his rental car.

Lyle's abrupt departure left a few loose ends, which Jade disliked. Restless and uncomfortable, she stood in the open doorway, lifted her chin, and let the cold wind blow away all lingering negativity.

Her spirit renewed, she withdrew to the soaring glass-and-stone conservatory that filled an entire wing of the house. There she sought a peaceful conclusion, to tie everything up in a neat package.

She selected a long white taper from a cabinet darkened with age, rubbed it with fragrant oil—one of her special blends—and sprinkled it with powdered orris root. Holding it in both hands, she closed her eyes and, working from the ease that came since practicing the Craft at her grandmother's side, quickly called her emotions to the surface.

Energy began to flow, to surge through her body like current through a wire. Jade directed that energy into the candle, charging it, focusing the powers of the universe on the matter at hand—Brenda's jilted fiancé—as she said,

"The all-seeing eye of fairness and love
Shines down and sees from far above
That whomever Brenda jilted, whatever his game,
He deserves someone better to take his name.

So no more heartache and no more trouble,
True love he finds, on the double!"

Jade set the taper into a niche in the stone wall
and lit it. The spell was done. Rarely did one of
hers require more involved ritual, though she often
embellished for paying guests. Over the years she'd
discovered that "elaborate" and "involved" were directly proportional to referrals, which is how she'd
dug Mystic Manor out of its financial quagmire after
her parents had passed the family home on to her.

If she'd left the conservatory then, everything
would have been perfect. But after the effort spent
on saving Lyle's romance, after seeing how his sister's
had progressed over the past year to impending moth-
erhood—well, it nagged at Jade, all of it. Pointed out
her shortcomings in the relationship/propagation department. Made her want to take control.

Some people cooked for others. Some sewed for
others. Jade cast spells, mostly for others. It was what
she did, how she gave back for the gift she'd been
given, and she enjoyed helping people, but now it was
time she did one for herself. Six years alone was long
enough. She and her husband had planned to have
children, and Doug was a sweetheart of a guy who
wouldn't want his unfortunate disappearance to pre-
vent her from having the family she always wanted.
It was time to at least open herself to the possibility
of a partner.

He, whoever he might be, had to be the right

man for her to marry. Trustworthy to a fault. A calm, even-tempered individual, able to deal with needy people traipsing in and out of Mystic Manor on any given day. Smart. Funny. Helpful. Really open-minded. Eager to have children, along with the ability; mustn't forget the ability. Loyal, truthful. Good-looking, much taller than her five-eight, sexy as all get-out—and why not? The universe held everything she wanted, as long as every step of her request was letter-perfect.

Timing couldn't be better; there was a new moon today. With the power of new beginnings behind this spell, she could meet and capture the heart of Mr. Right very soon.

Jade selected another taper, anointed it with oil, and rolled it in an herbal blend that felt personal to her, a combination of lavender, rosemary, and vanilla. During every step, she focused on all that she wanted and needed. For many witches she'd mentored over the years, focus was the crucial step that so many glossed over, with poor results.

Holding the candle, she closed her eyes and spoke from the heart.

> *"Spirits who see from far and near*
> *Know the values I hold dear.*
> *I am still here, alive and real.*
> *Enough time has passed for my heart to heal.*
> *It's time to love a man who is good*
> *So life can go on as it should.*
> *In this department, grant me every desire*

And send a man who lights my fire,
A man who is loyal and true."

Unbidden, an image popped into her head. Feeling a little impish, she grinned and impulsively agreed:

"A Pierce Brosnan clone will do."

Well, why the heck not? That's what wishes were for. If Mr. Right came in the perfect gift wrap, who was she to argue?

Match to wick, the second candle joined the first in the niche, along with a rose quartz. Finished, Jade walked away; the spells would work their magic without her presence.

No sooner had she closed the door to the conservatory than the spirits, normally so cooperative, added their own two cents. Hot wax breached the rims and began to drip down both tapers. Slowly at first, then faster as the heat was boosted with another wave and yet another, the white rivulets meandered across the stone base of the niche like lava seeking a path across rocky terrain.

At the midpoint, they pooled, intermingled, and solidified into one.

Chapter 2

Anthony searched high and low for Mason throughout Sunday and into Monday morning. He'd tried keeping tabs on him in the bar Saturday night, but at one point one of them had gone to the john, and they'd gotten separated.

Running out of places to search, and on the outside chance that Mason had been so bent he'd ended up in the honeymoon suite, Anthony finally checked the hotel.

"This is sick. You're sick," he said scathingly when he found Mason in the king-size bed, sound asleep, half-buried by a dozen satin pillows that ran the gamut from red, to white-with-red-hearts, to heart-shaped.

All froufrou; totally Brenda. All a man like Mason

wanted was one regular-size, same-as-he-grew-up-with pillow, and he was happy.

"Wake up!"

Mason stirred at last, unaccustomed to anyone entering his territory and shouting at him like a drill sergeant. He tossed frilly pillows adrift, completely oblivious to the metallic crunch of empty beer cans as he rolled over them.

Anthony wrinkled his nose. A honeymoon suite should smell like roses. This one rivaled a distillery.

"I can't believe you stayed here. What on earth were you thinking?"

Mason cracked his eyes open, squinting and throwing his arm up to block the midmorning light. "What the hell?"

"Exactly."

After they'd left the church, Anthony had decided that if his best friend and partner wasn't married, then his best friend and partner was going back to work. They'd both planned to take this week off, Mason on his honeymoon, Anthony skiing, but getting Mason back on his feet was more important. Even more important now that Anthony had seen how low he'd sunk.

"I've been lining up a job so you can get out of town and forget all this, and you've been"—Anthony scanned the suite with a disgusted scowl—*here*."

It quickly became apparent that Mason was far beyond inferring anything from whatever Anthony said or did as, arching his back, he slid his hand between it and the mattress and pulled out one minibar bottle after another. He tossed them carelessly, didn't bat an eye as they banged the wall and cracked the lamp. Seemed he didn't care much about anything except closing his eyes and passing out again.

"No way, man." Anthony shook him without success. Time to step up the assault. Poking through an assortment of clear and brown and green bottles, which clearly outnumbered the squashed cans, he barked, "Since when do you drink this stuff?"

Evidence said Mason had gone through a couple dozen, and those, all without caps, all empty, were just the ones currently visible.

"Get up. We're leaving."

"Must you keep shouting?"

"I'm not—" Anthony lowered his voice. "Get dressed. We have to be at the airport in an hour. My uncle got us a job. Surveillance."

Mason wasn't listening. He stuck a finger in his ear and wiggled it vigorously, as if he wasn't thinking clearly yet knew something was amiss. "You hear the shower?"

"Come on. Up, up, get dressed."

As Mason lay back and shoved more bottles and cans out of nose range, Anthony realized they weren't leaving anytime today unless he took charge. If the babe who'd been following Mason around Saturday night was using the shower now, well, there'd be no getting him out of this suite until he was darn good and ready—that could take a while after Brenda's crazy six weeks of enforced abstinence—so Anthony picked up one slightly damp shoe, prayed to

God it was liquor and not something yellow, and got down on his knees to look under the bed for the other.

He kept talking during this, hoping that as Mason heard details, his instincts would kick in and sober him up. No need to tell him just yet that the job was out of state.

"Three guys took out large life policies six years ago and then disappeared. Together. The county's issuing presumptive death certificates. A year late, which is curious, but I guess no one was in a hurry. Are you getting any of this?"

"Uh-huh."

"You'd better be, because we start today. My uncle already has teams on two of the widows. We're staking out the third. They're all friends, all still single, so to speak, and no surprise here, all have somewhat shady reputations in the community. The company's betting the alleged dead guys will sneak in just long enough to collect the checks. Maybe even the wives, who knows?"

Paying around-the-clock surveillance teams would be a lot cheaper than issuing three million in death benefits.

"What are you doing?" Mason asked, peering over the side of the bed at Anthony. Obviously no instincts kicking in there.

"Looking for your other shoe."

"Shouldn't I get dressed first?"

"Got it." Anthony whipped up the bottom of the sheet and crammed a shoe onto Mason's right foot.

"Ow. Hey, you got it on the wrong one."

"Trust me, after thirty years, I know the difference."

"It's too small."

"If you start whining, I'll quit feeling sorry for you." Anthony slapped on the second shoe. It was a tight fit, but he made it work. The shower stopped, and he said, "Let's get out of here."

"These shoes aren't right." Mason lifted his head off the pillow, but nothing else followed, so he just stared at his feet.

The bathroom door swung inward then, only it wasn't the beautiful babe standing there with a short towel draped around her. It wasn't even a pity date. Hairy chest, legs of steel—the guy looked vaguely familiar, but Anthony hadn't seen him half-naked before.

And then it came crystal clear.

"Well, you dog, you," Anthony said with a sly grin at Mason, who was blinking in confusion. "When I said the bartender was cute, I meant for me, not you."

With a horror-stricken expression, Mason shot out of bed, denying everything, but his foot caught in the tangled sheet and tumbled him flat on his face on the carpet.

Anthony nudged him to see if he was out. Had to be; a guy didn't gash his face on a bottle like that without knocking himself senseless. A little tape would hold the skin together. They could spin by Mason's condo, repack his bags for snow and ice, and still make the flight. Better get him to Missouri and in place before he sobered up, because he sure was gonna be pissed when he didn't wake up in Aruba.

Jade spent Monday morning removing the last of the Yule decorations throughout Mystic Manor, and a large part of the afternoon preparing for Imbolc, or Candlemas as West Bluff's church-loving population liked to call it. She was in and out of the conservatory numerous times, getting candles, placing them in every window and room of the house, ready to be lit at sunset. Never once did she feel that something was out of place until daylight began to wane. Then the hair on the back of her neck suddenly stood up.

Not a good sign.

She retraced her steps toward the conservatory until the feeling was strongest, right by the stone niche where, as a habit, she left dripless spell candles to burn. Right by the solidified pool of wax where there should have been nothing.

"No," Jade whispered. Her pulse skittered with alarm. She stared hard at the wax, struck immobile with a sense of disbelief.

Sure, she was unhappy with the mess, the way the wax had oozed into every dip and crevice and then hardened, but that paled in comparison to two different spell candles running together. How many times had Aunt Helen thumped her on the head and warned her that every misplaced word, every poorly calculated action, had consequences?

"How did this *happen?*"

More important, *How the heck do I undo it?*

All of Jade's tapers were supplied by Annie, one of her closest friends. They were hand-dipped and never dripped. Never. This had disaster written all over it. No way Jade could pretend there was no significance. The universe was too organized for things like this to happen without consequences.

She dug at the waxy white lump with her thumbnail and lifted off a small slab, but so what? The damage was done. The spell had more than enough time to begin to work. Possibly too long to break.

Nevertheless, she had to try to right it. She had to cast a strong, effective reverse spell immediately.

Though what spell? This wasn't something she had much practice at. Like, *none*. But every minute counted.

Clasping her crystal ring tightly, Jade put out a silent plea to Annie for help, which was really nothing less than a powerful, highly charged spell. Since Annie normally finished her candle dips in wax with a higher melting temperature so they wouldn't drip, and since she always was reversing her own spells-gone-awry, one could argue that Annie not only was somewhat accountable for this mess but would be an invaluable ally as well.

While she waited to hear from Annie, Jade rushed through the tunnel-like brick archway that led from the conservatory to the herb-drying room. There, in a closed cabinet, sat dozens of family grimoires, handwritten accounts of spells, charms, and remedies passed from one generation to another. She ran her fingers lightly over the gold-lettered spines, seeking guidance from the spirits before selecting one penned by Great-great-grandma, which seemed the most likely source because, as everyone in the family knew, Grandma Clarissa, poor thing, messed up as often as not.

An eclectic witch, Jade neither followed whatever traditions were in vogue nor favored one pantheon of spirits over another; she unashamedly sought help wherever most appropriate. Today she chose Cerridwen, as the Old One was the keeper of knowledge and transformation, and right now, Jade needed her expertise.

She laid the book flat and carefully thumbed through the delicate pages, preserved over the years from nibbling bugs with dried mugwort. Grandma's reversal spells focused on reversing hexes; maybe appropriate back in her day, but not so much now. Jade was just about to try another grimoire when Annie finally burst through the front door, shrieking Jade's name.

"Out here!" Jade called back.

Annie tore into the drying room, pink scarf flying behind her, shoulders and pixie-cut hair covered with snowflakes. Like Jade, she wore an abundance of silver rings, but otherwise she was her opposite, blond and short.

"What's wrong?" she gasped, breathless from rushing to Jade's side. "You're pale as a ghost. Whose grimoire is this? Is there something bad in it?"

When Jade didn't reply fast enough, Annie grabbed her and shook her until she did.

"Thank goodness you're here." Jade hugged Annie with relief, then thrust her to arm's length. "You have to help me. I need to reverse a spell."

Annie blinked. "You?"

Jade thumped Annie's arm so she'd stop grinning and recognize the seriousness of the situation. She explained what she'd done, even the Pierce Brosnan part and how the candles had dripped and—

"My candles? Dripped?"

"Annie, *concentrate.*"

"All right, already. Let me think. Take the wax, wrap it up—do you have some fabric handy?" Annie flinched as Jade grabbed her scarf and plunked the wax onto it. Annie snatched it back and glared at her.

"What? I'll make you a new one," Jade said.

"The heck you will. Courtney made it." Knowing the room well, Annie opened a drawer and pulled out a flannel square. She dropped the wax onto the center of it and took care to fold it away from Jade before handing it back.

"Now what?" If she hadn't been so flustered, so caught off guard, Jade wouldn't have asked at all, because even a toddler knew the answer to that. "Oh, I know. I bury it at a crossroad."

"At midnight."

"Midnight?" she wailed. "This can't wait another six hours."

"And sprinkle it with—"

"Annie!" Jade thumped her on the head this time. "Something I can do *now,* please. Something with a candle, maybe?"

Annie blinked, as if surprised she hadn't thought of that, since candle magic was the one thing that never backfired on her.

"Oh. Sure. You can burn a seven-knob candle. No, wait, that takes a whole week. Okay, I know. What do you have, a black candle, maybe? A silver one?"

Jade threw open a cabinet out in the main part of the conservatory, exposing shelves of tapers and pillars in a variety of colors, though predominantly white.

Annie pointed at the pillars. "Use one of those, it's easier. Get a knife."

Jade grabbed one and waited for further instructions.

"Now turn it upside down and expose the base of the wick."

"Of course!" Pleased with the simplicity and logic of this reversal spell, Jade made short work of preparing the candle to burn backward.

"Botanicals are your business," Annie said. "I leave the anointing to you."

"I'm not using what's in Great-grandma's grimoire, that's for sure."

"Don't have it?"

"Don't want to burn anything with pee on it."

"Eww."

"Maybe some arrowroot? And, hm, chamomile? Peppermint?" Jade said, not really asking Annie's advice but thinking aloud as she returned to the drying room and took stock of every precious dark-colored jar, selecting a few as she went. This was a concoction she'd have to make from scratch, then she'd oil the candle and roll it in the blend.

Annie said, "I'll scrape up the rest of the wax. When I'm finished, you want me to start lighting candles upstairs?"

"Thanks," Jade murmured, already turning words over in her mind, selecting and discarding several phrases one after the other.

It had been right to wish the best for Brenda's ex, so she didn't want to reverse that. Nor did she particularly want to reverse the part where she opened herself to a new love. But any parts that connected the first to the second had to go.

With her mission clearly outlined, Jade took a deep breath and concentrated on grinding the bad part of her inadvertently commingled spells to a screeching halt. For this one, she was pulling out all the stops.

A concealed drawer beneath the work counter housed several wands, most of them very old, each wrapped separately in sumptuous red silk. Jade selected a beautifully crafted eighteen-inch iron wand for extra power, one embellished with a crystal tip and black tourmaline. In moments, she raised her energy to a high level, because intent alone wasn't enough; spells didn't work without energy. She used the wand to cast a circle and hold all that power within. As she marked the four directions with stones, each in turn, she said,

> *"Guardians of the North, element of Earth,*
> *Two spells I cast; nurture them well,*
> *but smother any ties.*

Guardians of the East, element of Air,
Two spells I cast; separate is good, together not wise.
Guardians of the South, element of Fire,
Two spells I cast; that which unites, set to flames.
Guardians of the West, element of Water,
Two spells I cast; alone like islands, nothing the same."

Jade visualized Lyle calling one day soon, telling her that Brenda's ex was happy and settled with a family of his own. She took special care to clear her mind of that thought before moving on to visualize herself happy and glowing with a new love of her own.

That done, Jade lit the upside-down pillar.

Calmer now, she sighed with relief at a job well done, a catastrophe averted. She slipped her ruby ring off her finger and laid it by the candle; the color lent speed to spells, the setting of silver wings enhanced it further. Conversely, the ring also would absorb energy *from* the spell, without weakening it in any way, allowing her to carry that energy with her later, until the deed was done.

A spell was no good if she doubted herself, if she continued to worry about Lyle's ex-rival arriving in her life. She'd look back on this later and laugh. Next year, maybe. Right now, it was time to open the circle and leave the magic to work itself, and she did so promptly.

The sun had set while she'd been working, marking the beginning of Imbolc. The festival celebrated not spring, but the first stirring of it, when animals awakened from hibernation and crocuses began to peek through the snow. Jade lit a taper, left the conservatory, and began lighting candles in the back of the house.

"I skipped the office. Hope you don't mind," Annie said as their paths merged in the kitchen, and they continued toward the front rooms. "It's such a mess, I was afraid to light anything."

"No kidding. I didn't even put a candle in there."

Jade loved Imbolc. Her home took on the warm glow of candlelight, of flickering shadows and golden hues. Yule was over. The days were lengthening, the nights growing shorter. Soon it would be spring, bringing more clients for long, enlightening weekends.

Having guests was a mixed blessing. She couldn't have dug Mystic Manor out of debt without them, but some days she just liked to work in the drying room until lunchtime. Or wash her hair and lounge around in sweats all evening. It was, after all, her home, her refuge. It held the essence of generations of Delarues before her, and she didn't like just anybody traipsing through it.

"Feeling better?" Annie asked as they finished their circuit in the foyer.

"Yes," Jade said, able to smile now with real relief.

It didn't last long, only until the front door burst open and two men blew in and slammed it against the wind. Both were tall, bundled in dark parkas, and dusted with snow.

Forget positive thinking. It was too late for that. All Jade could do was stand there and gawk at the sum of what she'd wrought—

Pierce Brosnan's clone.

No, no, *no!*

The most she could do as she stared at him was gasp, and that didn't nearly echo the alarm she was feeling. She shouldn't be gawking. She should be shouting vile, horrible things that would make him back out the door and run away, escape into the night, but try as she might, she could barely breathe, let along put two coherent words together.

"Damn," she whispered at last. He was perfect; over six feet, with steel blue eyes, jet-black hair, the works.

"Yeah," Annie echoed.

"Guess I should've peed on the pillar."

"Yeah."

"Think it's too late?" That'd send any sane man running for the hills.

Though from the looks of him, he might not notice. Bloodshot eyes, a couple days' stubble on his face, and three white butterfly bandages closing a gash over his left cheekbone—what a sorry-looking double. The scowl didn't help either. As he did a visual 360 of the foyer and great hall, silently noting the candles burning in every window and in several wall sconces, he looked . . . *angry,* like a guy who wouldn't mind stuffing a body into a trunk right about now.

He also looked really, really good in candlelight.

* * *

"Whaddya think, wedding or funeral?" Mason had snarled a few minutes earlier, as a strong wind whipped Anthony and him up the flagstone steps to Mystic Manor.

Swear to God, there was a candle burning in every friggin' window. And this place had a lot of windows. All those flickering flames just reminded him of Brenda.

"Try to forget you're hungover and pissed off, okay?" Anthony said. They paused in front of the leaded-glass door and stomped snow off their hiking boots. "We're supposed to have been out eagle watching all day."

"It doesn't snow in Aruba. I could birdwatch in Aruba."

"Yeah, but you wouldn't get paid for it. Now shut up and make like a guy who's never seen anything as beautiful as a bald eagle."

Anthony opened the front door. They rushed in, both of them shouldering it closed against the howling wind just as Mason said, "You're only pissed because I slept with your boyfriend," in front of a stunned audience.

Two very striking women, staring at them, wide-eyed. Both holding burning candles. One in slim, curve-hugging jeans that made her legs look as long as his, the other in . . . something unimportant. They had their heads together, speaking softly.

While the number on the street side mailbox matched

their destination, there'd been no sign to identify this as anything other than a private residence.

"Ah, this is Mystic Manor, right?" Mason zeroed in on the taller one in stiletto-heeled boots. If there was a God in heaven, she'd be the subject. If not, if they were in the wrong house and had to stake out some other address, Anthony might have to find a new partner.

I am a trained professional, he reminded himself with anticipation. *And, I'll admit, a little slow on the uptake this evening. So I'll need to spend extra time familiarizing myself with every luscious inch of—*

"Yeah, we weren't sure," Anthony threw in, the sound of his voice forcefully reminding Mason that he was supposed to be working.

With the wind no longer numbing his senses, Mason glanced around, getting the lay of the land, so to speak. He took in lots of gleaming dark wood, richly colored Oriental carpets, and holy cow, at the far end of the foyer, a central staircase rose, split at a wide landing, and turned back on itself. The house was toned down from a mansion you'd see in the movies; more his idea of a luxurious hunting lodge where the weapons of choice were Jack Daniel's and a royal flush.

"Is that a Tiffany?" Anthony asked in a reverent tone. Unlike Mason, he was staring up at the large, ornate window topping the landing. Backlit for effect at night, its palette of jewel tones was nothing short of magnificent.

"Yes, he installed it himself." A little pride crept into Ms. Stiletto's voice, but it didn't last long. "Now, if you're looking for a place to stay, I can give you directions to several other establishments."

"Other" told Mason all he needed to know, which was good, because as soon as he'd once-overed the decor, he was back to studying the woman with fantastic taste in heels. He couldn't possibly be sober, or she wouldn't look like that. Perfect skin. Who had perfect skin these days, with pollution and junk food? Hers was flawless, swear to God.

Long, dark hair fell beyond her shoulders, twisting like a spiral staircase, which immediately led his thoughts right up to the bedroom. Those silky curls would snare a lover's hand, holding it captive, winding around his fingers like ribbons.

Eventually he got to her eyes. They tilted slightly at the corners, speaking of mysterious, exotic ancestry. Green. Mesmerizing. Magnetic. His brain was so muddled, he couldn't figure out if he was drawn to her like a mosquito to a bug zapper because he was still drunk, or if being so saved him from frying himself to an ignominious end.

Anthony cleared his throat pointedly. Mason took a long, deep breath to clear his head, thinking mystery was good—in a relationship, not a surveillance subject. Forced to concentrate on the job at hand, he realized Jade hadn't actually answered the question, a trait shared by most people with something to hide. He was better off focusing on the candle in her hand. That'd keep his head straight if he lived through it.

The flame was nothing less than a sharp pin constantly pricking his sore brain.

Anthony took the lead, nudging the registry on the kidney-shaped desk. "A guy down in town said this is a B&B. If you have any vacancies, we'd sure appreciate two rooms."

"At least Brenda didn't light them all at once," Mason muttered. Talk about déjà vu. Only the ribbons and flowers were missing.

"Excuse me?"

"Oh. Nothing," Mason said. A wave of his hand indicated all the burning candles. "Just wondering what the occasion is."

"Annie's birthday."

There it was. *Lie number one.* And it slid off her lips so easily.

If Annie was the blonde, then the raven-haired beauty who'd spoken had to be Jade Delarue, a.k.a. the Target. The name fit. He'd be hard put to say how exactly, but it did.

Didn't matter though, he thought, catching himself before he fell into her trap. There was a fifty-fifty chance Ms. Delarue had something to do with her husband's disappearance or knew something about it. Better than fifty-fifty. Three full-grown husbands, hers and those of her two best friends, didn't just go missing without leaving something to trace.

Annie was Team Two's target, which explained the dark van across the street. Mason didn't remember the third woman's name. Hell, he was doing well to remember there *was* a third.

"I'm sorry," Jade said, opening a desk drawer, extracting brochures. "I have a policy of booking advance reservations only—"

To Mason's surprise, Annie grabbed Jade by the arm and pulled her aside with a cute, apologetic, "One minute, okay?"

Anthony seized the opportunity to round on Mason and whisper, "Forget Brenda and the blasted candles for five minutes!"

"Look, I'm tired and I'm cold. I need to crawl into bed without worrying about the whole place burning to the ground around me, okay? Is that too much to ask?"

"Don't mess this up, Mason. You may not have little brothers and sisters depending on you for tuition, but I do, dammit, so be professional and stick to the plan."

"Okay, okay," he grumbled.

"I mean it. It can't get any easier than staying right under her roof."

"Chill, man. I promise."

That secured—Anthony knew Mason's word was ironclad—Anthony smoothly turned back to the women with his trademark disarming smile. Jade and Annie seemed to have resolved their issues just as quickly.

"It sure would be helpful if we could stay here," Anthony said. "You see, we're chronicling the increasing numbers of bald eagles wintering over along the Mississippi, and with this house perched on a bluff the way it is—"

"I guess I could make an exception for fellow nature lovers."

Jade smiled when she said it, but given her sudden change of heart, Mason didn't believe one enthusiastic note in her voice. *Lie number two.*

"I know just the rooms," she said. "You'll get the best views in the morning when the birds are more active."

"Great," Anthony said with an affable smile. "Isn't that great, Mason?"

"Great."

Anthony introduced them as freelance author/photographers, then smoothly took Jade into his confidence as he reached for his wallet. "I hate staying in hotels with all our equipment. Too many people in and out of the rooms to leave anything behind during the day, if you know what I mean. Do you take charges?"

"No, but a check will be fine."

Jade quoted a rate that had no business outside of New York or L.A. And when Anthony dropped the pen in surprise—not much surprised him, but the Mystic Manor web site had been all about botanicals and zip on the B&B—Annie stepped forward and said, "Ah, Jade, they'll be so busy doing their own thing, don't you think we could offer them the discounted rate?"

Jade's face went from *What discounted rate?* to *Oh. Sure.*

"Of course," she said, pasting on a smooth smile. "Annie's absolutely right."

Lie number three. In less than five minutes!

Mason could feel Anthony itching to get back to backgrounding, which, due to the haste in which they took this job, he hadn't had time to complete. Not their normal MO, but life didn't always work out by the book.

"Please, bring your things in and make yourselves at home. Mystic Manor prides itself on hospitality," Jade said with a warm smile, which faded a bit each time she looked Mason's way.

They had better than they'd hoped for—practically the run of the house. He and Anthony could be in and out all hours of the day and night. They could even wander into other rooms with no more explanation than, "An eagle flew this way. I thought maybe I could get a better shot from here."

As long as the rooms weren't rented, of course. But then, if Jade Delarue was hiding letters from a missing spouse, they wouldn't be in those rooms. Mason had to work on the assumption, though, that if he had been here anytime in the last six years, he might have left something behind. And that could be anywhere between the rafters and the cellar floor.

Or she could be hiding communication from a co-conspirator, because one thing was certain: Jade's husband hadn't disappeared alone.

When Mason unzipped his parka, Jade graced him with a smile, somewhat at his expense.

"What?" he asked.

"We're generally not so formal around here."

He looked down at himself, not a clue as to what she meant.

"The eagles don't expect a tux."

"The tux is for you, sweetheart," he said with a wink. He started a grin, too, until it pulled at the tender gash on his cheek.

"New style?" Jade cocked her head, her grin equally sassy.

Damn, he liked sassy. If he was going to have half a chance of seeing this job through, she needed to stop talking and let him get a good night's sleep to clear his head.

"Or do you always keep it rolled up in the trunk?"

Great. Witty banter, and he was at a distinct disadvantage.

Jade stepped very close, staring at the gash on his cheek. She smelled delicious, and it took all the willpower he could muster not to lean in and sniff her hair. He might have been dumped at the altar just hours ago—time spent unconscious didn't count—but he'd have to be dead not to take a minute to admire this lovely creature gazing up at him. And right now, he very much did not want to be dead.

"I'll make you something to put on that. It'll heal faster and won't leave a scar."

"I'm using one of those antibiotic creams."

She didn't roll her eyes but looked as if she wanted to.

"Up and to the left." Jade handed him a beaded

lanyard with an old-fashioned brass skeleton key and something else.

"What's this?"

"A mini dream catcher."

"Oh, goody. I'll dream about a mini fire instead of a big one."

This fire was as dangerous as it was magnetic. In Jade's presence, sporting a hangover to end all hangovers, Mason again felt like a stupid, misguided mosquito. If he wasn't careful, he'd land on her, fry his guts out, and bite the ground in a pile of dust. Not pretty.

He had to move away, get away, get his wits about him so he could deal with her. Bed. Alone. Sleep.

"Do you dream about fires often?"

"Forget it." Mason bounced the key in his hand and headed for the wide staircase.

"Your luggage?" Jade prompted.

"Warm bed," Mason replied.

Though sleep could be far from coming. Of the three women left behind on the same day six years ago, all had remained single—given their looks, what were the odds?—and two of them were in this house, right now.

It was going to be a pleasure getting close to Jade.

Chapter 3

Mason spent his first hour at Mystic Manor soaking up bone-melting heat in a gleaming, old-fashioned, claw-footed bathtub. The tiled bathroom was large, stocked with plush man-size towels in an assortment of browns and greens. A beribboned basket of small packages bearing Mystic Manor Botanicals labels offered bath salts for sleeping, dreaming (a choice of lucid or calm), and healing. Mason wondered what happened if you mixed them.

Also in the basket were MMB soaps, shampoo, lip balms, bath sachets for energy, peace, breaking habits—

"Give me a break," he muttered.

The tub filled while he poked through the basket. Nothing labeled Brenda Reject, Black Weekend from Hell, or Abducted to Siberia. One was for nightmares, though. If that didn't fit the bill, he didn't know what would, so he untied the ribbon and dumped it into the water. The white stuff disappeared and left behind little brown and green floaty things.

A candle had been left burning, same as in the bedroom. Mason had blown them out before he'd even turned on the water, thinking, *What, one insurance check isn't enough?* Now Ms. Delarue wanted to set fire to the house and blame it, oh so innocently, on a candle accident? The fire marshal would have a field day with the number of candlesticks left behind. From the foyer up to his bathroom, Mason had counted at least three dozen potential hazards.

As worn down as he was, he still wouldn't be able to sleep until he prowled the entire house later and blew out every goddam one.

Insurance money—what was wrong with people?

It wasn't as if Jade could just sell the property and leave the country on a yearlong round-the-world cruise, luxuriously ensconced in the Presidential Suite. A house like this, in this area, who'd buy it? Who could afford it? Add its total replacement value to the death benefit, though, and the sexy Ms. Delarue could relocate to Europe. Or a Caribbean island. Hell, she could buy a whole damn island and burn all the friggin' candles she wanted.

Although . . . Mason pictured Jade in a bikini, with him, on a sandy beach, and warmed up far beyond tub temperature. He had a great eye for detail, even if he was, at the moment, supplying instead of observing. He dressed her in a forest green bikini, to match her eyes. Then, hell, he figured a nude beach would be a lot more fun and ditched the suit.

It wasn't Aruba, but it beat running around in the snow in a two-day-old tux. He'd nearly had heart failure when he woke up in the hotel room with the naked bartender, but every pearly shirt stud had been in place, his cummerbund still on, and the bartender swore all they'd done was drink to broken hearts.

Mason topped off his water a couple times as it cooled down. He was fighting a chill from hours of standing out in the snow because Anthony said they had to at least look as if they'd been out doing their fake job.

This was a great idea. Already he felt more like himself. He didn't even mind the herbs sticking to his chest like brown and green freckles.

An hour later, he rooted through his suitcase and found his black warm-up suit; better for prowling around the house after Jade went to bed. He wasn't sure yet if this contract was on the up-and-up or a bullshit assignment designed to keep him busy until he was sober again. Whichever, he needed a nap before he got started. He'd just flopped onto the queen-size bed when Anthony delivered a deep bowl of homemade soup.

"Nice furniture," Anthony said. The bed and dressers were old and elegantly carved, yet heavy, not feminine and delicate. "My room, too. Bet these are original."

Mason couldn't have cared less. More alert now that he'd washed away two days of stink, he slipped into the pants and frowned at the bowl. Cream soup was for sissies, but other than a small bag of peanuts on the airplane, Mason wasn't sure when he'd eaten last. Anything that smelled that good had to be lethal.

"You think it's wise, eating her cooking?"

"It's not as if her husband dropped dead," Anthony reasoned.

"Who knows? Maybe she made their last meal before they left."

"Then there'd be a car. And bodies." Anthony wafted the soup beneath Mason's nose. "Taste it. You won't care."

"Still, it's cream soup."

"Come on, Jade ate from the same pot. Besides, she only just met us, and it's not as if my uncle advertised for a stakeout team. She couldn't be suspicious yet."

"What is it? Potato?" Mason leaned close and sniffed. "Clam chowder?"

"Doesn't matter. It's the herbs that make it." Anthony shrugged. "At least that's what she said. C'mon, man, you haven't eaten worth a damn. You'll need energy to search this place. It's huge. Probably has hidden passageways and hidey-holes. Maybe secret entrances. Hell, maybe even tunnels."

"What was his name again? Couldn't have been Delarue."

"Her husband? Doug Stockard. Now eat!" Anthony's phone vibrated on his belt, and he checked the caller ID. "For cripe's sake, call your sister, will you?"

"Tell her I'm okay."

"You're not okay."

"Then tell her I'm alive."

"I've talked to her five times, at least. She wants to hear it from you. C'mon, man, she won't quit leaving messages on my phone."

"Persistent, isn't she?"

"Yeah. Reminds me of someone. Where's your phone?"

Mason shrugged. He used just the tip of the spoon to taste the soup. That was all it took.

"Oh. Oh my." Mason took the bowl before Anthony decided he wanted seconds. "I'd say no wonder she charges so much, but no meal's worth those rates."

"True. What could she offer for—oh, hey, you think maybe we stumbled across a high-class bordello? And she's the madam?"

"I didn't think anything could beat Aruba," Mason said, grinning in spite of the pain beneath his eye. "I was wrong."

Mason pulled the corded phone onto the bed and settled against the pillows, warm and somewhat content after the soup. Physically, anyway. Emotionally was another matter, but he didn't want to go there. He'd talk to his sister for a few minutes and then crash.

"When you stormed out of the church, I couldn't tell if you were in a murderous rage or suicidal," Jen said when he called.

"Me either. I went to a bar to figure it out."

A soft sound of amusement traveled the wire. "Made everything come clear, did it?"

"For a while."

"You all right? You sound like a gruff old bear."

"Polar bear. Anthony says we're in Missouri, but I don't know. All this snow? Could be Alaska."

Jen sighed, knowing she'd get no more out of him on that score. "Do you hate Brenda?"

"I hired a hit man."

"Seriously, Mason. I have to see her at the Ladies' League meeting next month, and I don't know whether to say hello or bitch slap her."

"Damn, that sounds good. Can I come watch?"

Sometime in the course of his long soak, he'd decided he didn't hate Brenda. The big revelation was that he'd never loved her either. What she'd done and how she'd done it was pretty mean, but when it came right down to it, she'd started cutting the cord six weeks ago when she'd made him wait—not to mention the break before that—and then on Saturday night she'd severed it completely. He'd held up his end, putting on a tux, waiting at the church.

What the hell was I thinking?

She came to his room later that evening, when Mason was alone. By "she," he was hoping it was Jade knocking softly on his door, not Annie. Not that there was anything wrong with Annie, but how would he know since once he'd seen Jade, he'd barely looked in Annie's direction.

She didn't slip through his door without turning on the light, which would have been a great finish to the hooker fantasy he'd worked over in his mind after Anthony left. Instead, she waited quietly when he said, "Just a sec."

He was still in his running pants, still warm enough from the bath and the soup that he didn't need a shirt. Hey, if she found that erotic and wanted to run her nails over his bare chest, who was he to stop her?

She could be like a spider after its prey, the big kind, the ones that run it down and capture it, and hell if he didn't mind so much. That's how he knew he was in trouble. He didn't care. Even if she was a black widow who'd screw his brains out and then kill him, at least he'd die satisfied.

Widow. *Oh shit,* he thought as Anthony's briefing came back to him. Sure, sure, he was here to stake out her house and everyone in it, not enjoy the fringe benefits, but he'd been fasting for a long, long time.

If one could call this a house. He'd read the brochure, which wasn't an advertisement; more like a thank-you for staying here, and by the way, here's a little history about us. Mid eighteen hundreds, ancestor immigrated to this country, took up shipping on the Mississippi and Missouri Rivers, made a fortune in that and lumber, and so on. The first Mr. Delarue could have built along Millionaire Row in Hannibal with the other bigwigs, but "he and his new bride treasured their solitude" and chose this bluff instead, "where they could take advantage of the natural light needed for the conservatory."

Hannibal didn't have natural light? News to him. Probably news to all the Hannibalites, too.

Conservatory; sounded like a doozy of a plant room. Maybe the madam had orgies in there.

Mason opened the door, expecting to see exactly

who and what he got, except in his pruny, oversoaked condition, Jade's black curls shone like tempting tendrils, no, fingers really, curling at him, beckoning him to step closer, to cross the threshold and follow her to her room, which would be dimly lit with a romantic glow, a red scarf draped over a small lamp—

"I hope I didn't wake you," she said, staring at the left side of his face. "I noticed the light under your door."

She spoke quietly, as if there were other guests nearby whom she didn't want to disturb. That wasn't helping keep Mason's thoughts in check. She was still in snug, fashionable jeans and a very soft-looking sweater. Pink. Feminine. None of that helped either.

"It's best to start tonight," she said.

Mason swallowed hard and didn't realize for a couple seconds that she had something in her hand. She was holding it out for him to take, but it was only a small jar, and if he took it, she might leave, so he didn't.

When Jade reached out and touched his hand, lifting it from his side so she could give him the jar, Mason lost the power of speech. Oh, man, he was in trouble if things were starting out this way. The last time he'd felt like this, he'd been ten years old and found out the hard way that you have to learn how to swim *before* you jump in the deep end.

It was only because he had a hangover, because he'd drunk every meal since Saturday night, and then some. If he could last until tomorrow, he'd be fine. He'd be stronger tomorrow. He'd be himself. All business. All professional.

Jade's touch was soft, her skin silky. The tiny

jar that she set in his palm held her body heat and warmed his hand.

"There you go," she said with a small smile that fed his fantasies. "Just dab a little on that cut tonight and again in the morning."

He stared at the jar for a couple more seconds while he evaluated how helpless he could appear without overdoing it. Gashed face, two days of whiskers, but squeaky clean—he was guessing he could get away with a lot.

"How much is a dab?" he asked.

"A little bit."

"Yeah, but how little?"

Jade sighed. It was a good sigh, the kind a woman makes when she knows maybe her leg's being pulled but doesn't mind too much.

"I wouldn't want to mess up," Mason added, handing the jar back. He'd perfected the little grin, the little shrug of his shoulder that said, *I'm just a man. Help me.*

"You don't look so good." Jade's brow creased with concern as she slipped past him into the room. "Does your head hurt? You'd better lie down."

Okay, he was lying to himself. She'd said "sit." The quilt was already turned down and the bed rumpled. He didn't want to push his luck, so he chose one of the two upholstered chairs by the small round table at the window.

Jade disappeared into his bathroom, and Mason couldn't come up with any reason why except every lascivious scenario he'd already imagined, thanks to

Anthony, until she returned with a cotton swab and her hair bouncing about her shoulders.

She started to unscrew the lid, but stopped mid-turn. Mason followed her gaze to the table, to the dead candle.

"I need to relight that," she said. She gestured over her shoulder. "The one in the bathroom . . . ?"

"Don't bother relighting them."

"It's no bother. I just don't understand why they're not burning."

"I blew them out."

She looked alarmed. "You *blew* them out?"

"I cupped with my hand." He smoothed his fingers over the tablecloth. "See? No wax."

Jade's alarmed look dissipated, though in all honesty, Mason didn't think it was the no-wax comment.

"It's traditional to burn candles tonight," she said, turning her attention back to his gash. "It's a holiday."

"What? Isn't it, like, Groundhog Day or something? I don't like candles."

Jade grinned. "You never invited a woman over for dinner and lit a pair of tapers?"

"It's a recent issue."

When she opened the jar, he wrapped his fingers around her wrist and pulled her close—under the guise of smelling the ointment, of course. He didn't intend to get his face slapped. Man, that'd hurt.

"All right?" she asked, her breasts in very near approximation to his face, so the stuff could've smelled like a skunk and he wouldn't have cared.

"I don't know. What is it?"

"Healing Ointment."

"Nice generic name. Never heard of it."

Her eyes glowed with pride. "I make it."

"What's in it?"

"Alum, echinacea, goldenseal. Glad you asked?" she asked with a teasing grin that Mason wanted to kiss.

"Can't be too careful these days." He warned himself to back off. It wasn't working.

"The recipe's been in the family for generations. Nothing in here'll hurt a big strong man like you."

Okay, she may not have said "big" and "strong." So sue him. And the only thing in here now that could hurt him was her, because if in a moment of weakness he got lucky with the target and Anthony found out, it'd take more than hard liquor to dull the pain. Not to mention more than three butterflies to hold him together.

Jade dipped the tip of the swab into the jar and transferred a small amount to her index finger.

"You're tall, even without your boots." He grabbed her hand, stopping her as she reached for him.

Studying him, Jade tipped her head in a way he found too enchanting, too distracting.

Damn, he should have kept his mouth shut. Apparently alcohol numbed the discretion gene.

"Photographers notice those kinds of things," he said in his defense.

"Ones who can focus maybe."

"I haven't had a drink since last night."

"Let me guess. Last night ended well after the sun was up."

He grinned in spite of the pain. "Maybe even after I was on the plane." So nice of Anthony to have taken a long bathroom break.

"Let me do this."

"What's the rush?"

"I have to go hide the liquor."

Reluctantly, he released her hand. "I'm done drinking."

"Didn't help?"

"I'm really not much of a drinker."

"Could've fooled me. Hold still now."

She bent toward him and touched the gash under his eye with a soft, rhythmic, tapping motion.

"Do you have a license for this?" he asked, looking down her sweater.

"Dabbing 101. They teach it at the junior college."

"And you passed?"

"Hm, you know, when I saw you downstairs, I thought you fell on the ice or something. Now I'm thinking someone punched you."

As Jade leaned closer, Mason thought maybe he owed Brenda a big thank-you. A pale pink bra should look virginal, but Jade's was low-cut and cupped the nicest pair of breasts this side of the equator.

Her hair smelled herbal, but unlike something out of a commercial shampoo bottle, this scent was cleaner, more distinct and more subtle at the same time. Didn't make sense, but hey, she was inches away from finding herself tumbled on that big ol' bed over there, so forget clear thinking. Prolonged abstinence in conjunction with as much alcohol as he'd ingested over the weekend—he'd be lucky if he could get the job done right.

"Ow!" Mason's hand flew to his face, and his brain scrambled to figure out how Jade had slapped him without moving her arm. And how the hell she knew she should.

"Oh, that couldn't have hurt that much." Jade laid the stripped-off butterfly on the marble tabletop and had the gall to reach for his face again.

Mason didn't think she was coming at him with a sassy pat. He threw himself into Reverse, tipping the chair back on two legs until it hit the wall.

"Hm," Jade said, following, leaning close, but forget looking down her sweater.

"Stop! You pull off any more and it'll open up again."

Jade tilted her head sideways for a different perspective, her lips pursing in a little moue as she gave the matter some thought. "That wouldn't be all bad. You pulled it crooked, you know. Want me to fix it?"

"Get away!"

He must have looked horrified, because she laughed and said, "Just kidding. You looked so serious. How'd you do this anyway?"

He watched her warily, delaying his answer until he knew she wasn't just trying to distract him for another strip-and-run. Also, he had to make up something good.

"It was my own darn fault. I got in a hurry. You know how the eagles come in for a fish, wings open, talons spread. Great shot. Didn't want to miss it.

Wasn't watching where I was going and tripped." He fell silent.

"You were outside?" She frowned.

"You have an eagle that comes indoor and poses?"

"That's funny." She tipped her head the other way.

"That's me. Great sense of humor."

"No, I mean it looks funny. There's fiber in it, like carpet lint. You sure you fell in the snow?"

"I may have landed on a scarf."

Jade ripped off the second butterfly.

"Hey! That's not dabbing, it's torture."

"That's a 200-level class. I passed it, too. Come on, baby, one more."

"It's the last one holding my face together." He was smart enough to put his hand over it and leave it there.

"Your skin's already holding. We should get those fibers out, though."

Jade took hold of his wrist as if she could simply push his hand away, and he, with lightning speed, used the connection as leverage to throw her off-balance and tumble her onto his lap.

Okay, she was quicker than he was. If that didn't convince him to sober up the rest of the way—*fast*—nothing would. Jade didn't fall in his lap, but he was having fun lying to himself. She caught herself with her free hand on his bare chest, though, which was almost as good. Then she demonstrated there was some lightning speed in the room after all, but it was hers as she regained both feet a good yard from his knees.

"Sorry," he said. "Reflex action."

"Yeah. What's an eagle photographer without great reflexes?"

Mason could tell it was a point of honor with her not to run out the door like a scared girl. This was her house, after all. He was a guest who could be evicted at any moment; not something he wanted to explain to Anthony or his uncle.

"I haven't always been a photographer," Mason said, hoping for mysterious and just dangerous enough that she wouldn't ask questions. Because when it came right down to it, if he had to lie to get a job done, he would, but lies had a way of complicating things.

Jade studied him for a moment, and maybe because he kept his ass glued to the chair, she went off guard. She wasn't hanging around for round two, though.

"You know what a dab is now," she said, turning toward the door. "Keep the jar."

"Stupid, stupid, *stupid*." Alone in the hall outside Mason's room, Jade thumped herself upside the head.

She ran her index finger over the outside of his door, tracing a pentagram thereon as she said, "*Back to the way before; this shall be no more.*"

She was used to word-of-mouth guests, people who knew she had only their best interests at heart. Women liked her because she was candid. Men came with a well-defined goal they couldn't attain on their own and therefore looked at her as a means to an end instead of a member of the opposite sex.

She should have turned Mason away before he'd

brushed the snow off his collar. But Annie, whom she'd maim later, had pulled her to the side of the foyer and reasoned with her.

"It'll be easier to get rid of him if he stays here," she'd said.

"If he stays here, then he's *here*."

"I mean permanently. Think about it. He's right upstairs. You have total control over his room. His bed. Botanicals aren't my thing, Jade, but even I know there's something you can slip between the sheets—"

"Of course!"

Jade had several herbs that would do the trick. She had a pile of internet orders to fill tonight, but she'd bump this to Priority One. He'd be history by noon tomorrow.

"And if that doesn't work," Annie added, "there's always his food."

Jade had forced a smile on her face and welcome in her voice, and she'd let him stay. But as she'd discovered when she'd grasped his wrist moments ago, it wasn't only Mason she was fighting. She'd been so darned specific when she'd cast the spell.

A man who lights my fire.

Oh yeah, she'd gotten him all right. He was right there on the other side of the wall. Finally, after six years of waiting, her libido had perked up, her heart had sped up, and she'd probably radiated all kinds of pheromones that said, *Take me, I'm here, I haven't had sex in six years, and you look like the man who could make up for it.*

Too bad she had to send him packing.

Chapter 4

Why is Pierce Brosnan naked in the house?"

Jade wasn't the first Delarue to live on catnaps, so a middle-of-the-night phone call from her mother didn't take her by surprise. The naked part did, though; had her fingers pausing right over the keyboard while she wondered how her mother could possibly *know*.

Was Mason naked *right now*?

She touched the brown jasper on her desk, the small stone sitting there as of an hour ago to reduce stress over the whole Pierce-Brosnan, light-my-fire fiasco, as well as to strengthen her personal energy. Incense burned slowly on a censer on the file cabinet.

"Hello? Jade?"

"Is this a trick question?"

She shifted the cordless phone to her shoulder

and resumed her e-mail. Next weekend's guest had heard about the snowstorm and wondered whether he should go online and purchase Arctic wear before his arrival. She was *sooo* tempted to tell him she'd do a spell and make it all go away by then.

"I saw him in the bathtub," her mother stated.

"Congratulations. I see you're getting the hang of scrying." Not Mona's strong point.

"Finally. I met this lovely English gentleman— anyway, he's very good, don't change the subject. What kind of spell does a movie star need?"

"He's a clone, Mom."

Her mother chuckled. "Has to be in two places at once, huh? No wonder you charge so much for spell-casting. Well, I always like his movies, but you'll have to tell me which ones are the clone."

"The clone doesn't act."

"You know, that's interesting, because I got a sense that he isn't who he appears to be. I guess that's it. What does he do, then?"

"Photographs eagles. Some kind of freelance photo-journalist."

Her mother hummed. "No, that's not it."

Jade's fingers stilled on the keyboard as she consid-ered, then dismissed, the warning bell raised by her mother's certainty. "Yes, that's exactly it."

"Maybe you should look closer."

No way she was telling her mother she'd screwed up; not after that comment.

If she had to botch a spell, it was lucky she did it in February. When her parents had divorced, they'd handed off Mystic Manor to her—far be it from them to figure out how to save it from auction. They'd agreed to visit on alternate months. This was her father's month, to use or not; regardless, no mother.

"Maybe," Jade said, "you need more time on the crystal ball."

"I'm using water," Mona replied, too off in her own world to take offense. "I'll let you know what I see. Oh, before I go, I mailed you a package. Be sure it doesn't sit out in the weather when that horrid mailman finally gets there. It's, ah, something you don't have, if you get my drift."

Meaning, the importation of which would raise eyebrows, so her mother was being discreet.

"Now, just one last thing before you go back to your e-mail—"

How did she know? Jade's fingers shot off the keyboard before she realized her mother must have heard the keys clicking. That had to be it.

"Lucky guess."

"Whatever you say, darling. Now you know I'll be back the first of March, so if you have more clones up your sleeve, be a sweetheart, won't you, and get Sean Connery for me?"

Mason stole out of his room, dressed all in black, carrying a small flashlight. His head felt clearer now that he'd cleaned up, eaten, and caught a few hours of sleep. His steps were sure.

His sanity was in question. A stupid mosquito— what had he been thinking?

He hadn't been. Alcohol-induced fear was to blame, that's all. Jade was a Siren; beautiful, alluring, mesmerizing. If he wasn't careful, the end result could be the same, but at least this way it was a more interesting game.

Today's mission: find proof that Jade Delarue's husband was or was not dead. Then he'd fly straight out of this frozen wasteland and head for some quality dive time with a sunken wreck. He had a *date* with a wreck. Submerge. Forget everything.

Knowing where to search in the house wasn't a problem. It was amazing what people stuffed into their drawers. Mail they didn't have time for. Mail they meant to answer later. Receipts for things they never should have charged in the first place because charges left trails.

Fortunately, many crooks were a little light in the IQ department. Jade looked pretty smart, though. Mason doubted she'd leave a letter from a "dead" husband lying around, but you never knew. He'd look anyway because he was nothing if not thorough.

Was it legal? Was it admissible evidence? Hell, no. But it was a no-brainer that if he unearthed a postcard that said, "Tahiti's nice this time of year. Can't wait to see you. Bring the money," the widow would drop her claim. Simple leverage. If that didn't work, the insurance execs would pay him until he found something admissible, at which time they'd prosecute. Either way, they'd be a million dollars happier. Three million, if the postcard led to the others.

He'd slept like the dead, not stirring until almost

first light, hours past when he'd intended. Had to be the soup. Or the ointment. The Widow Delarue probably'd drugged him and rifled his gear to see if he was who he claimed to be. He'd been in no condition to pack for this trip, but Anthony would have done so accordingly: bird books, cameras and assorted photography paraphernalia, laptop, warm clothing, fake membership cards to writing organizations, fake letter from an editor. If she looked, Jade would find everything in order.

Creeping along the hall, he kept next to the wall where the floorboards were less likely to squeak. It almost didn't matter. He turned a corner and came upon a black dog standing guard. Huge was an understatement. This beast stood as tall as an Irish wolfhound and as broad as a bull mastiff. Possibly crossed with a buffalo.

Mason plastered himself against one of the built-ins that lined the hall, caught in a staring contest with an animal that showed no expression, that didn't squint at a flashlight beam shining in its face. Its bent-over ears didn't so much as twitch. Tail didn't wag; didn't even go up or down. It stood to reason that Mystic Manor couldn't stay in business if the dog ate the guests. Still, when he approached it, Mason used every precaution; gently, quietly, hand extended for a sniff. Show no fear.

Easier said than done when the dog dove for his crotch. He didn't think a sharp "No!" was going to cut it, and shooting it was out of the question, so he sort of danced past it sideways, twisting and turning, keeping one knee cocked and ready for a throat jab while doing a body slide along the wall.

He didn't breathe again until he was safely downstairs, and then not for long because there were clear sounds of someone moving around in the back of the house.

Mason went on instant alert as a drawer opened, closed. Then another. Dishes clattered, flatware jangled.

Too noisy to be Anthony, who wouldn't be searching the kitchen anyway. His job was backgrounding, and chatting up residents when he was "taking a break from the writing," as he'd tell them. Mason's generally was behind-the-scenes black bagging, because he attracted more attention, though he did do the occasional legwork. It wasn't his fault that people, when they saw him, tended to say, "Bond. James Bond," ask for his autograph, and question where his accent was.

Neither of them even suggested tapping Jade's phone. No way they'd violate federal wiretapping regulations just to save someone else's money.

Water turned on, gushing into the kitchen sink.

It was too much to hope for—the missing husband arrives in the middle of the night and roots around for the insurance check. Case solved.

Aruba, here I come!

Getting the check converted to cash before anyone was the wiser would pose little trouble for someone wily enough to vanish without a trace and stay hidden for six years. Especially with three involved.

It was no secret that the best way for three people to keep a secret was if two of them were dead.

Hours further removed from his alcohol-induced stupor, Mason recalled that the check hadn't been issued yet. And unless the dead guy hummed soprano and believed brewing coffee was key to going unnoticed, someone else was in the house.

Mason went into character, popping through the door like a freelance photojournalist intent on beating the sunrise.

"*Ahhh*, thought I smelled coffee," he said heartily.

The short woman emptying the dishwasher was about fifty, maybe sixty at the outside. She used blond highlights to camouflage the gray. She was very thin, probably from the amount of energy she burned as she flitted around the kitchen, exuding an eternally pleasant and helpful personality.

"Mornin'! Oh. Oh my!" She pulled a pen out of her apron and stretched out her arm, clearly indicating that he was to sign it in lieu of a piece of paper. "Heard you was here to photograph the eagles. Figured you'd be up early. Guess that's a cover story." She winked. Her perpetual smile grew wider, her eyes brighter. "Coffee's ready. Hope you like it strong."

"I'm not who you think—"

"If not, I can brew another pot. Won't take but a minute. Go on. Sign it."

Good Lord, if she didn't slow down, her head would start spinning. Hoping to calm her, he spoke slowly. "I'm Mason Kincaid."

She winked. "Sure you are."

"Really." He handed the pen back. "I am. I only sign autographs for people too stubborn to believe me."

She didn't look convinced.

Going full tilt, she had an insulated mug poured and in his hand before he could move a step, then produced real cream and a bowl of sugar, neither of which he used.

"Got stevia, too," she said. "It's a natural sweetener. Jade grows it right here in the conservatory."

"Black is fine, thanks."

"That's how I like it, too. You sure you're not— No, if you say you're not, I guess you aren't. You wouldn't be so foolish as to lie to Jade." She squinted at him. "You wouldn't, would you?"

"No, ma'am."

She cocked her head and studied him closer. "You know, now that you mention it, you are a little scruffy to be 007."

"I don't believe I mentioned that." One sip of coffee told Mason where the live wire got a good deal of her energy this early.

"'Cause let me warn you now, if you lie to her, she won't work with you. Not one bit, no, sir. So what would you like for breakfast? Waffles? Pancakes? French toast? Bacon and eggs? Anyway you like, over easy, poached, scrambled—"

Silence?

"—omelet. Any allergies?"

"No."

"How 'bout your friend?"

"No."

"Anything in particular you boys don't like?"

"Brussels sprouts."

"Oatmeal!" She clapped her hands together, then rubbed them briskly. "Oatmeal's good on a snowy morning like this, especially when you're gonna be outside. Sticks to your ribs longer."

Mason couldn't get a word in edgewise, so he held up his hand to see if that would stall her. It did. "Miss—?" he said, wondering if she was a relative of Jade's.

"Oh, my manners! Call me Weezy, everybody does."

"You up this early every day, Weezy?"

"Up, yes, but not here, my heavens, no. I just pop in when Jade has guests, and like I said, I heard you was here for the eagles—you know, besides the usual—so I came extra early."

The usual?

"My daughter, she lives just down the road. She sees lights in the guest rooms at night?—she gives me a heads up."

"Isn't that nice?" Mason graced her with his I'm-here-I'm-interested-tell-me-everything-you-know-about-the-target smile. "I hope Ms. Delarue lets you go home early to make up for your trouble."

"Oh, 'sno trouble. I go home when I want. I don't get paid none, so I set my own schedule."

There was an eat-in breakfast bar as well as a long plank table, durable but nicely finished. Weezy straightened the already-straight chairs, which lacked military precision by a mere millimeter. The canisters and toaster and blender suffered the same fate.

"Ms. Delarue can't afford to pay you?"

"Heavens, I couldn't *charge* her," Weezy said with an appalled gasp.

Mason rubbed the back of his neck. And here he'd thought all the alcohol was out of his system.

"Not a cent. After everything she did for me?— wouldn't be right. What kind of spell are you here for?"

"Excuse me?"

"Everyone stays for a spell."

Stay a spell. What colloquialism.

"A week, maybe two," he replied. "Whatever it takes."

"Oh." Weezy's smile wavered in a long moment of silence, then she darted toward the range and said, "So, what'll it be?"

Mason wasn't sure how he'd blown it, but he had. Weezy no longer wanted to talk, so he fell back on his original plan. If he could keep her in the kitchen for a while, maybe he could get some other room searched before Jade got up.

"Let's see." Mason sipped coffee while he plotted. "How about bacon, a couple sausage links if you have them, pancakes— Do you have something you can put in them? Like blueberries or pecans or chocolate chips?"

Weezy laughed with delight as she dragged out the griddle and slapped it on the range. "Just goes to show. Here I figured you for a plain pancake kinda man, just lookin' atcha. Chocolate chips! You're so naughty."

"It's the haircut. Fools everybody." With the dog upstairs and Weezy in the kitchen, Mason's thoughts returned to searching. An office, perhaps? Jade must have one. "I, ah, have to make a phone call," he began.

"This early?"

"Out of the country. Is there an office I can use?" he asked, hoping she wouldn't tell him the obvious, to go back and use his room.

"Upstairs, but Jade doesn't allow long-distance calls."

"I have a calling card."

"I guess that's okay then. If you get done before the pancakes, you can come back and visit with me. Or you're welcome to go out to the conservatory, but don't touch none of the plants in the far right corner. That's where the poisonous ones grow."

Mason paused a beat on his way out the door. People really shouldn't say the P word to an investigator working a man's disappearance.

"Where are you off to so early?" Jade asked.

She was sitting at the plank table across from Mason, gently stirring her herbal tea, watching the sky turn pink as church bells rang nearby. She'd been minding her own business, planning her day in her head, until he started slathering gobs of butter on his second stack of pancakes.

"I thought I'd start at the lock and dam. It's not far from here, right?"

"How do you . . . ?" She almost blurted, *How do you stay so fit eating like that?* but wisely decided she shouldn't mention that she noticed he was fit in the first place.

It felt good to have a man in the kitchen again, one who wasn't paying her, not for help anyway. One who had nothing to gain or lose riding on her skills. One who, when he looked at her with that sexy steel blue gaze, might just be interested in her for herself.

Sunrise, she thought. *Focus on the sunrise!*

Or the eagles. The birds liked feeding below the lock and dam. The churning water carried fish close to the surface, many of them stunned by the trip through the spillway. So of course that's where Mason would go to photograph, especially this time of morning.

"How do I what?" Mason paused with the syrup pitcher poised in midair.

With the full wattage of his attention on her, Jade's pulse skittered alarmingly. A ripple of excitement that she hadn't felt in far too long raced through her body, making her giddy and flushed and hoping he didn't notice.

He was staring at her, so Jade oh-so-innocently said, "What?"

"You just got that how-do-I-ask-him-for-his-autograph look."

She blinked. "Are you famous?"

"No."

"Then why would I ask for your autograph?"

Mason sighed. "Never mind."

"You know it's not open to the public, right? It's just a boat ramp."

"Boat ramp's fine. All I need's a place to park."

"Parking won't be the problem; getting in and out in this snow will. If you can, you should work somewhere else until all the roads are clear. I don't think Clarksville got as much as we did."

Mason broke out in a smile. "That's an interesting ring."

It should have been a totally unremarkable smile. She'd seen it hundreds of times on the big screen. But close up and in person, it was warm and friendly, and crinkled the corners of his eyes.

"It's an unusual setting. A pair of wings, is it?"

Jade glanced at her ruby, thinking, *My, he notices a lot.* Maybe too much. "It is. If you're feeling adventurous, you could snowshoe in."

Mason shuddered visibly, which made Jade laugh, and she said, "I have a pair if you change your mind."

"When hell freezes over."

"Haven't you heard? It did. Last night."

A flicker of amusement tipped one corner of his mouth upward, but Mason's easy smile was quickly hidden behind his coffee cup. Jade stared, waiting for it to come back, until she remembered she had no business waiting, and looked away.

"That's almost believable," he said, "but I'm still driving. I appreciate the advice. Clarksville it is."

"Be careful getting out of West Bluff. Our snowplows—and I use the term loosely—are two locals who put blades on their pickups and see who can get his half done faster. Chuck does a good enough job. Turner, though, he thinks everybody needs a little adventure in his life."

The possibility of Mason's sliding off the road into a tree worried Jade. If he landed in the hospital, he couldn't go home fast enough.

Yeah, that sounded plausible.

"My Jeep's better in the snow than a rental car." Jade tipped her head toward the hook by the back door. "The key's over there, on the ring with the tiger eye. I'm not going out today, so take it whenever you're ready."

"Jeeps are cold," Mason said.

"Yes, it's so much warmer in a ditch."

The corner of Mason's mouth twitched again, and Jade thought it might be the beginning of a smile— not that she cared, no no, not at all. When he pushed his plate away with a disgruntled sigh and glanced at the key, she knew he'd take the Jeep. It couldn't happen soon enough. She needed a few minutes alone in his room, and it wouldn't do to get caught.

Chapter 5

Through the big mullioned window in the study, Jade watched Mason cruise out of the snow-covered driveway. Her bright yellow Jeep slid sideways and came to rest in the front yard, brake lights glowing.

Great. So smart of her to lend her vehicle to a Floridian without asking if he'd ever driven in snow before. She wanted him gone, of course, but only back to Pensacola, not laid out by the side of the road.

As soon as Mason turned south onto the relatively clear street, Jade raced upstairs and threw open the door to his room.

"Whoa!" Anthony said, jumping back so as not to get bashed.

Jade halted in surprise, wondering what the heck she was supposed to say or do now that she'd been caught red-handed. "Oh! Sorry, I didn't know—"

"I came in to get this." Anthony held up a coiled cable. For a second, he looked suspicious, but that quickly changed to mildly curious. "Did you need something?"

She had no experience searching guests' rooms and wouldn't you know she'd run into trouble the very first time. She felt cross-examined. Tried and found guilty. And darn it, she hadn't done anything yet but open the door.

"I like to, ah, freshen up the bathrooms in the morning. Wipe down the sink. Make the bed. You know."

"Don't bother with mine, okay?"

Combined with his dark good looks, the smile Anthony flashed should have been romantic and distracting, but Jade felt oddly unaffected. Except for the guilt.

"Seriously, even if I'm out," he added. "I hate having my stuff moved. I promise I'm very neat, and you won't regret it."

As soon as Anthony was out of sight, Jade busied herself with making the bed, in case he popped right back in. While she did that, she looked around the room. She needed an article of clothing, something Mason had worn but not washed, and—didn't it just figure?—he turned out to be a guy who didn't throw his laundry in the nearest corner. Not so much as a pair of socks, which she was sure he wouldn't miss. After all, how many people counted their dirty socks when they packed up to go home?

She got down on her hands and knees and looked

under the bed, under the upholstered chairs, under everything, because the only alternative was to go through the drawers and his luggage, and if either of them walked in while she was doing that, it'd be impossible to explain. As would locking the door while she worked.

Turned out, Mason was the kind of guest who filled the bottom dresser drawer with two-day-old, drunk-in, slept-in, getting-married castoffs. Jade wrinkled her nose, averted her face to lessen the odor of booze and smoke and sweat lest she pass out, and poked through the remnants of Mason's wedding day. Pants, jacket, shirt—all too bulky. As she came across his briefs, she wished she'd thought to dig around with a pencil instead of her fingers, because this just seemed *way* too personal.

"Yes!" she said when she finally located his socks, still damp from being out in the snow yesterday.

She stuffed one into the front pocket of her jeans, shoved the drawer closed, and quickly ran down the back stairs to the kitchen. She was on a step stool, tearing through cabinets, when Weezy stopped beside her, arms akimbo. Weezy seldom stopped moving, so it was cause to notice that she was in her coat and hat, wearing a scarf that looked like a fat blue tire around her neck.

"It was a present from my middle granddaughter," she said proudly. "I taught her to crochet. See you in the morning."

"Thanks, Weezy. You know, if it's too cold for you to go out tomorrow, I can feed the guests."

Jade always offered; Weezy always brushed off her thanks. "Don't be silly. I enjoy it. You need help finding something afore I go?"

Jade pointed at Mason's sock, now lying on the floor in a crumpled wad. "I need something to put that in."

Weezy drawled, "Washing machine might be good."

"I'm going to throw it in the river, so it needs to float." Jade explained everything, how burning the candle backward hadn't worked in time, her plan to banish Mason from Missouri. "I need his sock to float downstream. If I don't put it in something, it'll just snag on a stick and hang around forever."

"Bet that feels odd. Spending all that time like you did trying to find your man, and now you're working to send another one away."

"True. But trust me, it has to be done."

Weezy opened a drawer and offered up a tall Tupperware cup and lid. "How 'bout this? Maybe someone'll pull it out and toss it in the trash. Could be pretty ripe afore they see it, though, depending on how far south it goes. Hope they don't open it."

"Eww. I'll write a warning on the outside."

Jade had a special pen for occasions like this. Over generations, the family had acquired many mismatched table knives. Uncle Henry discarded the blades, reworked the silver handles into beautiful ink pens, and charmed them for magical work. Jade used hers to print PENSACOLA on a piece of paper and dropped it into the cup—as long as she was sending Mason away, she might as well aim for his home. In went the sock and Banishing Powder. Once the lid was secure, she used an indelible marker to print DO NOT OPEN on the outside and, just for kicks, below that she drew a skull and crossbones.

Now, to give it a proper send-off.

Warm in a long, midnight blue wool cape, Jade walked out to the backyard, through snow that had been heavily tracked by both Mason and deer. Mystic Manor was situated on top of a bluff, and as usual, it was breezy. She stood still for a long, calming moment, lifted her chin, and let the cold wind blow away any lingering negativity.

Feeling free and reenergized, she added a few rocks to the cup to weight it against the wind. It'd take a good, hard throw to ensure that it safely cleared snags on the bluff, railroad tracks at the very bottom, a few feet of shore beyond, and ice along the edge. It wouldn't do to have it hang up anywhere; Mason might never leave.

Under any other circumstances, that wouldn't be a bad thing. He hadn't been around long enough for her to see the positive inner qualities she'd wished for, but as successful as her spell work was, there was no doubt he had them.

Still, he had to go.

Her stiletto heels dug into the snow like ski poles, anchoring her as she knew they would, but still, after practicing with a couple snowballs, it was clear that she needed a better plan. She tried again, using a snowshoe as a launching pad, swinging it like a tennis racket so she'd get more range. By the third try, she was confident that Mason soon would be on his way.

There was enough energy and intent behind the whole process of getting this spell ready that no words were necessary. Still, Jade closed her eyes and envisioned Mason walking in the front door at the end of the day, glowing because he'd gotten all the photos he needed, calling the airport, catching the next plane south. She'd even lend him her computer so he could print his ticket.

"So mote it be," she murmured, then bent down, intending to pick up the cup and launch it on its way.

"I thought snowball fights were hand-to-hand," Mason said.

Startled, Jade snapped up and wheeled around, having enough presence of mind to kick snow over the cup, though it didn't totally hide it.

Mason probably looked good in an unwrinkled tux—she'd never know—but without a doubt, he looked darn fine in jeans and boots. Mighty darn fine. It was a struggle to remember that was a bad thing. The strong pull she felt toward him weakened her focus.

Opting for offense, the better to steer her attention away from him and his attention away from the incriminating evidence on the ground, she said, "Don't *do* that!"

He appeared taken aback and came no closer. "What?"

"Don't sneak up on me."

"Sorry." He grinned, and Jade knew he hadn't noticed the cup at all. "Occupational hazard. I get better shots that way. Besides, the snow muffles everything."

"Funny, it crunches when I walk on it."

"Practice. Sometimes I lie still for hours on end and wait for them to come to me."

Jade wasn't altogether sure he was talking about birds.

Mason tipped his head toward her boots. "Careful you don't break your neck in those."

"You'd be surprised how stable a heel is when it's spiked into deep snow. I didn't hear the Jeep."

"Probably for all the church bells."

Jade cocked her head and listened to the silence.

Point taken, Mason said, "They're done now. What do they do—ring every hour on the hour?"

"West Bluff has a lot of churches." She didn't add that they had an equally large number of narrow-minded members because, who knew, maybe Mason was a Bible-toting regular himself, and the thought of offending him made her uncomfortable. "Was the road closed?"

"No, I had to come back for an extra memory card. And then I saw you out here lobbing snowballs with— Is that a snowshoe? Do people really walk on those?"

Jade barely nodded, moving into position to block his view of the cup as he stepped closer.

"I thought so. I just had to come out and ask. I

mean, my friends in Pensacola are never going to believe— Look out!"

He reached her so fast, Jade didn't have time to dart away.

"You almost tripped over this." He picked up the Tupperware.

Blast. Jade plucked it from his hand, relieved that his stolen sock wasn't out in the open between them. She tucked it safely beneath her cape.

"Something wrong?"

"It's, ah, delicate. I don't want the lid to pop off by accident."

"Really?"

Mason looked so unconvinced, Jade simply said, "Mm-hm."

He studied her for a long moment, mostly in the vicinity of the split arm opening through which the cup had disappeared. He noted the snowshoe, the river valley to the east. Rubbing the back of his neck, he said, "Kind of a new twist on a message in a bottle, isn't it?"

Pretty good at putting two and two together, Jade thought. Even if he didn't come up with four, he was too close for comfort. *Smart*, just as she'd requested.

"It's an experiment," she said vaguely, leaving it at that.

Mason nodded slowly, then shrugged as if that made perfect sense, and if not, he was too polite to say so. "I've got a pretty good arm. You want me to throw it for you?"

Would the spell work if he threw his own sock in

the current? No reason why not. As a spell, it was foolproof, unless the spirits had other plans. They were always the unknown factor.

"You do want it in the river, right?" he asked. "You're not aiming for the train or anything?"

"The river."

Helpful, too. What was he doing? Working his way through her list?

Mason swung his right arm in broad circles, warming up. He held out his hand. "Well, come on, hand it over."

She'd look petulant if she refused. "You sure you can throw that far?"

"I have to audition?"

"I can get it pretty far with the snowshoe. What if you're no good?"

He chuckled at that, leading her to believe he was good at everything. She stifled a sudden urge to unbutton her cape and flap it to bring her temp down.

"Is this right?" he asked.

While she'd been wondering how good he was, he'd packed a snowball for her inspection.

"You never played in the snow?"

"Just long enough to learn it's cold, wet, and I don't like it."

She nodded at the snowball. "It's good."

Mason stepped closer to the precipice.

"It's a long way down," Jade cautioned. "One slip, and you'd better have a good swan dive."

He glanced over his shoulder. "You live up here, and you're afraid of heights?"

"No. Just landing."

Mason held her gaze with twinkling eyes that heated her up even more and made her think twice about sending him away. But of course she had to.

He wound up like a pitcher, all grace and strength and ease, in spite of the bulky parka and heavy boots. The snowball flew twice as far as anything she'd lobbed, so she handed over the Tupperware.

When he glanced at it, she said, "It's not polite to read other people's mail," and he smiled and didn't look any closer, just wound up again and threw it even farther than the snowball.

"That okay?" he asked, looking rather proud of himself as he brushed snow off his hands.

"Looks good from here, thanks." Time to break this off before she got herself in trouble. She pretended to feel the cold, shivering and stomping her feet as if to get warm.

Mason chuckled. "Yeah, that's how I've felt since the plane crossed over Atlanta."

He has a nice laugh, Jade decided. A strong smile, not perfectly symmetrical, but showing some character. Straight teeth. But it was his eyes that made her smile back, even when a little voice inside her said not to encourage him. But how could she help it? It wasn't the shade of unweathered steel that attracted her, but the way they sparkled as he tipped his head and focused all his attention on her.

"You'd better go in and warm up," he said.

As Jade shuffled through the snow and up the wooden porch steps, she felt Mason's gaze on her back. She didn't have to turn and look. In fact, she refused to turn and look. She knew.

She stomped her feet on the mat both to distract herself and to knock off the snow before opening the door.

"You'll let me know if it works?" Mason called out.

Jade lost the battle. She turned back to him, and couldn't help smiling when she said, "I promise, you'll be the first to know."

"What the hell?" Mason muttered.

He'd spent the day knocking around Clarksville and all stops in between, capturing images of eagles, both bald and golden, from different points. They were quite amazing, really. Once, for five whole minutes, he'd forgotten he was cold, and how turned on he'd been watching a woman launch snowballs at the river. A woman he was investigating, and not for romantic reasons.

Between stops, he'd collected information on Mystic Manor. He had to be out and about to establish his cover anyway, so he talked to antique shop owners, waitresses at small cafés and tearooms, and local shop owners who liked to chat and knew the area well enough to make recommendations. And what had he learned? That brochures on Mystic Manor were virtually nonexistent, so how did Jade attract enough business to stay in business? That many claimed the property was haunted, cursed, or something equally unkind, while others smiled warmly and said nice things about Jade and her parents, how they'd helped them or a family member in the past. Though when asked for specifics, there was a lot of hemming and hawing, and no one would say how exactly.

He'd finished his day by returning to Mystic Manor with more questions than answers, no new information about the missing husband, and now *this*.

He leaned closer and peered intently at the notebook computer sitting on the small table in Anthony's room. Sure enough, that was Jade on the monitor, crawling around his room on her hands and knees. Not that he was surprised to discover she'd been in his room. Guilty people had a habit of being where they weren't supposed to be.

One thing for sure, he no longer thought this assignment was designed solely to keep his mind off recent relationship issues.

"That's nothing," Anthony said.

"It gets worse?"

"What's wrong with your voice?"

"Throat's scratchy," Mason said quietly, demonstrating an onset of laryngitis to go with it. He needed palm trees and sunshine and waves lapping on a sandy beach. He'd never before given a second thought to his neighbors' colorful flowers, but suddenly he missed them.

"Keep watching," Anthony said, gesturing toward the screen.

Mason shot his partner a glance, hoping the camera hadn't caught him flirting with Jade the night before. Keeping in mind that Anthony was still a little put out over the bartender non-incident, he made sure there wasn't an ounce of accusation in his tone when he asked, "Since when do you wire my room?"

Anthony grinned broadly. "Hey, a guy's gotta test new equipment."

Mason elected not to expound on the legal concept of expectation of privacy. Instead he folded his arms, taking extra care to hide just how interesting he thought Jade's cute tush was, poking up in the air as she crawled along the side of his bed, peering underneath. Black jeans hugged her rear and thighs like a glove. And if she continued to wear boots with stiletto heels on a daily basis, he was going to have a helluva time keeping his mind on business.

"I installed mine last night, yours this morning while you ate breakfast," Anthony said.

Mason relaxed a bit, that fear put to rest.

"You're looking better today." Anthony leaned close and sniffed. "Smell better, too. You been eating oranges?"

"It's the soap."

"Yeah? Which one smelled like that?"

"Luck Soap." Mason shrugged. "Figured it couldn't hurt. How about you? What'd you use?"

"Scorpio."

"I'd rather have luck than scorpions."

"It doesn't mean scorpions. It's for people with their suns in Scorpio. Forget it. You know what? You don't look better after all. You want a refresher on Jade's background?"

"Admit it, you're just mad about the bartender."

"Forget the bartender."

"Believe me, I'd like to."

"Are you ready now?"

"Shoot."

"Don't tempt me." Anthony consulted his notes. "Jade's twenty-eight. Local girl, as you know. Attended one year of college in Columbia, Missouri. At nineteen, she began Mystic Manor Botanicals. Which is a good thing, because when her parents divorced and decided to leave the house to her instead of fighting over it, it was heavily in debt, and she was able to show the IRS that she had a chance at turning it around. At twenty, she started the B&B. Now that we've seen how much she charges, I understand. Sort of.

"At twenty-one, she married our good friend, the missing Doug Stockard, whom she met in college. Kept her name; family tradition from way back. A year later, he disappeared. No children. She didn't do much the first year after that, but then she beefed up the business, put Mystic Manor in the black, and even has a nice nest egg."

"So she doesn't need the death benefit," Mason said.

"Would've come in real handy six years ago, though."

"No other family?"

"There's an uncle somewhere. I'm looking into that. Her in-laws live in Hannibal, both on disability. Her husband's brother lives with them, no visible means of support."

Mason was taking it all in, filing it away to take

out and examine later when he didn't have something as interesting as Jade to look at. Crawling across the screen, her hair tumbled forward, long, dark curls spilling over her neck and shoulders, trailing onto the carpet, getting in her way. She flicked it back absently with her hand. At one point, a long spiral caught on her pale yellow sweater, and if she'd been in this room, he couldn't have stopped himself from reaching out and putting it right.

"You all right?" Anthony asked.

"Fine. Why?"

"Well, if we'd just come up from a dive, I'd think you look like you have the bends."

"Hm." Mason shrugged. "Must be the cold. Is she active in the community?"

Anthony studied him a moment longer before letting it go. "I talked to some of the residents." He blew out an exasperated breath.

"Let me guess. Shady reputation?"

"A mixed bag, let me tell you, and strong feelings all around. Have you heard the church bells?"

"Kind of hard to miss them." They brought back warm memories of childhood summers, when he and his brothers and sisters had lived behind a church and had the whole playground to themselves, except on Sundays.

"You sure you're okay?" Anthony asked. "Now you're grinning kind of goofy."

"I'm fine. Go on."

Anthony didn't look convinced, but he continued. "There's Group A: church ladies who aren't too happy when someone turns up her nose at joining a congregation. They don't even care which congregation, just pick one. And not just Jade, but Annie, as well. Group B, on the other hand, likes Jade because she's ecology-minded and eagle-friendly. When I told them I was working on an article on the birds wintering over here, they were eager to talk to me."

Mason nearly groaned in envy. "What'd you do—sit in a toasty warm McDonald's? Drink hot coffee all day?"

"West Bluff doesn't have a McDonald's. No fast-food places."

"At all?"

"*Nada*. There's more. When I mentioned that I'm staying here, at Mystic Manor, the dynamics got really complicated. I got a lot of those square-shouldered, we're-a-small-town-don't-mess-with-one-of-ours looks. You know the one I mean. But then there were the others. Group C. Swear to God, Mase, they moved away so fast, I expected them to whip out wooden crosses."

Anthony shivered at the run-ins he'd had. Mason wouldn't have been surprised to see him suddenly cross himself.

"I'll get out again tomorrow, but I thought it was best I back off for a while. I also made contact with the other two stakeout teams. We divided up the work, so there aren't three strangers in town suddenly asking questions."

"Good idea. Hey, you should talk to Weezy. She won't run away."

Anthony grinned broadly. "Energetic little thing, isn't she? Good cook, too."

"Yeah, she could get paid for that anywhere. So why does she get up before dawn and cook breakfast for a couple of strangers for free?"

"Free, huh?" Anthony was quiet a moment, mentally reviewing items he'd learned since they'd begun the investigation. "Mystic Manor's solvent now. Jade should be able to pay her help."

"Weezy says it's voluntary. Says there's no way she'd accept pay for helping Jade, and that's a direct quote."

"Interesting. I heard that more than once today, how she's helped people. Maybe she's helping Stockard get rich." Anthony jotted a note to follow up.

Fascinated by Jade's activities on-screen, Mason continued to observe her quadrupedal path through his room. "Maybe she's checking for dust bunnies."

"Uh-huh. Keep watching."

Within seconds, Jade was rummaging through his dresser drawers.

"What's next? My suitcase?"

"Keep watching."

"My *laundry*?"

Dumbfounded, Mason leaned closer to the screen and replayed the segment. From the way Jade scrunched up her face, it could be that she'd gone into his room to find the source of a terrible odor and finally located it, but he didn't think so. His jaw dropped when she stuffed his dirty sock into her pocket.

Probably the closest I'll get to being in her pants.

"Still think it's dust bunnies she's looking for?" Anthony drawled.

"When was this taken?"

"About thirty seconds after you turned out of the driveway this morning. Nice set of wheels, by the way."

"It was cold and rough and drafty," Mason griped, then grinned ruefully as he dropped into a chair. "And kept me out of the ditch more than once. Jade talked me into going to Clarksville today."

"Because?"

"I'm not sure exactly. Maybe because the road to the lock and dam is low on the snowplow's to-do list. I checked; she was right about that." He related everything he'd learned out of town, then indicated the playback. "But after seeing this, I'm thinking maybe she wanted me off the premises for a good long while. When I came back for a memory card, I caught her throwing Tupperware off the bluff into the river."

Anthony's brow shot up. "Evidence?"

"I don't think she was unhappy with the product."

"How big was it?"

"Tall cup, twelve to sixteen ounce capacity. Sealed, so it'd float. Skull and crossbones drawn on it, which brings up another item. According to Weezy, Jade grows poisonous plants in the conservatory."

"Think that's a ruse for ones the DEA would be interested in?"

"Possibly. But why float them downriver?"

Mason rubbed the back of his neck, knowing he

was about to suggest crossing the line in a big way, but rationalizing that surely the plain view doctrine covered indoor, public areas of a B&B.

"How many cameras do you have?" he asked.

"I'll go into Hannibal and get more."

Mason glanced at Jade's image one final time, looking forward to reviewing new footage of her shenanigans at the end of each day. "Can you send copies to my computer as you get them?"

"No problem."

He looked forward to viewing them in private.

Chapter 6

You say you're staying up at Mystic Manor?"

The local hardware store was long and narrow, with rough wood floors. It smelled of sawdust, old metal parts, and oil.

Anthony had stopped in to ask about a map of the area. It was one of his favorite gambits in a small town where everyone knew everyone else. After that, he generally hung around, letting people get used to him. It never took long before someone turned to him, and said, "You're new in town."

Once Mystic Manor was mentioned, he was practically home free.

"Big place for one woman," he said, steering the conversation toward the Delarue family and friends. He discreetly switched on the digital recorder he carried. Later he'd send a highlighted copy to Mason's computer.

First guy to bite was gray, stoop-shouldered, and in no apparent hurry to do whatever it was people did when they retired and bought a business to keep from being bored.

"Worked on the heating system there once, don'tcha know?" the owner said. "Long time ago. Miz Delarue's grandfather was alive at the time. Yessir, called me up from St. Louis to work on it. Took forever. Dang near needed a set of blueprints to keep everything straight and find my way around. Found one, too. On a wall in a bedroom. Don't that beat all?

"Loved the town and came back here to retire, don'tcha know? Didn't see too much of the old man after that. Not that he was antisocial or anything. A lot of the Delarues kept to themselves. Like the one who lives there now. Jade, is it? I think that's right. She was in here last month ordering wallpaper, don'tcha know? She keeps pretty much to herself.

"Seems odd for a B&B owner, don'tcha think?"

Anthony glanced at the display of bird feeders, both hanging and pole-mounted. "Do you know if Mystic Manor has a feeder?"

"Yep. But she won't take to you feeding them birds just anything."

Anthony looked in the different bins, unable to identify anything except sunflower seeds. "She's particular, huh?"

"Well, I guess you oughta know, seeing's how she's

letting you stay there. You people have to pass some sort of written test or something?"

"Us people?" Anthony asked.

"You'n your friend."

"No, no test," he said slowly, trying to figure out where this was going. "My partner and I just blew through her front door when it was snowing."

"Huh! And she let you stay? Now this here's what she bought when she was in to order wallpaper." He scooped ten pounds of seeds into a brown bag and stapled it shut. "My cousin came into town last year, and she wouldn't let him stay there. Said he had to have an *ad*vance reservation, even though she was empty at the time. Seems odd for a B&B owner, don'tcha think?"

"Mm, it's toasty in here," Annie said as she poked her head around the doorjamb the next afternoon.

She was one of the few people Jade allowed in the drying room, and for good reason. This was the heart of her craft. The spicy-sweet fragrance of frankincense, burned daily for months and then years to bring their men home, still lingered.

This was the room that held the family grimoires, the books of remedies and spells they'd pored over after their husbands disappeared. It was the only time she, Courtney, and Jade had worked hand in hand. For months, they'd tried every spell, old and new, designed to relocate people, pets, objects. No method of divination had gone untried. They'd gotten discouraged after so much effort expended over such a long period, their own spirits flagged, and as the effort drained their energy, they'd finally had to taper off. Nothing could work without energy.

Directly across from the deep entry arch was a stone fireplace that never sat cold, not even in the middle of summer. It must have seen more duty in its lifetime than all the fireplaces in the county put together. Presently, the black cauldron in it was hanging above a low flame, its contents rising to a gentle boil. The mantel held two white tapers, both burning, each with a remnant of black ribbon tied around it.

Annie was always awed by this old house, all the history, all the memories. Over generations, the drying room had accumulated many tools of the trade: a variety of mortars and pestles; nonmetallic mixing bowls, pans, spoons, funnels; censers; jars, most with cork stoppers; and on and on. More than once, Jade had donated a no-longer-used item to someone who would value and appreciate it. It was how Annie had acquired her first cauldron.

Jade's hands were buried in a bowl of herbs, oils, and tragacanth glue, mixing it to a stiff, doughy texture. She'd been at it a while; hundreds of incense cones lined the table, drying on waxed paper.

Annie stepped across the threshold, moving around, checking shelves and baskets and bundles of herbs drying overhead to see what was new. She'd give anything to be half as good at the Craft as Jade. A quarter as good. No, make that one-tenth. Jade was her role model. Jade kept telling her she needed to believe in herself more, but shoot, all Annie's spells except the candle ones kept blowing up in her face, so how was she supposed to believe in herself? Maybe the spirits didn't *want* her doing anything but candles. Even the Delarues, as good at spellcasting as they were, had to bow to what the spirits wanted.

There was one thing she could do well, though.

"I brought you something. It should help." She pulled a silk pouch out of her purse and, from that, extracted a black seven-knob candle, one knob to be burned for each day of a seven-day banishing spell.

"Oh, Annie, that's wonderful!"

"I made it with the right intention, but of course you'll add your own. Inscribe each knob with Mason's name, then do what you do best."

"I'd better use symbols since he's staying in the house. I'll start it right after I finish up here." Jade tipped her head first to one side, then the other, stretching her neck.

"Have you been in here all day?" Annie asked with concern.

"Since about three."

She knew Jade meant A.M. "You know, of all people, you have the ability to whip up a sleeping potion."

"Grandma said . . ."

"I know, I know, spare me," Annie said with a chuckle. "'Everything will come right when you find the right man.' Sometimes I wonder if she was making a prediction or casting a spell."

"It suits me to be up at night. I get a lot done."

Jade's hair had come loose and was in danger of falling into the sticky mess, so Annie stepped behind her and retied the narrow ribbon holding it back. "You still believe it? Even though you couldn't sleep when Doug was here either?"

Jade grinned over her shoulder. "You're trying to give me advice again."

"If I were trying to give you advice, I'd remind you of one of the first things you taught me: that the spirits sometimes block our energy for a reason, or work against it, even, to give us what's best for us. So maybe we're not supposed to know what happened to the guys. Not yet anyway."

"Thank you, Alanna."

Annie shrugged it off good-naturedly. She used Jade's office to bang out the syndicated *Dear Alanna* advice column that she penned under someone else's household name. All very hush-hush to anyone outside their circle of friends. She'd fallen into the job with a bit of luck and a well-timed spell that actually had worked. If everyone in town thought she was a lazy do-nothing with no visible means of support other than selling a few candles, so be it. She had food on the table and a roof over her head.

"There's a letter I'd like to run by you when you have time," she said. "I know what I want to say, but I'd like your take on it."

"Now is fine."

Annie pulled the copy out of her back pocket and unfolded it.

Dear Alanna,

*Recently I invited my best friend and her hus-
band to stay with me while they were in town
looking for a new home. I know they love their
little dogs to pieces, but I was totally shocked
when they showed up at my door with them. I
have a small home, and she knows I have allergies, but she never even asked if it was okay. She
just said they'd bathed them in special shampoo
and everything would be fine. It wasn't. I had
to use my inhaler around the clock. She's my
best friend in the whole world and I wouldn't
hurt her feelings for anything, but what can
I do to keep this from happening when they
come back to close on the house?*

Annie refolded the letter. "So what would you
say?"

"Before or after I told her to grow a spine and stand
up for herself?"

"Yeah, that's kind of what I thought. But my editor's been telling me to tone it down."

Jade's jaw dropped. "But that's why people like
Dear Alanna. 'Tone it down' isn't in her vocabulary."

Movement outside the window caught their attention, Annie's especially.

"Jumpy," Jade commented.

"You should see the dog lurking around in the
woods by my house."

"Lurking?"

"Darn thing's as big as a black bear. Annoys the cat no end."

"This is awfully bad weather for someone's pet to be out."

"Pet? Think Cujo on steroids."

The glass panes were original and a little wavy, but Annie was able to make out the scowl on Mason's face as he trudged through snow, camera in hand. She had to fan herself; grumpy or not, he was still a hottie.

"I see he's still here."

Jade hummed, but the true meaning of that hum was as yet indecipherable. "The weather's certainly cooperating—for me. From the looks of him, he won't last much longer."

"For a guy who just got dumped, he sure has thrown himself into his work." Annie watched Mason pause to photograph bright red cardinals crowding around the feeder. "I don't know, me, I think I'd have to spend a week in bed first."

"Maybe his ex told him she was carrying another man's child."

"No! He said that?"

"Lyle told me. Mason's probably feeling lucky to break up sooner rather than later. Or," Jade mused as she watched Mason raise his camera, "maybe photographing eagles soothes a troubled soul."

Annie observed her friend. As an eagle soared from the river valley and up over the bluff, right over his head, Mason's scowl softened. He raised his camera halfway, but then his mouth fell open, and he forgot to take a picture. He tracked the eagle, gazing at it intently, and as he did so, Jade's actions mirrored his, only she didn't have the excuse that she was watching one of nature's most awesome creatures. Though Mason was pretty awesome.

It wasn't the cursory glance of a host toward a guest. It wasn't even the calculating glance of a witch looking for any signs that her reversal spell was working. Instead, it was the watchful eye of a woman staring at a man whose every movement caught her attention and held it far longer than necessary.

"Earth to Jade."

"Hm? Oh, sorry. I was, umm, calculating the next mixture. This is Business Incense. For a guy in Colorado."

"You know," Annie began slowly, treading her way carefully. "There's a reason I'm good at giving advice."

"Yeah?" Jade said absently, forming more cones.

"I'm good at reading people."

"Uh-huh."

Annie leaned close, lowering her voice. "Your mind may be telling you to get rid of him, but the rest of you is screaming, 'I'm tired of being alone. Come help me sleep.'"

Jade's laugh sounded false. "Don't be silly."

"I might not be as gifted or practiced as you, girlfriend, but silly, I'm not."

"I'm telling you—"

"Yeah? What have you done to get rid of him today?"

Jade inclined her head toward a small plastic bag lying to the side. "Cotton balls, soaked in Banishing Oil. One for his coat pocket. The others . . . I'm thinking his camera bag and inside his pillowcase."

"Oh." Maybe she'd read Jade wrong. "That ought to cover every minute of his day, I guess. What about the other one?"

"Anthony? They're partners. If one goes, they should both go, right? So I've made enough for him, too. If something doesn't work, and I mean *fast*, I'm going to have to start putting things away around here."

That puzzled Annie. The only messy room in the entire house was the office. "You're going to clean house?"

"Good grief, no." Jade's laugh was momentary, then she was all serious again. "Mason's a professional, right? With a camera. All I need is for the inside of Mystic Manor to end up in a coffee table book on eagles. I already locked up my parents' room, but there's so much of me in plain sight everywhere else, so much of what I do, things I don't want to reveal to just anyone and everyone—"

"Especially not the saints of West Bluff," Annie finished dryly.

"Exactly."

The majority of religious residents were rather paranoid about anything outside their parameters.

To the casual guest going in or out of the house, Mystic Manor's pentacles were just a few stars, as unobtrusive as dentil molding, purely part of the architectural charm. The original Delarues wanted them for protection, of course, but at the same time, they didn't want to scream, "Here we are, come burn us." Family baggage like that got handed down. From the cradle, Jade had been taught to be circumspect.

Photographs of Mystic Manor, published in a big, glossy book, lying open on a coffee table to be perused, would jump out and scream *witch*. Pentacles were embedded in the glass in the front door. A huge one was carved into the stone floor of the conservatory. A book like that in the hands of West Bluff residents, many generations of whom had heard rumors about the Delarues, would be all the proof they needed to further ostracize Jade.

Oh, Jade wouldn't mind for herself so much. Annie admired her strength that way. But she wanted to have a child and raise her at Mystic Manor, the same as she had been, to carry on traditions of the Craft. She wanted her to go to school in and be a part of the community.

What she didn't want was for her to go to the first day of kindergarten and get a pointy black hat slapped on her head.

Worse, over the years, the city limits had expanded to include Mystic Manor. Witchcraft, astrology, psychic readings, tarot, and everything else deemed non-Christian by those in power, was illegal within the city limits. Jade regularly cast protection spells to guard against intolerant people who would wish her harm, but Annie worried about her getting closed down, maybe run out.

"Correct me if I'm wrong," Annie said, "but aren't you the one who always says, 'Cast a spell and leave it be'?"

Jade sighed. "Yes."

"Then why are you supplementing with cotton balls and Banishing Oil?"

"Because it's not working fast enough."

"And the candles on the mantel?"

"One represents me, the other, Mason. The cut ribbon between them is symbolic of cutting the tie that binds."

They were both staring out the window again, but only Jade jumped when Mason suddenly turned and stared right back.

"Did you notice he shaved?" Jade mused aloud. "Good thing I don't have neighbors living right on top of me. They'd be running over here for autographs."

Mason's hand waved about in the air, miming a request to join them.

"It's about time," Jade said, nodding in agreement. "See? Cast a spell and leave it be. He wants to come in and tell me good-bye."

Not *us*, Annie noted with interest. *Me*. Showed where Jade's thoughts were, and if it was that obvious to her, a mere mortal, then she doubted Jade's good-riddance-Mason spells were packing much punch with the spirits.

Annie didn't want to be in the way. She uttered a hasty farewell, rushed out the deep arch, through the conservatory and into the kitchen, where she ran into

Mason struggling with frozen bootlaces and growling about the weather.

She tossed one end of her pink scarf over her shoulder. "You don't like a little snow?"

"A *little*?" He shivered inside his parka and grumbled. "When's it warm up around here? How long's it take all that to melt?"

"It's just a few inches. Six to eight at the most."

"I saw a foot and a half."

Annie chuckled. "Yeah, maybe where the snowplow pushed it. Anyway, the kids love it."

Mason's laugh was colder than ice. "Little monsters. They run up and down those slopes at the speed of light! I'm always a half second from falling on my ass. What're their mothers thinking? They should keep them inside. Being out in record lows can't be healthy for them."

His run of grouchiness tickled Annie's sense of humor. "What record lows? It's almost thirty."

The disgusted look he shot her was colder.

"You should come back in the summer. It's pretty then." That would be all right. Fair. His free will to do so then, because Jade's spell was for *now*.

If Mason came back in the summer, Jade would have no reason to send him away.

Standing outside the door to the conservatory, all Mason could see through clear and etched leaded glass was an inviting collage of light and green. It was doubly welcome after being loaded down with two cameras, a pair of binoculars, several layers of clothes, a tripod, a camera bag, and having spent hours tramping through white death.

Snowdrifts; as a concept, they sounded innocent enough. Maybe even pretty. In reality, they were sneaky sons of bitches, lying in wait for unsuspecting photographers generally looking the opposite direction, *up*. All in all, he'd rather take his chances with a shark.

The closer he got to the conservatory, the warmer the ambient temperature beckoning him forward.

He'd avoided this wing so far only because it was exactly that, a separate wing. It seemed private, even though Weezy'd said otherwise, and considering that he had his own secrets to keep, he didn't want to appear to be a nosy guest and arouse suspicion if there was any chance he'd be caught in the act. But now Jade had waved him in.

All of his senses came alive as he pushed through the double doors. Humid, earthy aroma of rich soil. Every shade of green imaginable. Twittering black-and-yellow finches.

"Holy shit. I didn't know you could grow a jungle inside a house," he said, momentarily distracted from the splendor by Jade, waiting just inside. Waiting for him.

What the hell—why not just admit that she aroused him more than Brenda and her two predecessors put together, all of whom had tried to rush him into marriage? There was nothing wrong in getting turned on. Jade was a sexy woman; he was healthy. If he got any healthier, he wouldn't be able to walk.

He quickly forgot that he was fighting a cold and short on sleep, that he'd spent hours snooping through Mystic Manor in the middle of the night. The kitchen drawers were safe another day, as Jade had been up, too, and he'd had to be content with searching the attic.

"I thought the eagles were awesome, but this . . ."

Finally, a warm spot in the midst of all the snow. Mason circled a few paces, corralling his libido, looking up, around, all around.

"This is like stepping into the tropics. All it needs is a surf— Wait, is that a waterfall I hear? How big *is* this?"

It felt right. It smelled right. But son of a bitch, there were at least a dozen tall cabinets set into the stone walls, between windows. If he was going to black bag this area—and he was—he'd have to be creative. One way in, one way out, probably Jade's favorite area. Already it was his.

"I took a sketching class last year," he improvised, raising his camera, snapping off a dozen pictures, constantly moving, changing angles, catching a few shots of Jade. The heat, while welcome, made him sleepy after being out in the cold, and he struggled against a yawn. "Would you mind if I come in sometime and practice? All these leaves, the shapes, the textures."

"There's a hook in the wall if you want to take off your jacket," Jade said.

"I'm fine, thanks."

"Are you losing your voice?"

"'Fraid so."

"Sore throat?"

"Not so far."

"Um, Mason? I'd appreciate it if you don't take photographs inside," she said nicely.

"Oh. Sure." He shut off his camera with a boyish, been-caught grin, one of a small but effective repertoire. "Secret plants?"

"Secret house," she shot back mysteriously.

No lie there. Last night in the attic, Mason had discovered that when one family, such as the Delarues, lived in a house for over 130 years and never moved, there was little incentive to throw away anything. But really, they should have. A lock of hair was a simple memento. Same with a favorite doll. But when the doll was wax and hidden in a dusty trunk, with human hair glued to its head and a pin stuck in its gut, come on, somebody was up to something.

He knew very little about voodoo or anything like it. The doll hadn't looked like him, but even though it was meant for someone else, would he start getting sick simply because he'd looked at it? Professional or not, if he started throwing up or running to the john, he was outta there for good.

There was more. Saving photographs of the family pet was okay, but this family saved the damn pet! He'd nearly had a heart attack when he'd opened a box and found a black cat. A real one, stuffed, back arched, tail up, its neck circled with a jeweled collar. His suspicions were confirmed when he opened a brittle diary and read how this particular familiar had assisted in magic rituals.

Did Jade know that one or more of her ancestors had practiced witchcraft? Should he be worried?

Nah. Witches didn't come in stiletto heels and fuzzy sweaters, green with white snowflakes today. Besides, all that stuff had been packed away forever.

Had any other Delarue spouses mysteriously disappeared?

He should check out more of the conservatory while he had the chance, especially the poisonous corner.

"That *is* a waterfall I hear," he declared. He craned his neck this way and that, searching for the path that would lead him to it, as excited over the discovery as he was eager to take care of business.

"You'll get overheated back there with your coat on," Jade warned.

"Me?" Mason did a double take, but she looked perfectly serious. "No way. Sounds like heaven."

"Okay, but the paramedics hate it when people pass out in the back. They charge double."

It was almost worth shedding his coat just to see what the heck she was up to, but he only unzipped it. He had naturally broad shoulders and he worked out regularly, but come on, she couldn't be so sex-starved that she'd make up excuses to get him out of his clothes.

He *wished*.

"This way?" he asked.

Jade helpfully pointed to the left, and Mason set off along the meandering flagstones. While he should have wanted to be alone so he could photograph the plants and check them out later, he was, in fact, inordinately happy to hear Jade following him. Sneakers would have softened her steps; that *tap tap* could only be made by tiny heels on stone. Eventually the tapping was drowned out by the splash of cascading water.

It wasn't a huge fall by any standards, but indoors, it was pretty magnificent. Taller than he, nestled beneath a canopy of trees, it slipped over the edges of dark rocks and tumbled into a shallow pool. A turtle lurched off a boulder and swam away, following the pond as it narrowed and meandered through verdant vegetation.

Anthony had joked that this area might be used for orgies. Mason was rapidly approaching critical condition, a romp for two in mind.

It was out of the question of course. He was a professional. He was here to work. But he couldn't be arrested for fantasizing about Jade, himself, and the rock ledge. He could cushion it with the very coat she'd wanted him to leave behind.

Jade bumped into him when he stopped, though it hadn't been abrupt at all. Not so sudden that she had to catch herself by putting her hand on his hip. Call him nuts, but first she tried to get him out of his jacket and then she picked his pocket?

How could she possibly suspect he wasn't what he claimed? Not one single item had come with him that didn't support his cover. Except the Glock, but she hadn't seen that.

He turned and reached for her, as if to steady her on her feet. She jumped away quickly and remained at arm's length, affecting a wide-eyed, innocent look.

Mason wanted to put her at ease—he'd say the job demanded it, but that wasn't the half of it—so he revved up the boyish grin in preparation to say something clever and amusing. He was born knowing how to charm women, and in truth, he'd honed the skill until it was child's play for him to get information out of the most recalcitrant females.

"If I'd known this pond was here, I would've packed my snorkel and—"

He began all right, but then choked like never before in his experience. Whatever he'd been about to say was lost beneath the intensity of her gaze, the green of her eyes. He closed his mouth before he said something stupid, like how the color was a perfect match for the dark leaves all around them. Or how, if she kept it up, she'd stare a hole straight through him.

He could no longer blame this weakness where Jade was concerned on the Black Weekend. His head no longer pounded or threatened to split open at the slightest sound. His gut no longer roiled with every movement. Sweat no longer oozed out of his pores at ninety proof.

The first rule of investigative work was *never get involved*.

He was so close to breaking it. *Shattering* it.

"Are you all right?" Jade asked.

The way she was looking up at him, eyes full of

concern, Mason figured he hadn't blown it—not yet. He could cover his ass and claim he was feeling over-heated after all, but she might call 911. He had to do better.

"I, ah . . . just remembered. I was expecting a doc-ument, but I had trouble with my computer, and I was going to ask to borrow yours, but you weren't around at the time, so I went out and started taking pictures . . ."

He was babbling, but Jade didn't seem to notice. In fact, she looked inexplicably overjoyed when she said, "You want to borrow my computer?"

Was he professional or what? If that wasn't permis-sion to take a look at her files, he didn't know what was.

Chapter 7

ystic Manor. You're staying there? Nice place."

Anthony put his feet up on the bed and listened to the day's recording, thoughtful about what he'd heard in line at the grocery store. Not that he needed to buy snacks, but sometimes, if the line was long enough, people got bored and talked, like the guy who'd been behind him. He'd looked like a salesman, with carefully styled hair and a nice suit under a tailored topcoat.

"That Jade, she's some looker, isn't she? I thought about asking her out—who hasn't? But she never attends any of the Friday night singles functions, and I got to wondering why she doesn't go to church. Because she's done something wrong, and she's going to hell anyway, so why bother?

"I'm not saying she did. Just wondering.

"Far as I know, none of the others have asked her out either. Though maybe they did. Maybe she turned them down, and they just don't want anyone to know.

"Know why, don't you? You heard about her husband disappearing? Newspaper reporter's been going around interviewing people. Told her what I know. You'll want to keep your eye open for that.

"Guy like you, traveling all the time, you have enough insurance? You know, if you travel out of network and get sick or injured, your out-of-pocket expenses can get out of hand. Here's my card. Stop by the office later, and we'll talk."

When it became evident that Mason and his partner weren't leaving by midweek, Jade invited them to dinner for a little extra oomph on the riddance scale. What she wouldn't give for a fourth-quarter moon, the absolute best phase for getting rid of anything, including men who were there by mistake.

The dining room looked bare since she'd removed every Craft-related knickknack, right down to the hand-carved trivets made by Great-uncle Norman, each displaying a different Nordic rune.

To minimize the bare spots, she dialed down the chandelier and wall sconces. She'd find something else later to fill in the spots. Maybe her old snowman collection. She'd packed it away when she'd gotten engaged to Doug because it seemed the grown-up thing to do at the time.

An eye-popping bouquet of long-stemmed calla lilies and blue iris had arrived a short while ago. Jade placed that on the table, off to the side where it wouldn't block anyone's view.

She set two tall white tapers on the long rectangular table and was just about to cast a spell on the salt when the phone rang. Ordinarily she wouldn't interrupt a spell to answer it, but it was Courtney, the men would be here any minute, and Jade had a huge favor to ask.

"Hello," she answered quickly, eager to skip the social niceties and get right to the point.

"He's dead," Courtney said, just as abruptly.

"Mason?" Jade clutched the back of a chair, frightened that she'd made another mistake, a horrible one this time, but only because she'd just been thinking about him.

"Don't be a smart-ass," Courtney said, her dry tone dispelling Jade's qualms. "This is the part where you always say, 'He could be missing,' and I always say, 'A week is missing. A month is missing. Six years is dead. And if he isn't dead, I'm going to kill him when he gets home.' And then I could tell you the news."

Jade regained her composure and said, "Guess you're not worried about anyone listening in."

"Yeah, the mystery is *sooo* current."

"Let's pretend we said all that then. Just go ahead and give me the news."

"It's official. We're widows. The county's issued presumptive death certificates on all three of them. The insurance company will cut the checks any day now."

"How're you doing?"

Courtney's sigh was a little ragged. "I always thought I'd know if he was dead. You know, feel it somehow. I still don't. I get a feeling of foul play, but not death. And I realize—it happens every day in this country right?—we might never know."

"Six years." Jade slid onto one of the chairs, lost in thought.

When had she finally given up on Doug's return? Or finding out what had happened to him? She'd never cared about the red tape, the legal delays in pronouncing him finally, irrevocably deceased. For a long time, if it wasn't official, she didn't have to believe it.

"I guess it's not as if we didn't expect this."

"Time moves on," Courtney agreed.

"You ever wonder how comes none of us has? Moved on, I mean. We're all young, intelligent, healthy, self-supporting—"

"Simple. Men are nervous as cats around intelligent, self-supporting, pretty women who can't explain what happened to their husbands. Anyway, that's all I have. You called earlier?"

Jade blinked, rapidly switching gears back to the reason she'd called in the first place. "I have a huge favor to ask."

Most friends would say, *Sure, anything.* But there was one thing Courtney didn't like to do at all, not for anyone. Not even for herself. Especially not since the guys went missing.

"What?" she asked warily.

Jade explained the whole Pierce Brosnan-clone mess. "Please, Courtney, I wouldn't ask if it wasn't really important. I'm not having any luck putting things right on my own. I can make a talisman, but . . ." She left the suggestion hanging in the air.

"But you want me to make one for you."

"Mine aren't as powerful as yours. You know I wouldn't ask if I weren't desperate, but the longer Mason's here, the harder it'll be to break this spell."

"I don't know," Courtney said, drawing it out, stalling for time. "Seems like you could repel the man if you try hard enough. Don't brush your teeth until he leaves."

"*Ew-ww.*"

"That's the point. If you're afraid he's falling for you, make yourself less approachable."

"I have limits." She had a pair of sweats she saved for wallpapering and painting. A man'd have to be insane to think she was desirable in those.

"So do I," Courtney said.

"Please?" Jade wasn't above begging, not for something this important.

"Well . . ." Courtney fell silent, and Jade realized she was going to have to pay up big time. "Valentine's Day is coming up. Jazzy's teacher's looking for volunteers to make treats for the class party."

That wasn't so bad. "I can bake."

Jazzy wasn't six yet; Courtney'd found out she was pregnant just days after the guys had gone missing.

"You have to stick to tradition, though," Courtney warned. "Pink hearts. Cupids with arrows, not broomsticks. No moons, no stars."

She was going to do it!

"Thankyouthankyouthankyou," Jade said in one breath, giddy with relief. If she'd been religious, she would've crossed herself. "No moons, no stars; I'll try to contain myself."

"You *will* contain yourself."

"Okay, promise. Hey, listen, I just heard the clone come in the back door. I have to go."

"I'll drop it by soon."

Time was growing short as Jade hung up; Mason could stroll into the dining room at any moment. With a talisman from Courtney, she probably didn't need to do any more spell work, but she was just stubborn and proud enough to want to fix her mistake on her own. Besides, anything she learned in the process would go in her grimoire, to be passed down to future generations.

The sooner she got rid of Mason, the sooner she could get to work on finding the right man to help with that. She'd rerun the same spell later, only with an escape clause.

Jade slid the saltshaker into position in front of the candles and laid her hand on it while she affirmed her intention, the same one she'd use on the wine and honey, too, just to be sure Mason got a dose.

"The moon isn't perfect and neither am I,
But we must quickly fix what has gone awry.

Salt you are and salt you'll stay;
When consumed by my mistake, you'll send him away."

Mason was ravenous. Something about freezing his ass off all week to support his cover made him hungry, and the inside of Mystic Manor smelled as if a gourmet chef had moved into the kitchen and worked since dawn.

When he entered the richly paneled dining room, he couldn't help thinking Jade looked just as tasty. Which was saying a lot considering his teeth were still chattering, and there was a crackling fire calling him toward the hearth. Just looking at her standing beside the table in curve-hugging jeans and a peach sweater heated something else he thought he'd frozen off.

"Wonderful," he said with his new raspy voice, trying not to drool.

"It's a great room, isn't it?" Jade said, misunderstanding his comment. Just as well. "My ancestors settled here at the beginning of the lumber boom. This room's walnut."

His ancestors had been indecisive, moving from New York to Wisconsin, Kansas, and finally Florida. For his money, they could've skipped Plymouth Rock and landed in the Caribbean.

Mason made a beeline for the fire to warm parts resistant to Jade, like his knees. "I hope you didn't go to too much trouble. Anthony can't make it. He says to tell you he's sorry."

Jade gazed at the table set for three, looking perplexed for just a moment before she lit the candles and regained her cheerful composure. "I guess it'll still work."

"Sorry. Did we mess you up?"

"Ah, I was thinking it's a big table for just the two of us, but we'll be fine."

"Nice flowers."

The card was right in front of him, though tucked deep inside the greenery, and he peeked when Jade wasn't looking. Not that he expected it to say, "Miss you, babe, can't wait until we're together again. Love, your other half," but he had to check. He certainly didn't expect what he read, either.

Many thanks, Lyle and Brenda.

"Pretty, aren't they?" Jade said.

Mason coughed. It was that or stammer out something stupid.

Lyle and Brenda? How—?

They knew Jade? She knew them?

"You okay?"

Mason felt as if he'd just been harpooned. He thumped his chest, making sure his heart was still beating. "There, that's better."

Jade wiped her palms on her jeans, drawing his eyes to unsafe territory. "Cold settling in your chest?"

"Mm. Yeah. My throat, too."

"Try this."

She poured from a china teapot and handed him the warm cup. Mason had always thought tea, like cream soup, was for women. He'd been wrong about the soup. And this brew smelled really, really good.

He leaned over the cup for a closer sniff, and the aroma alone began to soothe his scratchy throat.

Just shoot me now, he thought, because he'd do almost anything to stop a cold. Hell, if she'd poisoned the tea, and he fell over dead, at least his throat wouldn't hurt. And there would be flowers.

"I'll be right back with our dinner."

Mason watched Jade leave the room, one second wondering if her ass was really that nice or if it was just the jeans, the next realizing that once she was out of sight, the room felt lonely. And . . . something else. Bare—that was it. There'd been knickknacks when he'd walked through the other day. Now the mantel was empty. Nail heads stuck out of the paneling, nothing on them. The built-in china cabinet displayed several patterns, but if he wasn't mistaken—and he rarely was—a whole set of goblets was missing.

He couldn't afford to linger by the fire. Jade was getting their meal, and since he oughtn't risk eating food that he didn't know came out of the same pot, he hurried through the butler's panty and into the kitchen in time to see her ladle up both servings.

"Can I help?" he offered, a sharp eye on the lookout for any extraneous herb sprinkling, especially over his bowl. Just because he wanted to strip her naked and throw her down in front of the fire didn't mean he'd completely lost his senses. "Mm, what is that?"

"Stew."

"I've had stew. It never smelled like that." He stepped behind Jade for a closer whiff. He was drawn closer, involuntarily, until he was leaning over her shoulder, and it wasn't because dinner smelled so good.

"It's the herbs," Jade said, drawing him back to the subject of food.

"Can I help?"

"Sure, you can bring the honey and wine. They're on that counter over there, by the candle."

Mason gathered up the wine bottle and the jar of honey, then, because they were leaving the room, he leaned forward to blow out the candle. It was an unusual one, black knobs stacked one on the other, with scratches on the side.

"I hope you like it," Jade said. "It's locally— No!"

Mason snapped upright. "What?"

"Never blow out a candle. You should snuff it, or pinch it."

"*Why?*"

"It's bad luck."

"Oh. I used to blow Brenda's out all the time."

"Who's Brenda?"

"The woman who jilted me Saturday night."

"Well, see?"

Mason didn't know what he'd expected. Sympathy, maybe? Surprise? Heightened sexual interest in salving his wounded psyche?—that would be nice. At the rate he was striking out, he didn't have to worry about Anthony finding out there was a part of him that wanted to get very involved with this subject.

"Yeah, she ran off with some guy named Lyle." Giving her time to, oh, *come clean* and say, "That's funny, I know a couple named Lyle and Brenda, too," he set the wine down briefly, licked his fingers, and reached for the candle.

"Let it burn."

She was so smooth with her lies, he'd lost count. "But we won't be in the room."

"It's in a safe spot. Don't worry about it."

It did look safe, sitting on a heavy glass plate far from anything flammable, so Mason let it be and followed Jade to the dining room, still mulling over her nonreaction to his getting left at the altar three days ago. Women didn't ignore a situation like that. Women commiserated with a jilted man. They couldn't help it; they were built that way. They wanted to comfort— or find out what he'd done wrong so they could bawl him out a second time.

Jade was doing neither, and for one very simple reason. If she knew Lyle and Brenda, she knew about him. Yeah, sure, there *could* be another couple with the same names, but if it was all that innocent, she wouldn't be keeping that to herself, now would she? So why were they thanking her?

Maybe if he kept filling her wineglass and kept her talking, she'd eventually let something slip. Not admirable, but eminently effective.

As they set their bowls on the table, he said, "Don't take this the wrong way, but why do women like candles so much?"

"I think a better question is why do you dislike them so much? Would you like me to take them off?"

If she removed them, she'd probably turn up the lights, dispelling the cozy atmosphere, and then she wouldn't be as likely to confide in him. Or she'd see the gash on his cheek and move in to check it out, and while he wanted her close, oh man, did he ever, he knew his limits.

"They're fine. Leave them."

"You're sure? Because that took quite a while for you to decide."

She grinned, slow and cute, glancing at him from beneath lowered lashes as she rotated one of the candles until it was just so. Probably giving him time to change his mind.

"I was just thinking you need some of this tea, too, but you don't have a cup." Mason opened the china cabinet and set a matching one out for her. Only after she'd had a couple sips did he savor the warm liquid on his throat and murmur, "Oh, man, that feels good."

"I made enough so you can reheat another cup before you go to bed."

"How come herbalists don't put doctors out of business?"

"Doctors have their place." Jade took the tiniest little taste of her stew and made a face. "I forgot to salt it," she said, and pushed the saltshaker across the table toward him.

Mason looked at it. He looked at her. "Ladies first."

"But you're company."

"My mother would roll over in her grave."

"Well, we couldn't have that, could we?"

She gave in and went first, which would have eased Mason's mind except that when she was finished, she set the shaker close to him. And then pushed it even closer.

He debated whether a person could successfully poison the salt below the top layer and not suffer any ill effects from the first helping. Impossible, of course, so he bit the bullet and seasoned his stew while Jade stared at every grain that fell into his bowl. He scooped up a bite, then with it halfway to his mouth, he paused.

Jade's gaze was riveted to his spoon.

"Aren't you going to eat?" he asked.

"Oh," she said, flustered. She looked as if she might have blushed, but in this light, who could tell? "Yes! I'm famished. I hope you like it."

After his first bite, Mason said, "Mm, you were right. Here," and, in challenge, pushed the biscuits toward her.

She took one and bit into it, so then he didn't know what to think, except that maybe he was letting his imagination run wild. But he'd staked out some real scumbags since he'd partnered with Anthony five years ago. People were capable of anything. You never could tell; some of them masqueraded as cute and innocent for years before they were caught.

"Do you like honey? It's local. It's very good." She pushed the jar toward him. "The wine's local, too."

The table was starting to look unbalanced with everything getting shoved his way. He got in the last word, though, as he filled her glass. "Ladies first."

"You're a guest."

"Please. My mother raised me to be a perfect gentleman, and if you make me go first, then all that hard work goes to waste."

Jade's eyes twinkled in the candlelight as she held up her glass and said, "Can't argue with that. To mothers who raise perfect gentlemen."

As sound a plan as it was to get Jade tipsy and talking, she didn't cooperate. Mason figured she knew what he had in mind. She must. That or she wasn't much of a drinker. But the food and the fire and the ambiance was working anyway, and they talked about everything else through dinner, then lingered over a dark chocolate mousse. To-die-for mousse.

He hoped that wasn't literal, but what a way to go. Beautiful, intelligent woman. Low lighting. Crackling fire.

"Are there herbs in this, too?" he asked, trying to get his mind out of the romance gutter.

Sharing a cozy meal with Jade should not make him long for bouncing a little girl of his own on his knee. Chrissakes, he'd never sat with Brenda and imagined having a child with her. He just missed Lily, that's all. In his rush to leave the church, he hadn't said good-bye. He should call her.

Damn. Jade licked her spoon like a kid licked a brownie mix spatula, only a helluva lot sexier. Mason's mouth went dry as he watched every little dart of her tongue, up the spoon, down the spoon, around the friggin' spoon, until it was clean, even though she had half a bowl left. After that demonstration of dexterity—he was a hundred percent certain that Jade had no idea how sexy she was, or how provocative, which just made her hotter—he had no recourse but to chug the rest of his wine.

Willpower—ha! He'd sworn off alcohol two days ago, and if he didn't drink himself senseless in the next thirty seconds, he wasn't going to be responsible for reaching across the table and doing a little licking of his own.

He was startled back to sensible when Jade said, "No herbs. Why?"

"Oh, just wondering."

"It's dark chocolate, though. Dark's healthy."

"Do you hear bells?" For once, it wasn't church bells.

Jade was already scooting her chair away from the table. "It's the side door."

On the opposite side of the house from the conservatory, Mason recalled, the door led out to a porte cochère, where carriages used to pause so guests could enter in bad weather without getting wet.

"You expecting guests?" he asked.

"Enjoy the fire as long as you like. Just close the screen when you leave the room, okay?"

Now she was ignoring questions. It beat lying. Maybe.

"You're not coming back?"

"Sometimes these things take a while." She dropped her napkin beside her bowl.

Eyeing her half-eaten dessert, Mason asked, "Anything I can do?"

"Do and you die." She obviously thought the temptation was too much, because after the slightest hesitation, she grabbed the bowl and took it with her.

Mason felt dismissed—utterly, completely dismissed. The possibility of her words being a threat never entered his mind, because the thought of Jade's rushing off to let her husband in sobered him up faster than throwing him out bare-ass naked into the snow.

But, hell, her husband wouldn't ring the bell. So who would? She'd gone to answer the door as if used to receiving visitors on cold, dark nights on the outskirts of West Bluff. What was so important?

Mason didn't know if Anthony had a camera on the side door, so he followed quietly, keeping his distance. By the time he'd parked himself behind a tall potted tree in the unlit music room adjoining the side foyer, Jade was deep in conversation with the two men she'd let inside. Big guys, rough-looking. Insulated coveralls, insulated coats, heavy boots.

Weight and hair color could change. Eyeglasses and beards came and went. But both these guys were too tall to be the dead husband. That didn't mean they didn't know anything about where he was, though, so Mason listened closely.

"Nathan, you didn't drive all the way from Keokuk tonight, did you?" Jade said, sounding surprised at what they'd told her so far.

She should be, if she meant Keokuk, Iowa. It wasn't as if there was a four-lane highway connecting it to West Bluff. What they had was two lanes, unlit, with snow, black ice, and headlight-crazed deer.

Nudged by his buddy, Nathan whipped off his bright orange knitted hat, turning it over and over in his hands. "Sure did, Miz Delarue. Uncle Noah's been tellin' me to come here for days, but my wife, she wouldn't have none of it. But now she's got herself all worked up over this, and with her expectin' and all . . ."

Jade appeared comfortable with their arriving after dark, and apparently they knew someone in common. Mason made a note to ask Anthony who Noah was.

"The first for-sale sign kinda got lost, if you know what I mean," Nathan continued to explain his plight.

Mason wasn't sure he caught that accurately, because the guy had a speech impediment, most likely due to the wad of tobacco he kept working. Mason leaned as close as he dared, risking personal eye injury from a tree branch.

"But the owner, he come along and put another one up. He'll get suspicious if I keep takin' 'em down. But we got no other place to live, so what'm I 'spose to do? So Uncle Noah, he says you can help."

"You don't have a rental agreement?"

"No, ma'am."

"So, can you? Help?" the other guy said, softer but easier to understand. Then he whipped his hat off, too.

"I believe so," Jade said.

Mason could tell she was thinking. About what, he didn't know. How to approach their landlord and talk him out of selling his rental property? Ways to convince a local motel to put the family up until they could find an apartment? Anthony hadn't relayed any pertinent background on Jade that gave a clue as to how she could be of assistance.

"Thank you, ma'am. I 'preciate it, really I do."

"Why don't you two go on into the dining room while I put something together?" Jade said warmly. "There's a nice fire in there. Mason'll show you the way."

Mason froze behind the tree. He just flat out quit breathing. Jade was talking in general terms; she couldn't *know* he was there.

She turned and stared straight at him. "Okay, Mason?"

He figured he had about fifteen seconds to come up with an explanation good enough to keep from getting booted out on his ass.

Chapter 8

Mason had been *eavesdropping*? What was up with that?

The night air was cool and crisp. It was snowing again, big fluffy flakes that fell softly, refreshing the landscape with a fresh coat of white.

Jade pulled up the hood on her cape, tugging it with unnecessary force, a sure sign that Mason was getting to her, and she didn't mean just the fact that he was still at Mystic Manor. Sure, he was an eaves-dropping slug, but, silly her, she hadn't specified that she wanted someone who didn't listen in on things that were none of his business. She'd asked for a man who lit her fire, and Mason did that so well, just thinking about the way he looked at her had her sucking in freezing air to cool her insides.

Focus.

She should be thinking ahead to helping Nathan and his family keep their home a little longer, not self-combusting over the clone.

Better yet, she should be watching where she was going. The five-day-old moon was obscured by clouds, leaving only a few dim landscape lights to illuminate the walk to the drive. There were icy patches, even though Henry had shoveled it recently. Her uncle could go for days without being seen, but he seldom missed a chance to do something sweet like this. He didn't like to make a big deal about helping with the house and property, or packaging up her botanical shipments in the dead of night. Henry pretty much kept to himself.

Jade paused on the walk, taking a moment to face the bluff's edge, to let the breeze wash over her and blow away the negativity she was harboring over the eavesdropping incident.

Refreshed, she moved on.

The spell she was preparing to do for Nathan didn't require much in the line of supplies, not for her part. Witchcraft was all about intention and belief and trust. She could buy his family extra time as long as they believed in what she did. But people expected a witch to pull out a wand and cast a magic circle for every little thing, and if they didn't get what they expected, their negative energy worked against her efforts. So, draped from Jade's shoulder was her trusty carryall bag, holding an athame, a wand, and a few other items she "needed" to take with her tonight.

Well, everything except her mind. *That* should

have been thinking ahead, forming an ironclad, impossible-to-misunderstand intention, but in spite of every effort to stay clearly focused, a certain sexy eagle photographer kept winging into her thoughts.

And her line of sight. As if she'd conjured him up, she found Mason leaning against the front of the Jeep, shivering in spite of his hat, his coat, and the engine rumbling beneath his butt.

"Want some company?" he asked.

No way he could continue to stay at Mystic Manor, not with clients arriving for the weekend. Having him on the premises made it easier to tuck banishing herbs into his pillowcase, but for what they were paying, her clients expected privacy and discretion with their spells, not an outsider lurking behind potted trees. Mason would have to be gone by Friday afternoon.

Geez, that was tomorrow already. She'd give him until evening.

Jade intended to glare at him, the better to get across the message that he'd done wrong and wasn't welcome here, but shoot, how was she supposed to look at Pierce Brosnan, even a faux one, and not melt at his feet? Mason was every bit as sexy, in spite of the shivering. Maybe more so, because he was here, in person, someone she could talk to and touch—if she wanted, not that she intended to touch, no, no, that wouldn't be right at all.

How could she give the cold shoulder to a man who appreciated eagles and put up with weather conditions he hated, just to bring them to life in glossy pictures for thousands to enjoy?

How could she ignore a guy who didn't press for more information on why she'd been lobbing Tupperware off the bluff—and one marked with a skull and crossbones, at that? Who volunteered his strong right arm to help, and was comfortable enough in his own skin to joke about auditioning for pitching services?

Mason didn't look the least bit uncomfortable beneath her gaze, so Jade figured she'd failed horribly with the glare. Odd, but if she didn't know he was a photographer, she would have guessed he'd lean toward a more exciting career, maybe even something dangerous. He just had that look about him, the way he held himself, always so poised and yet ready for more. *Anticipating* more.

He levered himself away from the Jeep and walked toward her in no apparent hurry, seemingly oblivious to snowflakes accumulating on his dark collar and across his broad shoulders.

She felt like lingering as well, but Nathan and his brother were in their truck, idling in the porte cochère, waiting for her.

"Keokuk's an hour each way," Mason said, his voice stronger since he'd had a healthy dose of her tea.

She shouldn't be analyzing his voice. She should go. Right now. Just get in the Jeep and go.

He cocked his head to one side, seeming concerned about the long drive she had ahead of her. "Maybe more. There could snowy patches on the road. Black ice."

With a deep breath of frigid air to stiffen her resolve, Jade opened the driver's door and tossed her bag inside, careful to remain silent until she could trust herself not to gush and give the impression he was welcome to stay.

"I came out to shovel the walk," he said. "Somebody beat me to it."

Persistent devil, especially considering how much he hated the cold and snow.

"So I thought I'd warm the Jeep for you."

See, just one more reason to like him. It had been parked in the unattached garage, but would've been freezing just the same.

He stopped in front of her, looking protective and, again, just a little bit fierce. "You don't know these guys."

"And you know that how?"

His grin said, *Okay, so I was bad. But I admit it, and I'm a helluva cute guy, so you'll forgive me.*

And her heart, blast it, did a little pitter-patter and made her think, *How can I be mad at him when it's my fault he's here?*

"If a guy was at my sister's house for dinner," he said, "and two strangers showed up after dark and asked her to drive off with them, I'd sure want him to check them out."

"Sure, you say that now, but—"

"Hell." He blew out a breath. "I'd want him to pack a gun and go with her."

Mason wasn't looking at her the way a man looks at his sister, but Jade wasn't about to say so, because then he might move toward her with a line like, *Yeah, how'm I looking at you?* or *I was speaking hypotheti-*

cally, but now that you mention it . . . She wanted him thinking about leaving, not putting the moves on her.

Instead, Mason took her by the shoulders and softly kissed her cheek, his breath warm and moist on her skin, and damn, in spite of all her resolve to the contrary, she didn't have the wherewithal to spring away from him.

She felt herself nuzzle against him. He lingered close until she whispered, "What's that for?"

"Dinner." His voice was gruff, and not all attributable to his cold. He put two inches of space between them.

Jade gazed up into his eyes, trying to read him, but it was too dark, and he was too close.

Then, probably because she'd been too surprised to lurch away from him, he slowly pulled her back toward him, closing the gap until he held her firmly against his chest. He was tall and big, and had no trouble wrapping his arms around her in a warm, secure hold that made her remember what she'd been missing, and would take weeks to forget.

When he oh-so-slowly relaxed his hug, still allowing only a couple inches of space between them, she whispered, "What was that for?"

"To warm you up."

She wanted to lie and say it didn't work. She wanted him to embrace her again, only longer, so she'd have more to remember. So she could dream of how close she'd come to getting it right.

She didn't dare. Instead, she forced herself to ease out of his arms, to turn away and stumble into the Jeep and slide behind the wheel.

The problem with continuously developing and casting spells to get rid of Mason was that she was always aware of him. Always evaluating his face and mood—did he look or sound unhappy enough to leave? Everything he said and did. Was he any closer to leaving? Or further from it?

As a result, Mason was always on her mind, and she noticed the little things about him that ordinarily might have passed unnoticed. The little smiles tugging at the corners of his mouth when he was amused by something she said or did. The heat in his eyes, which he quickly masked whenever she turned to him, but not quickly enough. The promising sizzle behind a kiss on the cheek.

Fine. He could stay until Saturday morning, but that was it.

Nathan's truck died. Jade experienced a surge of incredible joy, thinking she might not have to leave just yet. Quickly followed by the voice of reason and Nathan's truck revving back to life.

Jade saw Mason's brow crease. He probably was thinking, *Great, their truck'll die out on the road, she'll give them a lift and never be seen again.*

"Don't worry about them," Jade said. "They're Noah's nephews."

"And Noah is?"

"The milkman. He's practically family." And had been ever since her grandmother had helped his father with a Steady Business spell. When Weezy was in the kitchen, Noah left extra yogurt in the refrigerator and hung out for an hour. "Watch your toes."

She shut the door and threw the Jeep into gear, not leaving any time for Mason to talk his way into the passenger seat. She was often called out at odd hours to help someone. Even if she wanted to talk to Mason on the long drive, she sure didn't want him seeing what she did once she got there. Noah wouldn't have told his nephews she was a witch if he didn't know they could be trusted; no one she knew could vouch for Mason.

It was miles before Jade felt the cold again, miles during which she drove like a robot, following Nathan's taillights through the snowy night as she re-lived Mason's kiss, the touch of his lips, the pull of his arms. The heat in his eyes.

Focus.

She didn't need to go to Nathan's place, not technically. She could have handed the sea salt-valerian mix to him with explicit instructions on what to do, but his family's situation hit a little too close to home. When Mystic Manor had been heavily in debt, there'd been talk about the town taking it over, charging tourists to traipse through her historic house and touch her furniture and carry negative energy into her conservatory while a local guide explained how riverboat shipping and a lumber boom had made a tycoon of Sebastian Delarue. While her living situation and Nathan's were vastly different, the underlying stress was the same. It had been a difficult time for her, and she hadn't been pregnant, like Nathan's wife. For all concerned, Jade wanted to handle this herself and get it done quickly.

As the air inside the Jeep warmed, Jade noticed a hint of oranges and nutmeg. She grinned to herself, then, because she knew Mason, who'd driven it for hours today, had chosen Luck Soap from the assortment in his bathroom.

So, he felt he needed a little luck, hm? A little extra help from the spirits to move his book smoothly through publishing channels, perhaps?

He didn't have to know the soap was charmed to make it work; all he had to do was think about what kind of luck he wanted while he was washing, and, barring any negative thoughts he might harbor to the contrary, the energy he sent out would do the rest.

Funny he'd passed over the Love Soap. Maybe he'd given up on love for a while. Not that she could blame him, after being dumped like that.

Darn, there I go again, thinking about Mason.

Jade wiggled in her seat, mentally grounding herself to the here and now, concentrating on the swoosh of the wipers and the winding road instead of Mason in the shower with her soap. Geez, she hoped he didn't think it was "Get Lucky" Soap. The way he looked at her sometimes, it was as if he wanted to gobble her up.

How could a kiss demand so much attention when no lips had met? That was silly. Ridiculous.

It was all the more special because it was different. She reached up and touched her cheek, right where Mason's lips had caressed her skin. She wanted him to do it again, only mouth to mouth next time.

Good grief, she was in big trouble. No wonder he

hadn't left Mystic Manor! The powerful attraction between them had overridden all her attempts to send him back. No spell to get rid of him was going to work if she wasn't a hundred percent behind it. The same went for the one she planned to do for Nathan.

She smacked the steering wheel with her palm. *Concentrate!* She could figure out what to do about Mason later. Right now, Nathan needed her help.

This spell was a simple one, but her intention had to be clear. She'd sprinkle the sea salt-valerian mixture in a circle around the rental, focusing on how Nathan's family needed that house to live in a while longer. It would buy extra time for them to find another place. A nicer place. With lower rent. Closer to his job. In a nice neighborhood.

Now she was cooking!

The perfect number of bedrooms and bathrooms to fit their situation. Low maintenance. Good, safe appliances. No hidden detriments or dangers. A perfect place for Nathan's wife to nest. That was a different spell. She had everything she needed for that one, too.

Maybe she could spend a *little* time thinking about Mason.

"Mystic Manor, huh?"

Anthony reviewed another recording, this one made at the local computer repair shop that afternoon. He always carried a busted laptop to break the ice. The tech had gone right to tapping buttons, bringing up screens that Anthony had no idea how to access.

"Buddy of mine used to live there. Five, six years

ago. No, a little more, I guess. Man, I sure miss him. Used to play poker together a couple times a month. You know, rotated where we played. But we never played there. Mm, this doesn't look so good.

"Lucky bastard. Never met anyone could win as often as he did. He even won my bird dog once. Dog never was the same after that. Slept for a week when I got him back, then woke up and looked at me kinda like, Oh, man, *you again*. Like he was depressed to be home or something.

"You met the old man yet?"

That caught Anthony's attention.

"Ah-hah! You've got spyware on here. I can fix it. Give me a day or two."

"So what excuse did you give Jade?" Anthony asked when Mason related the postdinner, potted-tree fiasco.

"Right then? Nothing. I froze, plain and simple."

Had Jade pressed, his only recourse might have been to pull out his Glock and shoot himself, but that would necessitate even more explanations, at which, apparently, he wasn't very adept.

He wouldn't be any better at explaining why he was in her closet at three in the morning. With her off at Nathan's, and Annie and Weezy not likely to pop in, he'd had the run of Mystic Manor all evening and into the night. He'd heard someone in the kitchen once, but since he hadn't seen anybody when he went to investigate, he blamed King Kong and counted himself lucky.

He'd searched every guest room; every box, tin, and

trunk; every closet, cabinet, and drawer on both floors, except for the conservatory, which he'd get to later.

Only one room had been locked, and it was a doozy. Talk about War of the Witches! Two altars stood on opposite sides of the blue room, and even though they both held candles, incense burners, and various small items, such as crystals, they couldn't have been more different. One was simply a scarf-covered dresser, without a speck of dust. The other was a marble-topped table, and who'd notice the dust on it with a crystal ball the size of a bowling ball sitting on the tabletop? Oh yeah, Jade knew she had witches in the family.

Clothes in the closet and drawers belonged to a man and a woman, and it definitely wasn't the room Jade had shared with her husband, then locked up when he went missing. All the sizes and styles were wrong.

Tables held bowls of salt. He'd have to get back on the internet and find out what that was about. Family photos covered the walls, along with a framed collage of Mystic Manor during various stages of construction. Not exactly the blueprints he'd heard about in Anthony's update, but maybe the old guy at the hardware store had embellished.

Nothing was revealed about Jade's missing husband, so Mason had moved on to her office. He spent a lot of time going through hanging folders, trying to discern what devious method she used for filing, only to throw up his hands and conclude there was none. After that, when a quick scan showed six hundred thousand files on one computer alone, filed by the same devious method, he installed wireless network adapters in both of them. With Jade's odd hours, and Annie and Weezy coming and going whenever they pleased, the only way he'd be able to examine those files thoroughly was from the privacy of his room.

And that had brought him to her room. Mason's flashlight lay on a shelf, and as he took a moment to rotate it toward a stack of shoeboxes, he caught a familiar smell. It wasn't the first time he'd smelled cigarette smoke in the house, but he'd yet to see anyone light up.

"Hey, Anthony, you smoking out there?"

Anthony was slouched on his tailbone on a chair. He'd kicked off his shoes and propped his feet on the windowsill on the far side of Jade's queen-size bed, keeping an eye on the driveway as he listened to snatches of conversation he'd recorded, sharing pertinent details with Mason after each one.

"Yeah, I took it up five minutes ago. Figured after thirty years of clean lungs, I owed myself a treat."

"You can't smell it?"

"No. I thought you had a cold."

Mason paused in surprise. "Hey. Wow."

"What?"

"Jade made me some tea. I guess it worked. My throat's better, too. Which reminds me, you need to send your mother some flowers."

"I do?"

He told Anthony about the bouquet from Lyle and Brenda.

"I'll do it first thing tomorrow," Anthony said. "If Lyle stopped in and chatted, I might get something, but if he just called it in, well . . ."

Mason checked his watch often, hoping Jade would be home soon, even if it meant he had to quit for the night, because the longer she was out with those two bozos, the more he worried about her safety.

"What do you know about Noah?"

"The milkman?" Anthony said. "Took over the business at fourteen when his father died. So, clear this up for me—you just walked out from behind the tree and led the guys into the dining room to enjoy the fire?"

"That's about it."

Bingo! Letters from the dead husband in a shoebox. Undated, so Mason had to read them. Stockard wasn't much of a writer, and it was easy to see these were written before Jade had married him.

He went through every shoebox. Lots of stiletto heels. Even strappy sandal ones; man, what he wouldn't give to see Jade in those and a short skirt. Thinking about her in the red pair made him forget he'd been awake since dawn.

"You couldn't come up with a reasonable excuse," Anthony said around a yawn, "because you always think you'll never get caught."

"Never have been."

"Until now. You'd better have a good story by the time she gets back."

"Nah, I covered my ass in the driveway. Told her, 'come on, a woman living alone in a relatively remote area, answering the door in the dark of night—what man wouldn't be concerned for your safety? If you were my sister, I'd want me to check out the guys at the door.' I think she bought it. Plus, I warmed up the Jeep for her."

"I don't know, Mase. You give a woman hours to mull over something like that, she's bound to come back angry."

"Anybody who loves chocolate as much as she does and leaves it behind to go help two strangers—which, by the way, is nuts; you have to try some of her mousse. Anyway, someone who can do that isn't the type to hold a grudge."

"You have to remember, this is a small town."

"Say, did you see who shoveled the walk?"

"I figured you did."

Mason leaned around the jamb and stared at Anthony.

"Right. What was I thinking?"

"We need a camera out there."

"I don't know about you, but if I were playing dead," Anthony said, "I wouldn't shovel my wife's walk."

"You might if you were in town to pick up a million dollars."

"Are you about done? I can hardly keep my eyes open."

Mason closed the lid on the red sandals and returned the box to the stack. "Do you mind? I'm being thorough."

"Yeah? What've you found? Hey, you're not trying on her bras and panties, are you?"

"Very funny."

Mason snooped through built-in drawers next, suddenly engrossed in trying *not* to picture Jade in silky lingerie. His fingers slipped through stacks of it, searching for anything below the skimpy items. Some slinky. Some lacy. All sexy. It was several minutes before he realized Anthony hadn't said anything.

"You still awake out there?"

"Yeah, just thinking. Is that why you didn't become a spy when you had the chance? You were afraid you'd freeze up like you did downstairs?"

"Hell no. Spies get sent places they don't want to go. Cold places." Mason shivered just thinking about it. "And they get shot at."

"You've been shot at."

"Yeah, but they were all amateurs."

"That's not it. You're a risk taker. Like scuba diving—most people go down to see fish; you're not happy unless you're exploring wrecks. And what you did in Jade's office—how are you going to explain networking cards in her computers?"

"There's enough wires under there to hold up a bridge. She'll never notice."

"But if she does."

"Then what's to say *I* put them there?" Mason pulled a pink-flowered hatbox off the topmost shelf, disturbing the layer of dust on the lid as little as possible as he lifted it off. "Hey, found something."

Anthony strolled over to the closet door. "Anything good? Knife with dried blood? Murder pact signed by all three women? Love letters dated last month?"

Mason spread the contents on the carpet, sorting through what was left behind when a husband disappears.

"Passport. Birthday cards. Anniversary cards. Wedding photos. Same guy as in the pictures scattered downstairs. Three guys, hunting, fishing, a boat. Nice boat. I could live on a boat like that."

"They owned it together."

"I guess so—a cruiser like that isn't cheap. What happened to it?"

"It was in their names; the husbands'. It sat on a lift for a year, then the wives leased it out. What else do we have?"

"Pocketknife. Yo-yo. Wedding band; too small to be his. High-school diploma. College diploma. Hey, wait." Mason fanned through birthday and anniversary cards, taking a closer look. "These are *to* him, mostly from Jade. Some are from his parents. This is the kind of stuff you save for somebody else, in case they come back. She didn't kill him."

He felt it in his bones, as sure of her as he was of his own name. He'd wanted to kiss her deeply by the Jeep. At the last minute, common sense had grabbed hold of him and steered him to safer territory. If there was any chance of enjoying Jade's arms around him, the gun had to go. Fortunately he was carrying the baby Glock and could move it to an ankle holster.

He fanned through the contents again. No love letters from Jade to Stockard. He couldn't believe she hadn't written any. Jade was a font of feelings, of emotions. A woman who'd love deeply and passionately and have no qualms about committing those feelings to ink.

The slimeball hadn't kept them. In that instant, Mason decided he didn't like Stockard. Dead or alive, didn't matter, even if the guy had met some untimely horrible fate and wasn't guilty of insurance fraud, he just plain didn't like him.

Stockard better hope he was dead, because if he was alive and had left Jade to think he was dead, to find out the man she'd loved hadn't loved her back, it'd take more than Anthony to hold Mason back from punching the guy out.

"Uh-oh."

"What uh-oh?" Mason stared at the splayed contents to see what he'd missed.

"Jade's back."

Mason began replacing items in the box methodically.

"*Really* back. As in she's in the house."

"Some lookout you are." Mason threw everything back into the hatbox, stuffed it back up on the shelf, and darted for the door. "Time for bed, Goldilocks."

"Don't go out there," Anthony whispered frantically. He dove deeper into the closet.

"I'm not staying in here. I'd snore and give myself away." Or Jade would undress in the closet, he'd whimper, and that'd give him away.

Mason could have made it out of the room in time, if not for King Kong blocking the door.

"Shoo," he whispered, waving his hands.

The dog didn't budge, just studied him with an expressionless gaze that could've been, *Oh, brother, another human for dinner* or *Hey, I'd better dispose of the idiot snooping through my mistress's belongings.*

Mason didn't think Jade would still be angry about the eavesdropping incident, but if she caught him in another compromising position, say, *her bedroom*, she'd throw him out for sure.

Unless she found the dog's teeth wrapped around his arm. *Yeah!* He could claim that he was in the hall, minding his own business, when the dog grabbed hold of him for no apparent reason and dragged him into her room. He was a huge dog. With big teeth. Not only would Jade buy it, she'd be too upset to suspect a little creative ass-covering.

"Here, boy. Nice dog. C'mere." Mason bent down to the dog's level.

Man, if the CIA could see him now.

Jade's cell phone rang, and she said, "Hi, Daddy," from a lot closer than he'd expected.

Mason checked over his shoulder to find the dog had disappeared. As covers went, it hadn't been a very good story, but it was all he'd had, and now it was gone.

"Think you'll make it later this month?" Jade asked, nearing the top of the stairs. In fact, Mason could see the top of her head.

He dove into the closet.

Chapter 9

Anthony huddled beneath a bottom row of Jade's soft sweaters as Mason barrel-rolled across the floor and crashed into him. He scooted against the wall, giving them more room to hide.

Mason sucked in his breath and said, "The light."

"I unscrewed the bulbs."

"Way to go."

"Hey, just because I don't like getting caught in a woman's closet doesn't mean I don't know what to do when I am."

They froze as Jade walked in, flicked the switch several times, and muttered a soft curse. They both breathed a sigh of relief that she didn't think, *Hm, what are the chances of two bulbs burning out at the same time?* and try tightening them.

She rummaged through the shelves, found what she wanted, and returned to the well-lit bedroom. Anthony peeked over Mason's shoulder and through the clothes just long enough to see Jade strip out of her sweater and bra and toss them onto the comforter. Not much left to the imagination. Not that he was interested, but he could tell by the stiff set of Mason's back that he was all eyes.

"See anything dangerous?" Anthony whispered, settling back and leaving the show to his partner. "A gun? A knife? Little vials of poison?"

Mason groaned, and muttered something about smooth skin and perfect breasts.

"Bet you're loving this," Anthony said, more than happy to goad his partner. "If she were that cute bartender you slept with, I'd be loving this."

"Oh for the love of— I didn't sleep with him."

"Has she taken off her jeans yet? I'll bet her naked legs look really long. Is she wearing skimpy little panties?"

Mason jabbed his elbow backward, connecting with Anthony's gut, but he was ready for it.

"I bet she'd look good in high-cut panties."

"Have you called him yet?"

"Who?"

"The bartender."

"Are you kidding? I was so busy keeping an eye on you so you didn't jump out the window that I never even got to talk to him."

"And he was very upset about it."

"He was?"

"I was drinking because Brenda jilted me. He was drinking because you ignored him."

"Damn." Anthony punched Mason in the kidney, "I knew I was right to be mad at you."

"So call him."

"Move forward."

"No. Why?" Mason asked.

"I want to kick you, and there's not enough room."

"Didn't I give you his number?"

"*What?*"

"I told him you said he was cute, and he gave it to me."

"You *told* him I said that? Really? What did he say?"

Mason groaned again and mimed banging his head on the floor. "He gave me his number, idiot."

"Where is it?"

"Will you shut up? All this talking's ruining the view."

Anthony slipped both hands around Mason's neck and squeezed.

Mason croaked, "I'll look for it."

She was in one piece, thank God.

Mason felt like throwing his arms around Jade and hugging her again, and not because she looked tired and was dragging in with her eyes half-open, because neither was true. She looked as fresh and mysterious as ever, and he was prevented from grabbing her and kissing her right this time only by Anthony's fingers sunk in his windpipe. Damn near killed his erection.

Smooth skin. High, perfect breasts. Man, oh, man, he could lie here for an hour with this view, if not for Anthony. But when Jade went into her bathroom, Anthony darted out, and after a moment Mason figured he, too, was better off taking his chances at escape.

King Kong was in the hall again, only this time Mason wasn't playing his game. He'd nearly slipped sideways past him when the dog lowered his head and came up between his legs. Not a good thing. Mason cupped himself for protection, too late. He ended up in a fetal position on the Oriental runner, with tears in his eyes.

"Mason?" Jade said from the doorway, sounding confused to find him there. She might have said more, but he wasn't hearing too well, and through his tears, he saw she'd gotten dressed.

When he could speak, he said, "I tripped over the dog."

"Uh-huh." She crouched beside him and felt his forehead.

"That's not what hurts."

"I can see that. But since there's no dog, I'm suspecting head injury."

Mason let go of himself and rolled onto his back so he didn't look so pathetic, though he still couldn't straighten his legs. "Maybe you have some wonderful home remedy?"

Jade's brow rose, even as her eyes dipped south. "An ice bag?"

"I was thinking herbs." *Hand-applied, please.*

"I think that was a four-hundred-level course."

"I could be your lab rat."

"What are you doing up anyway? It's after three. Don't tell me you were sleepwalking."

Her tone was light, but there was an undercurrent that warned him she wouldn't buy that overused cliché. No, he'd have to do better.

"That'd be right out of a one-star movie, wouldn't it?" he said, buying time to think.

"Yes. It would."

She waited, and he came up with, "I, ah, don't sleep."

"You don't sleep?"

"Nope," he said decisively, invoking another rule of investigative work: Choose a plausible cover and stick to it. "My laundry's piling up, so I thought I'd look around for a washer and dryer."

A smile spread across Jade's face then, lighting up the whole hall as she sat on the floor beside him, and it was very easy to imagine how wonderful life would be if he deserved that smile.

"Do you mind it?" she asked.

"Doing laundry?"

"Not sleeping."

"You get used to it after a while."

"It's terribly hard on most people's bodies. Unhealthy, in fact."

"I feel fine."

She snickered. "Yeah, you look it."

"I must be healthy." He pointed at his cheek. "Look, you can hardly see the cut anymore."

She rested her elbow on her thigh, chin on her palm, clearly comfortable as she tipped her head and studied him. "I've never known a man with insomnia."

"As opposed to women?" he joked, slowly rising until he was cross-legged on the rug, facing her. They had this whole huge house they could sit and visit in, but they stayed right where they were, and it felt intimate because there were no extraneous distractions, just each other.

"That's right. It runs in my family."

A sense of dread rose up and slammed Mason in the head. Ever cool and composed, though, he said, "Really?" and remembered another rule: Be flexible.

"Mm-hm," Jade hummed.

"Let me guess. You?"

"Personally, I find it great. I get so much more done than people who sleep all night. Don't you find that? Sure you do. That's why you're trying to do your wash in the middle of the night. And your eagle book—I'm sure you'll get it done in no time and move on to your next project."

Jade seemed overly happy about that, Mason thought.

"Washer and dryer are at the other end of the hall. Those double doors down there."

He'd already found those, of course. Aiming to withdraw more information, *any* information, he said, "Must be small to fit in there."

Jade's brow arched playfully. "You're planning on doing the blankets?"

"Just marveling at the plumbing it took to accomplish that."

He shut up while he was ahead. Though he wasn't sure he was ahead at all. There had to be a cellar somewhere; he still hadn't a clue how to get to it.

"Weezy's son-in-law's pretty handy," Jade said. "I'm glad we had this chat." Meaning she was done sitting in the middle of her hall, entertaining a man until he could walk again. "Because now that I know you don't sleep, I won't worry about disturbing you if I knock on your door in the middle of the night."

Yes, yes, *yes*. Mason pictured himself never sleeping again—not at Mystic Manor anyway—and in a good way. First thing in the morning, he was quitting this case. Anthony would understand. Well, no he wouldn't, but he'd be afraid his recently jilted partner would take to the bottle again if he got all bent out of shape about it, so he'd cut him some slack.

"UPS finally delivered the wallpaper I've been waiting for," Jade said. "I need to do your bathroom."

"No need to knock."

"I wouldn't think of going in without knocking first."

Was she grinning? Sure she was. The corner of her mouth was tipped up. Just a little. Enough to qualify as a grin. "Are you flirting with me?"

Jade jumped to her feet. "How about breakfast? I'm always famished after, ah, a long drive. Let's go cook up a banquet."

"I'm not all that hungry." Not for food anyway.

"Oh, but you have to eat something," Jade said. "I can't give you bad news on an empty stomach."

Mason looked wary. Jade needed to stand firm, to tell him he had to pack up and leave for the weekend, but the words weren't coming out.

He had insomnia, too! How perfect was that?

Her husband had been a light sleeper. Jade remembered tiptoeing around at night so she wouldn't disturb him. And unplugging the phone after ten o'clock so calls from her mother wouldn't wake him. Like Mason, Doug usually asked her not to leave when someone interrupted their dinner, but he generally had ulterior, husbandly motives and tried to make her feel guilty for neglecting him. He never once stayed up until she returned.

This was so different. Tonight, when she'd come in from the long, cold drive and found Mason still up, Jade had felt instantly warm, cozy inside and out, as if she'd finally come home to what she'd always wanted.

How could something be wrong when it felt this right?

True, he hadn't looked too good lying on the floor with his hands between his legs and his knees drawn up to his chest, but the point was, he'd been worried about her when she left, and he was up when she returned.

And now, poor baby, she was going to reward him by tossing him out into the cold.

She'd spent the entire drive home staring through

whooshing wipers, trying to get up the backbone to ask him to leave for the weekend. Trying to convince herself that the only reason she didn't want him to go was because, if he stayed, she could keep fresh Banishing Herbs hidden inside his pillow. That's how she was *supposed* to feel. But look at him, standing there like a kicked puppy, waiting for the bad news.

How could asking him to go be right when it felt this wrong?

She'd relit the knob candle in the kitchen on her way in. She was tempted to go back down and snuff it out. But she couldn't. She needed a moment, needed space between them to lessen the attraction, so instead of giving him the bad news right off, she said, "Just let me check my messages first," and ducked into her office.

Mason followed slowly. "The phone rang a lot right after you left."

Jade stared at her answering machine. "Six messages. That can't be good." She punched the PLAY button.

"Ms. Delarue, this is Fred Smith. I heard you're having a blizzard up there. Just hang on to my deposit, and we'll reschedule when it's warmer."

Jade punched ERASE. She should be ticked; she wasn't. "Good news, Mason. No bad news."

"I don't have to leave?"

"What are you, psychic?" He wasn't more than a foot behind her. She turned slowly, studying him to see whether he was guessing or knew more than she'd given him credit for.

The machine waited for no man and started on the next message. "Mrs. Delarue, this is Tricia Sherwood from *West Bluff News*. I'm calling to do a follow-up story on your husband. I'd like to schedule a time—"

Jade punched ERASE, noticing Mason's attention was now riveted on her machine.

"Mrs. Delarue, this is Tricia—"

ERASE. Jade used her vintage knife pen to jot Tricia Sherwood's name on a piece of plain brown paper; she'd do something special with that later.

"Mrs. Delarue—"

ERASE.

"Mrs.—"

ERASE.

"You're married?"

Mason sounded surprised and just a little bit worried. After all, Jade recalled, he'd gotten familiar with her in the driveway. A nice guy might be worried about the mystery husband coming home and knocking out a few teeth.

She debated whether to tell him her husband was away on business, but if Mason talked to anyone or read the newspaper, he'd soon know the truth anyway.

"Widowed," she said.

It was the first time she'd said it to someone who hadn't heard about the infamous West Bluff Widows, the first time she'd said it out loud since it became official. She had mixed feelings. Bad that it had to happen, of course; relieved that the slate was clear and she could move forward. Especially since Mason was standing close enough for her to feel his body heat, and if she were still married, she'd have no business feeling the things she was feeling now.

Lust for him, sure; look at him—what was not to lust over?

Like, definitely. He was easy to be around, and always had a twinkle in his eyes for her, which didn't hurt.

Attraction, oh yeah. But she'd covered that ground already.

"Sorry to hear that." Mason stepped away, rubbing the back of his neck like a man who'd stuck his foot in his mouth and didn't quite know how to extricate it gracefully. She had to hand it to him, though. He tried. "Not recently, I hope. I mean, Anthony and I practically barged in here, and if this isn't a good time, we can go."

Jade's heart skipped a beat. "Back to Florida?"

"No, we'd have to stay around here."

Damn. Couldn't have been that easy, could it?

"The book's going slower than I thought it would. I don't have the right pictures yet. More sunshine would be nice."

"Might as well stay here then."

Maybe if she let him think it was recent, he'd quit looking at her like a hungry wolf. Maybe then she could get a rein on her own libido.

"Doug's been gone six years," popped out before she could stop herself.

Surprise flickered across Mason's face, while Jade warred with herself over the implications of what she'd just said.

Why the heck does he have to look exactly like I specified?

It wasn't that she had to have a man who looked like Pierce Brosnan, but the fact that he did tied his arrival directly to her commingled spells, reminding her she'd made a mistake, and he wasn't fair game.

"The media's still interested after all this time?" he asked.

"It's a yearly thing." Jade closed her eyes and tried to picture him short, fat, and bald. It didn't work; she still liked him. She hadn't seen every quality she'd asked for yet, but so far he was right on the mark.

"You okay?" he asked.

Why the heck does he have to be so considerate?

Maybe if she did something to repulse him. Or offend him.

"Yearly? Like an anniversary? What was he, mayor or something important like that?"

Or scare him.

"No, nothing like that." Frustrated, determined, she blew out a breath and plunged ahead. "They just want to know where I buried the body."

Chapter 10

"ystic Manor? Say, we're sort of in the same business. Tricia Sherwood. You're working on a story about eagles, I'm working on a story about the owner."

The twentysomething reporter wore a black beret over short red hair, Anthony noted. He toyed with the idea of introducing her to Mason, just to get him out of his mood, especially when she asked if he was available.

Come to think of it, Mason's mood had picked up since they'd arrived. He'd seen and heard him flirting with Jade, a dangerous prospect, but on the other hand, he hadn't mentioned Aruba in, oh, *hours*, so he might not be a flight risk anymore.

"She's a widow, you know," Tricia said. "Next couple days, she's going to be a millionaire. You know if she's doing anything special to celebrate? Throwing a party? Inviting famous people? I always wanted to write for the society section, but nothing big ever happens here."

"Haven't heard about any party," Anthony said. "But it's not a story. It's research."

"Oh. Will it be a best seller? Maybe I should interview you now."

On second thought, Mason was doing just fine on his own.

Courtney strolled into Mystic Manor on Saturday morning to find Weezy holding court, cleaning, and cooking all at the same time. The atmosphere in the kitchen was bar-friendly, as usual when guests were in residence. Jade didn't mind, and Weezy and the clients seemed to love it.

Noah was standing at the open refrigerator, personally replacing aged dairy products with fresh. Not his job, but everyone in West Bluff knew the third-generation milkman had a thing for Weezy.

"Brought you a pound of fresh butter, Weezy."

"Good Lord, what'll I do with a whole pound?"

"Sour cream, too. I remember you make a mean stroganoff."

"Have you ever heard of cholesterol?"

"He thinks fiber protects him from cholesterol." Buzz, the mailman, ate over the sink so he wouldn't have to bother about coffee cake crumbs. When he saw Courtney come in, he held up the coffeepot with a question in his eyes.

"Oh, yes, please," Courtney gushed, hugging herself against the winter chill. She'd had enough of winter, the snow, the long, hard freeze. At least the sun was peeking out today.

Weezy plucked a recipe book off a shelf, muttering, "Butter, butter," as if it would help her find what she was looking for.

Then again, in this house, it might.

"I got aged cheddar, too. Five years. Can you imagine that with a good bottle of wine?"

"You delivering wine, too?" Weezy asked, her back to him as she turned pages.

Noah looked at her hopefully and said, "I could," but Weezy didn't pick up on it. Or if she did, she ignored it.

By the time Courtney'd peeled off her coat and all the winter accouterments that went with it, regulars plus one were in stitches over a story about one of Weezy's granddaughters, and a mug of hot coffee was waiting on the counter. She blew on it and sipped it, turned to the newbie sitting at the long plank table, and said, "Hi, I'm Courtney."

"Mason." He stood up and offered his hand; *very* impressive. Dead ringer for Brosnan, too. Damn, Jade was good.

The only thing Jade had ever wished for that she hadn't gotten, as far as Courtney knew anyway, was the safe return of their husbands. When the guys had gone missing, and the officials were doing their own search, she, Annie, and Jade had tried everything magical they could to find them. When they'd given up on that, Jade had cast spells for information on what had happened to them. Again, nothing. It was almost as if someone was working against her. But that was just silly. This anniversary thing had her imagination running wild.

It was one of the few times Courtney shook hands with someone where she wished she could read the vibes. Wouldn't it be great to know if someone was good or bad just by touching him? But *nooo*, she had to be stuck with the other side of the coin, leaving her vibes all over every gosh darn thing she touched.

"I'll bet people ask for your autograph a lot," Courtney said.

"I recognized him first," Buzz said.

"Did not," Noah objected.

They both whipped out fresh autographs, whereupon Courtney grinned at Mason and said, "You didn't."

"Can you believe he tried to lie his way out of it?" Noah stared at Mason and shook his head, as if to shame him.

Mason just grinned unapologetically and shrugged one shoulder, and Courtney thought if Jade didn't want him, she wouldn't mind talking to him for a while and see if he had an emotional block against single mothers.

"Someone just pulled in the driveway," Buzz announced, meaning he didn't recognize the car.

"Probably that damn reporter." Courtney rushed one last sip before she set her mug in the sink and prepared to get very busy. "She's been following me. If she comes to the door, don't answer it."

"You want us to take her out on the playground and give her a noogie?" Noah teased.

"Why don't you just slip her a . . . gift?" Weezy's glance in Mason's direction was fleeting.

"There's a thought," Courtney muttered. "Is Jade in the conservatory?"

"Try the study."

Courtney caught up to Jade going from room to room, pulling snowmen from a dusty box, placing them on shelves, hanging them on walls. It was an eclectic collection, from Old World to whimsical, figurines to needlework.

"Hey, these are cute." Courtney picked up a salt-and-pepper set, enchanted by their carrot noses and corncob pipes. "Did you get them at that little antique shop on Main?"

"You never saw them? They come with a story." Jade unwrapped a snowman ornament and set it in the china cabinet. "My great-great-great-grandmother Jade—I'm named for her, obviously—was married here, at Mystic Manor, in the dead of winter. There was a storm that evening, so they couldn't leave on their honeymoon, and guests had to stay over. The next morning, all the trees were dripping with icicles, which I'm sure was very beautiful, but that kind of got eclipsed by what the wedding party had done during the night."

"Wait. Is this some kind of legend or something?"

"I read it in her diary."

"Okay, I'll bite. What'd they do?" Courtney settled on a chair to listen.

"They made snowmen. Or more accurately, a snowman and snowwoman consummating their marriage. If that wasn't scandalous enough, she was anatomically correct and on top."

"In the *1800s?*"

"Mm-hm. So you can see why her father built a bonfire and melted it. *But* not before the spectacle had drawn a lot of attention. So the next year, on their anniversary, my great-great-great-grandfather gave her a snowman as a reminder. And then one every year after that. But not always statues."

"What a romantic. I can't believe I never heard this story."

"Then when I was, oh, I don't know, five, I guess, Mom gave me the one that started it all. This one."

Jade handed it to her, but Courtney was so afraid of breaking it, she set it on the table right away.

"I liked it so much, she gave me more of the collection each winter. I put them away when I got engaged to Doug, though. I guess that was right before you moved here. I thought it was the mature"—she emphasized with finger quotes—"thing to do."

"Jazzy'd love to see them."

"You should bring her over. I have two more boxes. Mugs, candles, bells, storybooks."

"She's asking about spells."

"I swear, Courtney, I never—"

"I know, I know." She sighed, making a decision. "Maybe you should. She watched a Harry Potter movie at her friend's house, and I swear when she came home, I could see little witchy wheels turning in her head, remembering every little thing we've said over the years when we didn't think she was old enough to understand. And there was that time she saw a wand on your kitchen table."

"She was three."

"She remembers."

Jade patted Courtney's arm, but she didn't feel very comforted by it. Jade was comfortable being a witch, and someday when she had kids, she'd never hide the truth from them. But that hadn't been Courtney's plan. Wasn't much she could do about it, though, when she laid down her hairbrush or a fork or a key, and Jazzy picked it up just to "feel" it.

"Better she learns it from you than Annie, I guess. Or worse, stumbles around in the dark on her own and sets the house on fire."

"I'll help her. Tell her to wait until you bring her over."

"Thanks, I will."

Jade stood back and assessed what she'd done. Courtney did likewise and said, "The snowmen trivets show up really nice on the wood."

"I don't know. Do you think they're too immature?"

"No, a collection is special. This one's so romantic, and it says something about you. How tied you are to your family's history."

Jade chuckled. "Yeah, that's exactly why I put away all the black cats and broomsticks."

"But you've always wanted to keep that side private. I never understood why you put those things out in the first place."

"They were gifts."

"So?"

Jade's sigh was wistful. "You're right. I used to leave the snowmen out all year. I didn't realize how much I missed seeing them."

"There you go. By the way, I came in through the kitchen. Met Mason." Courtney fanned herself and raised her eyebrows questioningly. "Sure you still want the talisman?"

"He has to go."

"Ooh, positive thought; that's good."

"I tried to scare him away last night. Earlier this morning, really. I had a bunch of messages on the answering machine from Tricia Sherwood."

"I know. She's calling all of us."

"Yeah, well, Mason heard them, and I wanted him to back off, so I sort of mentioned that she wanted to know where I'd buried the body."

Courtney laughed. "What did he do?"

"Suddenly remembered something he needed to do. At three in the morning. I thought he was going to pack, but he's still here."

"He has a nice laugh."

Jade shrugged as if to say it was nothing special, then a second later, the corner of her mouth tipped up, and she nodded in agreement.

"Noah's in there," Courtney said, "charming Weezy as usual, and Mason's just sitting back enjoying the show. You're absolutely sure?"

"*He has to go.*"

Courtney held up her hands in surrender. "Okay,

okay. Just checking to make sure this is what you really want." She reached into her purse and pulled out a small box, wood with an inlaid top, no bigger than the palm of her hand.

"That's beautiful." Jade admired it, but only briefly because she knew the box wasn't the important part. "Now open it and let me see."

"You don't need to see it."

"What?" she asked, affronted.

"You know better. I'm going to hide it in his room. You are not to go looking for it. I'll pick it up after he's gone."

"I can take it up." Jade reached for the box.

"Don't make me slap your hand, girlfriend. And pouting won't work either. Now, Jazzy's teacher wants five dozen assorted treats by ten o'clock on Valentine's Day. That's A.M. for people like you who live around the clock. And Jazzy asks if you'll please, please, please—that's just how she said it—if you'll please, please, please make a special one for her to give to a little boy she likes."

Jade's eyebrows arched. "She's *five*."

"I know, I know." Courtney knew her daughter and waved away any concern. "Go ahead and do it, or I'll never hear the end of it."

"Is she requesting a charm on it?"

"Over my dead body."

Anthony was rummaging through Mason's drawers, searching for the bartender's phone number, when a knock sounded on the door. It was perfunctory, closely followed by a woman's entrance. While he hadn't met her, from her photo, he knew it was Courtney, the third widow.

Abandoned wife. Whatever.

Jade was raven-haired and mysterious, tall, exotic, with a penchant for stiletto heels. Annie was a blond pixie. Both stood out in their own way, while Courtney seemed to do everything to maximize normalcy, to try to blend in. Average weight, simple makeup, brown hair tucked behind her ears.

"Oh," she said in surprise, immediately reversing, pulling the door behind her as she went. "Sorry. Wrong room."

Anthony closed one drawer and tackled another.

"Ah-hah!" The phone number was jotted inside a matchbook cover, and the matchbook was from a bar. Had to be it.

He snatched his cell off his belt, giving no more thought to why Courtney would enter Mason's room by mistake.

Annie grabbed Courtney in the kitchen before she could get out the door. "We're meeting in the drying room," she said.

Awareness and alarm skittered across Courtney's face. "No . . . I have to . . ."

"You have to do this," Annie said, combining empathy with a no-nonsense attitude that kept readers clamoring for more of Dear Alanna. "It's time to help the guys transition properly. It'll help us move on."

"I'm fine. Really."

"Then do it for Jade. She's got a man right here who's hot for her, and I think she needs us to show her that it's all right to fall in love again. That her world won't end if she does."

"What about you?" Courtney followed, albeit reluctantly.

"I need this, too. I need to say good-bye, with my two best friends beside me."

Normally Jade would work in the conservatory, but with traffic in the house the way it was, she'd elected to withdraw to the privacy of the drying room.

Unlike the others, Annie was short enough that she didn't feel the need to duck the curved lintel into the drying room, which felt cozy and intimate with flickering white candles, soft music, and the spicy-sweet fragrance of burning frankincense for protection.

Jade looped an arm around Courtney's shoulders and spoke with gratitude. "I'm glad you're staying for this. It would feel incomplete without you."

What she didn't say, Annie knew, was that Jade worried about Courtney blocking what came natural to her.

There was a cushion on the natural stone floor for each of them, and they settled in, triangulated around a small portable altar covered with a white cloth. On that sat a silver tray with the incense, a photograph of their husbands on the deck of their cruiser, three small pots of earth, and a bowl of tiny bulbs.

"Tell me everything," Annie said, eager as ever to learn.

"Psychopomps are the spirits who guide souls between the realms of the living and the dead," Jade began. "We're here to share a favorite memory of our men in life, then send them on their way in death so they can be reborn at another time. We'll keep it brief so the spirits don't think we're asking to let them stay. Who wants to go first?"

"You," Annie and Courtney said in unison.

Jade took a deep, calming breath, then smiled softly. "I remember the day they bought the boat. How proud they all looked, as if they'd built it with their own hands. How they wanted to share the moment with us and insisted we all sleep on it the first night."

Annie liked the boat topic and decided to stick with it. It seemed appropriate, since it was going to check on the boat that took her husband away. She took a deep, cleansing breath, then chuckled. "I remember the champagne they bought to celebrate. I wasn't sure if the boat was rocking or if it was me. And after that first night, I remember the stories they'd tell when they came home on Sunday evenings, mostly of the fish that got away."

"I remember how they seemed closer than brothers," Courtney said. "That first summer, they started finishing each other's stories. And laughed at the same things. And trusted each other. How spending time together restored their energy and centered them. They made better husbands when they came home."

They each took time to sit with private thoughts,

and when no one said anything more, Jade proceeded. "We should add a few things to the altar. Let's play to our strengths. Annie, you're good with candles. If you light this one, it'll symbolize a torch leading the way on their journey."

Annie took a few moments to add her intention to the votive before she lit it and set it on the tray.

"Courtney, if you add a key, it'll symbolize opening the door to the next realm."

Courtney fished out a key, held it in her hand a moment, then laid it on the tray.

Lastly, Jade added a small knife and said, simply, "To cut the ties that bind."

They reached for each other spontaneously, holding hands, completing the circle, each meditating on her own memories, her own hopes for her husband's peaceful repose.

"I chose white daffodils," Jade said, explaining the bulbs. "Floriferous seemed appropriate, because they produce several blossoms on each stem. We can each plant one now, signifying putting the men to rest, because we never were able to do that with their bodies. Later we'll plant the bulbs in our yards, so every spring they'll come up and visit with us for a while, and we'll remember how close they were, and how they died together, doing something they loved."

With only the soft sound of flutes floating on the air around them, each woman planted a small bulb in a pot.

They closed the circle together and, united with her

sisters-in-craft, they embraced. Each went her own way, to place her bulb in a safe spot, to be nurtured until planting time.

By the time the moon finished its first quarter, Jade was beginning to think nothing would work on Mason. Nothing could be worse for a witch than to doubt herself. Negativity bred negative results.

But then she ran into Sarah at the gym. Once or twice a year, she asked Jade to cast a spell for her. Not always simple, but always successful. And Becca. She'd had a big problem with a mean husband until Weezy, who was her mother, had asked for Jade's help. He was gone for good within three days.

When Jade finished her errands and returned home, she went into drying room and pulled out the diaries where she logged all the spells she did, for herself as well as for others, both locally and long-distance. She'd cast a lot of spells over the years. She'd helped a lot of people. She was *good*, damn it, so why wasn't Mason leaving?

Maybe Courtney had been onto something when she'd suggested Jade not brush her teeth until Mason moved out. She couldn't do that, yuck, but she did have a last resort—baggy old sweats stained with wallpaper paste and paint.

Wallpapering didn't pay the bills, though; botanicals did. So Jade spent the evening in the drying room blending oils to fill mail-order requests, working late into the night. When she was finished, she left the final packing for Henry, who crabbed at her if she didn't leave something for him to do to be helpful.

Time to wallpaper.

She changed into paint-splattered purple sweats; gold from the kitchen, blue from the room her parents "shared" on alternate months, brick and tan from other guest rooms she'd either done or touched up. Did she have to do this while Mason was in the room? No. But he wasn't paying full rate, she wanted him gone, and she looked repulsive enough to send him running out into the night.

She gathered up all the tools she'd need, then set them down and, for good measure, mussed her hair. Then she carefully balanced the full load again and knocked on Mason's door, not caring if he was deeply focused on the eagle book. If she interrupted his concentration enough, he'd have to find a better place to work.

Not for a minute did she stop to think he wouldn't be decent.

There were two things on Mason's body when he opened the door: a few drops of water glistening on his smooth, broad chest, probably because he'd heard her knock after his shower and had been in a hurry to answer the door; and the towel, slung loosely around his hips.

Jade didn't move. She couldn't raise so much as a voluntary muscle twitch. Not to turn and run away. Not to stop her eyes from roaming over his well-muscled chest, down to a very impressive six-pack. Not to swallow and ask if she could come in and get the job done, which was good, because he'd probably grin and ask "What job?" with a lot of innuendo that would leave her struggling for a coherent answer.

He grinned at her, lopsided, the way a man does when he appreciates being ogled, but isn't conceited about it. The way a man does when he's returning the favor.

It was going to be very difficult to hang wallpaper straight.

Chapter 11

Mason stood on his side of the threshold with one hand on his hip, securing the towel. He didn't need a trained glance to log Jade's balancing two rolls of wallpaper, a folded drop cloth, four-foot straight-edge, sponges, and a bucket overflowing with tools.

More interesting, especially at this time of night and in his doorway, she was staring at his chest with a stunned look, uncertain whether to reach out and touch, or bolt.

No problem; he kept in good shape and didn't mind showing off, especially if the one looking happened to be Jade. He skimmed his hand over bare skin, right where she was staring a hole, and innocently—yeah, right—asked, "Did I miss something?"

She sort of hummed in the back of her throat. Oh yeah, she wanted to touch.

"Jade?"

"Hm? Oh." The straightedge slipped to the left, the drop cloth to the right, and the rolls of paper took on a life of their own. He reached out to help, but she yelped, "No! Keep your hands where they are. Please."

Obviously mortified to mention that she'd noticed the hand holding the towel together was the only thing keeping him decent, she turned bright pink and overjuggled everything until half of it landed on the floor at her feet.

No stilettos tonight, Mason noted with regret as he tucked in the end of the towel. As substitutes went, her ratty old sneakers had no laces and, overall, were in pretty bad shape. Her socks didn't match; one white, one gray, they didn't even come close. And moving up rapidly because all the good stuff was hidden behind the accessories she'd regathered in a jumbled pile, what was with her hair? Her perpetually seductive, come-to-my-boudoir spirals were twisted and caught in each other like dozens of kinked telephone cords.

"Hard night?" he asked.

Grinning was out of the question. If she wanted to sweep him out of her life with ugly clothes, frightening hair, and talk of missing bodies, she was going to have to work a whole lot harder to scare him.

He was walking a fine line, though; a curious investigator on the sly, impersonating a wary guest.

She glanced at his towel, then tried to look as if she hadn't. "I should . . . come back later."

He quickly stepped back, wanting to reassure her

so she wouldn't disappear, acting as if he always wore nothing more than a towel while talking to hot women in the middle of the night.

"Don't be silly. I'll get dressed. I guess you were serious about wallpapering."

She headed straight for the bathroom, and he, sorry to say, was a sick, sick dog. Even though she was fully covered by the most abused set of sweats this side of the garment district, he stared at her ass the whole way across the room until it disappeared through the door and turned the corner. He'd been watching her for days now. He'd always thought the sex-kitten sway of her hips was due to the stilettos. He'd been wrong.

From the bathroom, Jade said, "I'm so glad I found out that you don't sleep either. I need to get this done, and now that you've settled into this room, I really didn't want to ask you to move. But if you're working tonight and you'd be more comfortable sitting with your laptop in one of the other rooms, feel free."

"No, no, that's fine." *Couldn't get me out of here with a crowbar.*

"Well, if I get too noisy, and you change your mind, feel free. I'll just close this and set up while you get dressed." Jade swung the bathroom door until it latched, leaving Mason in control of the door to the hall.

Leave it open? he wondered, rooted to the spot with indecision. Or close it?—just in case wallpapering was a ruse and what she really wanted was him.

He probably was grinning like a hound dog, too,

but he quickly masked all expression when Jade poked her head out of the bathroom a few minutes later and, noticing that he was safely covered in jeans and a flannel shirt, said, "How does a photographer work without a darkroom, anyway?"

"I shoot mostly digital."

"Oh, that's right. Memory card." She retreated, tramping across the drop cloth now covering the floor. "So you crop and touch up and everything right on the computer?"

"Just what I was about to do. I could put it off a few minutes, though, if you need anything first?"

She turned and smiled at him, and he thought, *Please, God, don't let it involve hanging wallpaper.*

"The ladder."

While it wasn't what he'd wanted to hear her say, it wasn't all bad; he'd yet to find access to a cellar in this monstrosity. "Tell me where it is. I'll get it."

"In the hall."

Damn. He muttered, "What am I? Cursed or something?" because he couldn't catch a break. This time, when he brought the ladder in, he swung the door to the hall closed. If she planned on making a move on him, it'd be one less thing to worry about.

He opened his photo-editing and word-processing programs, so if Jade stepped out to see what he was doing, he'd look like the author/photographer he claimed to be, hard at work. He sat at the far side of the table so he'd know when she was peeking at him.

He had a nice view of her body every time she bent

down to run a large sponge over each new strip of wallpaper. At least from that angle, the bag went out of the sweats, and he wasn't nearly as sleepy.

He minimized those programs and picked up Jade's office computer on the network. He started with e-mail, an easy way for a not-so-dead husband to keep in touch.

Dear Alanna,

My sister is getting married next year to a man of another religion. I am concerned for her spiritual well-being, and for those of their future children as well. When I bring up this subject, though, she just brushes it off and says not to worry, everything will take care of itself and work out in the end. I try to tell her that important issues are at stake here, issues that can make or break a long-term relationship, but she's not listening. What can I do to make her listen to reason?

What the hell? Mason thought. It was incoming mail, not outgoing. And there were more.

Dear Alanna,

Recently I invited my best friend and her husband to stay with me while they were in town looking for a new home." It finished with, *". . . what can I do to keep this from happening when they come back to close on the house?*

"Grow a spine?" Mason muttered, thinking it must be easier for men. If a friend of his was that rude, he'd simply say, "Hey, man, you're cramping my style. You have to find another place to stay. Want a beer?"

There were a hundred more e-mails just like those, in the Inbox. Thousands if he counted the ones filed away in folders.

There was a nationally syndicated Dear Alanna, of course. No reason Jade couldn't be moonlighting under a pseudonym. Interesting.

Mason looked beyond his screen and watched Jade carry a strip toward the ladder. If he had to miss a night's sleep, this wasn't all bad. Her whole body swayed rhythmically, and when he listened carefully, he heard her humming, soft and low. Too quiet to catch the tune, and he couldn't help wondering what it was, what kind of music she liked to listen to. It wasn't a professional thought. He was getting comfortable having nonprofessional thoughts about Jade.

When he refocused on the screen and moved on to another e-mail account, he found a history of e-mails addressed to Annie and none to Jade. So, this was the computer Annie used, which made *her* Dear Alanna.

He headed for Annie's word-processing files next, unsurprised from what he'd seen in the office that the files weren't organized in folders. None of them were even properly named, carrying only the program-assigned first few words of each document as a title, such as "If you have a troublesome neighbor.doc" and

"If you want to increase success.doc." He assumed they had something to do with the Dear Alanna letters until he started opening them and found recipes. And not normal recipes either.

"Carve a candle," he read under his breath. "And dress it with All Saints Oil—what? Nail a slice of bread to the front door? Cast a ritual circle?"

Ohhh. Annie's the witch.

Mason quickly sent an instant message to Anthony's computer. He examined the file names closely now, looking for something along the lines of "If you want to get rid of your husband.doc" or "How to collect buckets of life insurance.doc." No luck there, so he settled in and opened a lot of files.

He learned more about witches than he thought he'd ever want to know. Annie, anyway. And she made lots of follow-up notes, like "next time, try cinnamon." He'd never look at cinnamon the same way again. In fact, Weezy had put cinnamon on his French toast yesterday. He was debating eating breakfast out from now on when he heard Jade's cell ring.

"First of all, it's not *his* bathroom," was the first thing she said. "And I'm in it because I'm wallpapering it."

Not "Hello." Not "Hi." It piqued his curiosity, more so when she lowered her voice.

"What's the matter with them? I always wear these when I work around the house."

Mason developed a sudden need to consult, hm . . . Maps! Of course. Hannibal, Clarksville, West Bluff; they just happened to be across the room near the bathroom door, and he scooted right on over there.

"That's the point, Mom. Look, I have to go. Talk to you later."

She barreled out the door, stepped around Mason, who was instantly poring over a map spread out on the triple dresser, and slid her phone across the carpet all the way to the door.

"Looks like you've had a bit of practice at that."

"Mothers," she said disgustedly, ramming her fingers through her hair, mussing it even more. "I'd shut it off, but then I forget to turn it back on."

"She always call in the middle of the night? Oh wait, she has insomnia, too?" Mason had all he could do not to stare at Jade's hair. His fingers ached to pluck at that one hank over her right ear. Just to unhook it. Just to let it fall naturally. Would that be so wrong? To reach out and touch?

"What? What are you looking at?"

"Oh. Sorry."

"Do I have adhesive in my hair? Oh, tell me I don't—" She rushed into the bathroom and checked in the oval mirror she'd already rehung over the sink.

Mason followed, sure she'd freak out when she saw how she looked and would need a comforting pat on the back. Maybe a hug. Maybe something a lot more reassuring, like jumping on the bed and getting naked together.

"Nope, looks fine," she pronounced with a bright smile.

Their eyes caught in the mirror. Like everything else in Mystic Manor, its dark wood frame was old, carved, and lovingly preserved. In it, Jade looked like a beautiful Medusa.

"Sorry if I disturbed you," she said, turning around to face him.

"I needed a break anyway."

He couldn't help it; he reached out. Jade arched backward over the sink and said, "What?" as he discovered that her hair was as silky as it looked.

"It's just a little . . . wild. There, that's got it."

The bathroom seemed small with two in it. Or maybe it was just because it was the two of them. Warm from the lights and her working. Fragrant from whatever botanical soap and shampoo she used.

"Pinch me," he said. "I smell suntan lotion."

Jade made a face. "I was going for coconut. Maybe I need to reblend—"

"No, that's it," he said with excitement and, he supposed, longing. "It smells like a beach."

"Please. I prefer to be a bit more purist than commercial suntan lotion."

"Beaches remind me of Aruba."

Jade started picking up her tools. Mason bent down and helped, getting in her way when he could so she'd bump into him, because she had the sweetest way of putting her hand on his arm or his shoulder to fend off accidental body contact. If she had any idea it wasn't accidental or how much it turned him on, she'd shove him into the tub and turn on the cold water.

"You like Aruba?" she asked.

"Love it. I was supposed to be there this week. All

week. Seven whole days." He couldn't help a sigh. A woman would call it wistful; he called it regret. See if he changed his life for a woman again.

They folded the drop cloth together. After a moment's hesitation, Jade said, "Sorry. You must be devastated."

"Yeah. I had dives lined up almost every day. There's a wreck not too many people get to see, and I was going— What?"

She chewed the inside of her cheek; totally adorable as she chose her next words carefully. "I meant getting *dumped*."

"Oh." He put on his winning caught-with-his-hand-in-the-cookie-jar grin. "Brenda and I hadn't been getting on too well."

"Of course. That's why you were getting married."

"It made sense at the time."

Jade gathered up the folded drop cloth and some of the tools, then suddenly said, "Oh!" and froze halfway to picking up the bucket. She straightened up abruptly. "You mean you didn't *want* to get married?"

"Nope."

She not only looked concerned for his feelings, happy that he wasn't devastated, but more than all that, and this was a stumper, she looked a tad . . . relieved?

"Then *why*?"

He shrugged it off, but she stood there and stared at him and waited for an answer, which he wasn't really sure of himself. That would take close examination, maybe hours of it. He was a guy; he had better things to do. So sue him.

"Wow." Jade's eyes narrowed as she peered closer. "Did you stop breathing?"

"What can I say? She told me it was time to move to the next level, and I believed her."

"Because I never saw a guy freeze up like that over a simple question."

"It was a hard question. No simple answer."

She looked doubtful. No way to convince her but to hit her with an example. "You try it," he said. "Were you happily married?"

"Yes. See how easy that was?"

Probably because Annie cast a happy spell on the poor bastard.

Although, from the notes he'd seen in Annie's files, she wasn't too happy with her own results. There were a lot of try-this-instead-next-time and don't-attempt-this-one-again comments. Shit, maybe that little pixie had offed all three guys at once because she, what, used the wrong bottle of oil? Said the wrong words? Holy shit.

"There," Jade said. "You just did it again."

Was it too late to move out? Was Aruba far enough away, in case Annie tried a spell on him? Or got him by mistake?

Mason hadn't learned enough about witchcraft yet. If you'd asked him last week if he believed in it, he would've said he didn't know enough about it one way or the other. But after seeing all the witchy stuff in the attic, the altars in the locked room, and hundreds of web sites devoted to the Craft, he had to figure that if some people believed in it strongly enough, there must be something to it.

"If you don't blink soon, I'm going to try CPR," Jade said slowly.

Mason pulled the sponges off her pile and dropped them to the floor.

"What are you—"

Then the drop cloth.

"—doing?"

"I can't remember when I've had a better offer." He had to tug at the bucket of tools, but Jade smiled suddenly and let it go, and he said, "Are you any good at CPR?"

She splayed a hand on his chest. "I haven't had any complaints. Do you want to get married?"

"Right now?"

"It's not a proposal. Ever."

"No."

Her smile broadened, and her relief was palpable; not the reaction he expected from a woman pressing him backward, out the door, steering him on a straight path backward.

Mason gave in. He plunged his fingers into Jade's hair and smoothed it into something less frightening, though at this point, she could have turned green, and he wouldn't have cared.

They shuffled toe-to-toe to the bed. With his hands cupping her head, he tipped his and teased her lips with his mouth, the tip of his tongue, not going too fast, letting her know where they were headed.

Jade, bless her soul, never wavered. Never slowed on her path. She backed him right up against the mattress and pushed on his chest, sending him tumbling backward. He, athletic sort that he was, grabbed her and hauled her down with him.

The computer beeped once, and he prayed it wouldn't distract her.

Jade's green eyes bored into his, hot and twinkling and promising that he was finally going to get to see and touch what was beneath those hideous sweats.

"Get those ugly things off," he growled, reaching for her top.

"I wore them for you." She brushed his hands away.

"Don't do it again."

She laughed and bent forward and teased his mouth the way he'd done hers. It was easy to slip his hands under her shirt, more difficult to decide whether to palm her breasts or unhook her bra or drag her down on his chest. He wasn't used to being the bottom. Wasn't used to being the one not calling the play.

Wasn't used to hot smoldering kisses with the god-damn computer beeping in the background like a truck's backup alarm.

"Is that anything important?" Jade whispered breathlessly against his lips.

Mason answered by rolling her over and stripping off her sweatshirt in one move. He sunk his weight onto her, between her legs, pushing her into the mattress.

Jade started laughing.

Mason lifted his head, barely, not willing to lose

his place. Or give her time to change her mind. "What?"

"Do you have a fantasy of making love in a parking lot?"

"Don't move." He dipped his head and captured her lips for a long, slow, hot kiss before he levered himself off and stalked toward the computer.

He knew that beep. Only Anthony could instant-message him on this computer.

It hit him then, a crippling grip deep in his gut that killed the mood quicker than running out of air on a thirty-meter dive.

The video camera.

He'd forgotten to block it when he'd come in earlier. Anthony would have seen everything if he'd been monitoring, and apparently he had.

Hard evidence confirmed it. On the screen, in black and white and once for every beep, was a message that said it all: "Are you out of your fucking mind?"

This was his own fault, every bit of it. Normally he'd care, but not for the reasons he would have suspected. Normally, this would be exciting, like spotting a reef shark circling the dive site and taking pains to avoid it. This, though . . . this had no good end in sight.

If Jade ever discovered a camera in one of her rooms, if she ever knew someone on the other end had not only seen but recorded her half-undressed, if she even suspected someone had watched her jump him, she'd never talk to him again. Hell, if she discovered his Glock, she'd probably shoot him—and that was if he called it quits now. Imagine what she'd do to him if he went ahead and ravished every inch of her, which pretty much had been his plan.

He slammed the lid shut.

"Mason?"

"It's not you," he began, because he didn't know where to begin.

Jade's eyebrows arched, as if he had to be nuts to think that she might think it was. And she was right.

"It's me. We're, ah, moving too fast."

If she never spoke to him again, it'd make the don't-get-involved rule a lot easier to follow. Thinking about her never speaking to him again, though, just left a big, gaping hole in the center of him.

He didn't want to examine it any closer than that. He might not like what he saw. Or he might like it too much.

Chapter 12

"Well that was awkward."

Jade hadn't gotten into the hall on her own. Within a few short breaths, she found herself staring at the outside of Mason's door. Her sweatshirt was on inside out, maybe even backward, but frankly, her head was spinning with too much confusion to care.

She'd seen hardness in Mason's eyes, in the rigid way he'd turned back to her from the computer, in every atom of his body, quickly replaced by regret and determination. He'd batted items around on top of the dresser, then swept her to her feet, into her sweatshirt, and out the door.

His parting words had been, "You have to go."

Yes! The mixed-up spell was weakening. She'd thought so when he said he didn't want to get married. Now she was certain.

Wasn't it sweet? As much as he wanted her—that hadn't been a telephoto lens in his pants—he'd put on the brakes and called a halt. What determination. What chivalry!

What consideration, she thought with a sigh. Like any self-respecting woman, Jade wanted to be wanted for more than her body, but knowing a man thought she was hot after all this time was pretty darn nice, too.

And he'd clearly said he was off the market and not interested in getting married.

Spirits forgive me for rationalizing a bit here, but I've been without a lover for a long, long time, you know. Seemed that should make a short-term relationship acceptable, with the emphasis on short-term.

She could look for a serious relationship after Mason left. Call this a warm-up. Were her hormones waking up, or what!

Jade was still standing in the same spot in the hall when Mason yanked open his door and barreled out of the room.

"'Scuse me," he growled, brushing past. He rushed headlong down the hall, barged through Anthony's door without knocking, then ever so briefly turned back to Jade and said, "Don't come in. No matter what you hear. Even if you think I'm killing him."

"Are you going to—"

"Probably."

"But—"

"I'll tell you when to call 911," he said, slamming the door behind him.

* * *

Mason might have been able to sneak in a few hours of sleep after reaming Anthony a new one except that he was too keyed up. Not trying to figure out how to avoid any future sexual encounters with Jade; on the contrary, his hormones were working overtime on just the opposite.

Yes, it was wrong. But did he give a damn?

Ah, *nooo*.

He'd come *this close* to getting married a week ago, and it surprised him, shamed him even, that he hadn't felt then, for Brenda, what he was feeling now for Jade. Brenda had been simple—the relationship had been simple—until she'd started all that let's-take-a-break, wait-for-our-wedding-night shit. She'd been convenient.

Dammit all—and it really hurt to admit this—she'd been *right*.

His feelings for Jade were far different. More exciting. Like a deep wall dive with good visibility. Or being the first person to explore an uncharted wreck.

So even though he'd had a long day, there was no sleeping that night. And he couldn't nap around Mystic Manor during the day. Sure, he could lock his door, but if Jade knocked, he'd have to answer—if he woke up at all—and it'd be clear he'd been sleeping longer and deeper than a power nap. There'd go his insomnia cover. How could he talk his way around that?

No way around it; he had to get out of the house,

which unfortunately took him away from the computer, away from his main resource, the internet. Anthony had stormed out in a huff and taken their rental car, so Mason borrowed Jade's Jeep again. As destinations went, the library was looking pretty good. It'd be warm. They probably had computers. Seems he'd stumbled into a hotbed of witches, probably more than he knew, and he wanted to learn more so as not to overlook anything. If it was boring, he'd catch some shut-eye in the stacks.

He hadn't counted on a small-town library with small-town ways. Everyone stared at him upon his entrance; half a dozen people scattered among the tables and a man as old as dirt dusting the shelves. Instead of leaving Mason to his own devices, the overweight, middle-aged librarian abandoned her cart of returns, smoothed her full skirt, and approached him with a soft smile.

"May I help you find something?" she asked quietly.

Well, why the hell not? "I'm looking for books on—"

"Oh, you're that eagle photographer! You're the talk of West Bluff, don't you know."

"I am?" He squinted at her and lowered his voice. "What have you heard?"

She grinned with mature wisdom. "Depends on whether I'm listening to the men or the women."

"Well, don't believe everything you hear."

"That'd be a crying shame. Now, what can I do for you? Oh, of course, you need local color for your book. We have wonderful resources. Right this way."

He let her help him find what he didn't need. It was easier that way. Then when he was settled on a hard chair in the middle of the room at a table covered with local books, he said, "Mm, there is one more thing."

"Yes?"

"I've been in town several days now, and I've been hearing rumors."

"Woman my age, you learn not to believe everything you hear. Still," she said, the grin a little wicked now, "can't beat the fun of hearing it. You need me to clear up something?"

"I'm not sure. Maybe if I could get online, I could just surf around a little. It's about witches."

Her smile didn't just fade, it was wiped off the face of the earth, replaced by the coming of the next ice age. Mason stifled the impulse to shiver.

She gained two inches as her spine stiffened. "We're a God-fearing community, Mr.—?"

"Kincaid."

"That's not gossip, Mr. Kincaid. It's heresy."

"I see." He didn't, until he heard the peal of church bells not too far off in the distance. Anywhere else and he would've thought it was Sunday, not Tuesday morning. "Well, I'd like to understand more about it, so I'll, you know, recognize it if I see it."

"Not in these parts you won't."

"It's not here?"

"You won't see it. Not in town, not in our homes, and certainly not in our library."

Holy cow. "Any idea if the library in Hannibal—"

"I wouldn't know," she cut him off, her tone pure frost.

No wonder the guest room was locked and Annie didn't run around in a pointed hat.

Witches did rituals; he knew that much. But what else was there to see around Mystic Manor? Who was involved? And how might witchcraft have been used against three unsuspecting husbands?

As for the scores of candles burning around Mystic Manor on his first night?—probably ritual. Maybe Annie felt safer doing her thing away from her own home. If that was the case, then Jade knew. Shoot, being an herbalist, she probably supplied Annie with whatever herbs or oils or potions she used. All stuff he knew little about, but wouldn't it be nice to expand his working vocabulary on the subject?

Two altars in the locked room. He couldn't get online right now, so could he find a book on witchcraft and learn what the items on the altars were used for? Good or evil?

And if Jade was supplying Annie, then what about the damp cotton ball he'd found in his pocket shortly after she'd bumped into him in the conservatory? What was that all about?

He perused the local books so as not to offend the librarian, and also because word would get around town and substantiate his cover.

Driving down Main Street an hour later, he got a huge surprise when he saw Brenda walk into a needlework store. But then he realized that was nonsense; had to be a look-alike. Or sleep deprivation. Brenda had no ties to anyone in the Midwest, nor would she be shopping for needlework of any kind, so he pushed her out of his mind and moved on to the independent bookstore. Parking was at a premium, what with piles of snow plowed here and there, left to freeze in a giant maze. Again, no quiet corner with a chair, any chair, in which to sleep.

The librarian had been right; no witchcraft books there either. When asked for suggestions, the clerk looked left and right and over his bony shoulders, then leaned toward Mason and whispered, "Try the internet."

"How about Hannibal?" he asked, equally quiet.

"Um. Yeah. But you didn't hear it from me."

"Thanks. 'Preciate it."

Back out on the sunny sidewalk, the smell coming from next door reminded him it was lunchtime. Inside the café, the locals were hashing out the very popular missing husbands mystery. Theories abounded.

Samuel sneezed. Mason knew it was Samuel because a dozen people said, "Bless you, Samuel," and plowed right on with their conversations.

The counter was bracket-shaped, long side toward the front door. Out of twenty padded chrome stools, nineteen were occupied by coffee-drinking, cigarette-smoking, predominantly male customers, every last one in a logo-emblazoned ball cap. All branches of the armed services were represented, as well as the Lions Club, John Deere, and the local gun club. The latter had the floor.

"Heard now that time's up and the county's issued death certificates, them widdas're getting five million each."

Mason knew for a fact that was an exaggeration.

"Black widdas, if you ask me." This from Farmers' Co-op.

Mason accepted a heavy white mug of steaming coffee from the gal behind the counter. He wrapped his hands around it for warmth and looked over the dry-erase menu board while pretending not to be overly interested in the conversation bouncing around the Formica top.

"My cousin's wife's brother said he seen Doug— I forget his last name . . ."

"Stockard."

"Yeah, Stockard. He said he seen him in town night before last."

"Which one's that?"

"One lived up at Mystic Manor."

"Lot going on up there ain't right, you know what I mean."

"Aw, Jade's okay."

"Ain't saying she's not."

"Reuben's right. She has guests fly in to stay at her house, and how often do we see any of 'em in town?"

"They do tend to keep to themselves."

"Amen," the waitress said with conviction. She reached up and touched the cross hanging above the pickup window.

"What do you think's going on?"

"Something kinky, that's what I think."

"Sinful. Just sinful. Why I've a mind to—"

What Samuel had a mind to do remained a mystery as the waitress cleared her throat and coughed. All eyes turned to Mason, stared at him through the fog of smoke. He sipped his coffee and set his mug down, so tempted to jokingly share the bordello theory, only this bunch might take it as gospel, and then where would that leave Jade? If she was innocent of anything, he certainly didn't want to be the cause of further hard feelings toward her.

"You doing kinky stuff up there, son?"

"No, sir."

" 'Course, if you was, you wouldn't say so, now would you?"

Mason grinned good-naturedly, though nothing was going to change the fact that he was the outsider here. "No, sir. But truth is, I'm not doing anything except working on a book with my writing partner."

They didn't look as if they believed him.

"Freezing my ass off, too. Know where I can buy some sweaters?"

They gave him a couple options, one of which was in Hannibal. Speculation about Jade and Mystic Manor dropped off.

The special was baked spaghetti, canned green beans, small salad. Adequate, he supposed. No, better; it was nice not to worry about being poisoned. So nice, he was going to have to stop eating at Mystic Manor entirely. No more breakfast there for him. Too risky.

When he was finished, he left with a large coffee to go.

He bought half a dozen books on witchcraft at a bookstore in Hannibal, two sweaters, and a ball cap with a fish on it so he'd blend in better, then settled in near the boat ramp at the lock and dam.

The first bald eagle that flew overhead took away his breath. Did a person ever get used to seeing these birds in their own backyard? If Jade were with him now, he could ask. Then again, if Jade were with him now, chances were he wouldn't have noticed much outside the Jeep.

He called Anthony. "We've been friends a long time, right?"

"I'm on the other line with Ken. In light of our longtime friendship, can we make this fast?"

"Who's Ken? Oh, the bartender. Right. That's great."

"I was thinking faster."

"We need to talk. Face-to-face."

"Five seconds."

"Get that camera out of my room *now*. That fast enough for you?"

"Don't look now, but that damn ethical streak of yours is showing."

"Thought you were in a hurry."

"I've been watching you struggle with it since the night we arrived, when you promised you wouldn't do anything to screw this up."

"Exactly. That's why I'm resigning, so there's no conflict there."

Anthony was silent for a long moment. "I need you."

"This is a bullshit assignment, man. Seriously. Way below our capabilities."

"Seriously?" Anthony's tone was low and dangerous, leading Mason to believe that he was going to go off about something.

"Yeah," Mason said anyway.

"When I called my uncle about finding us this job," Anthony argued smoothly, "your *capabilities* were seriously in question."

"Mine? They're never in question."

"Mase, Mase, Mase. You left the church at 6:05, swearing you were going to have a drink for every year you'd wasted on Brenda. By 6:15, you'd called all our diving buddies, told them to ditch their dates and meet you at the bar. By 7:15, you'd had five shots and upped your vow to two drinks for every year."

"See? Shows how capable I am."

"Uh-huh. At ten, you asked a nun if she thought you'd be better off in the priesthood."

Mason grinned. He didn't remember it, but it sounded like something he'd do. "Wait a minute. You're making that up."

"Swear to God."

"What was a nun doing in a bar?"

"Bachelorette party for her sister. Biological, not religious. At midnight, you were arguing with a woman that you needed to use the ladies' restroom because it was cleaner than the men's."

"Again, good argument for me. Not making your point."

"Yeah, it sounded so lucid coming from a man with his head in a public toilet."

Disgruntled, Mason snapped, "Weren't you on the other line or something?"

"At one o'clock in the morning, you were taking out a hit on the candles left in Brenda's apartment."

"You are so goddamn detail-oriented."

"And you're damn good at what you do when you're sober. So if you think this job has been only a step above babysitting a five-year-old, I apologize. But the more you drank, the more I thought it was all you were going to be able to handle. And since I couldn't count on you for a more brain-intensive job, and since I knew you'd rather die than go skiing, and since I needed you to get back on the horse and not sabotage our professional reputation, I took it."

Mason didn't have a comeback.

"You've known Jade a week."

"Eight days." Mason winced; it sounded worse out loud.

"Give it more time."

He blew out an exasperated breath. "Hell, time's no guarantee. I gave Brenda five years. Look where it got me. I'm more sure of Jade now than I ever was with Brenda."

"I need you."

"I need her more."

"You want to talk about need? Parker—"

"Oh no, not with the kids," Mason groaned, because with the phone getting bumped around on the other end, he knew Anthony was going for his wallet.

Mason knew the photo well. Parker, the long-legged teenager, wearing a track uniform and a big grin.

"He wants to drop out of school and help with the rest of the children, but I keep telling him to leave that to me. If I can just keep him in school, he'll most likely win State again. They're scouting him already, you know. Full ride. That kind of money doesn't grow on trees, my friend."

"Neither do women like Jade." It felt damn good to say it, too.

"We're partners," Anthony continued, as unmoved as if Mason had said he needed a drink of water. "We're under contract to do a job. And we're going to finish this job right. The children are depending on me—"

"Oh, don't go there. I love those kids, too, you know."

"So wait. For their sake. Sleep with her after we're done."

"It's not just about that, sleeping with her. I don't expect you to understand this, hell, I don't expect anybody to understand this, but if I couldn't have sex with Jade for some reason, I'd still need to be with her."

Silence.

"I need her, man. Pure and simple. So bad, I can hardly breathe."

"Oh hell," Anthony said with the air of one who'd given up. "Gotta go."

The connection went dead, leaving Mason to his own thoughts as the wind shook the Jeep and the river flowed by.

Eagle watchers came, a car here, an SUV there. They watched from toasty warm interiors until they spotted what they'd come for. Mature bald eagles, standing so majestic on bare branches, their white heads glowing when the sunlight hit them. Juveniles, not bald yet, difficult to distinguish from the goldens. In Pensacola, it would've been seagulls and pelicans.

No, wait.

No, couldn't be. Here? *White* pelicans? With black wings? He focused and shot a flock flying over the river, just so he could zoom in later to see if he was hallucinating now. Maybe he was; the tourists didn't seem to notice them. Swathed in ski caps and knitted scarves, the ones who got out of their vehicles hunched down into thick coats. They peered at the eagles through binoculars and cameras until they could no longer stand the biting wind, which blew hard along the river. And then they were gone, soon to be replaced by the next carload of day-trippers smitten by the national bird.

Mason clicked a few photos himself, then turned to the material he'd brought along. To say the books were biased was an understatement. They were written by witches, for witches, and for people who thought they might want to be witches. Between yawns that had nothing to do with the material, he learned that contrary to what was depicted in movies and on sitcoms, witchcraft was not genetic. Witch adults didn't sit around waiting to see if their babies were going to wiggle their noses and make it rain in the dining room. The Craft could be learned. It could be practiced. It was a way of life. If you liked to follow rules, there was Wicca.

None of the books so far were antiwitchcraft, and little addressed how practicing the Craft could be bad.

He wasn't going back to enlighten the librarian. He looked forward to getting back to his room and burning the midnight oil on Google.

His whole body flinched once, and he realized he'd nodded off. He sat up straighter and thumbed through the pages, stopping abruptly when he saw the picture of a seven-knob candle, just like the one in the kitchen. Was Jade—?

Hadn't Weezy asked what kind of spell he was here for? It wasn't colloquialism, and she hadn't been asking for herself.

Jade's a witch?

Fuzzy sweaters, snug jeans, stiletto heels—well, hell, he didn't suppose witches had uniforms, but c'mon, there should have been some clue. Bat earrings or bad teeth or a cackling laugh. Not silver hoops, a perfect smile, and a laugh as sexy as it was arousing when she'd stripped off the butterfly bandages and dabbed goop on his face.

Annie *and* Jade? And, hell, probably Courtney, too.

The damp cotton ball in his pocket was making more sense. And maybe the little dried leaves in his pillowcase weren't something that came out of the wash.

Had they turned to witchcraft after exhausting all other means of finding their husbands?

Or had they cast a spell to rid themselves of excess baggage?

Annie took the call. It was that or tell the Dear Alanna letter writer that if her husband had been showering her with diamonds and rubies for ten years, then he was going to continue to do so no matter how much she complained about it, so boo-hoo, live with it.

"This is Mercy Hospital calling. Annie, is that you?"

Annie sat back in her chair, keyboard forgotten. "Gabby? What's wrong?" Though she knew Gabrielle from the gym, she worked as a nurse at the local hospital.

Gabby's laugh eased Annie's mind. "Not too much, if you know what I mean. We've had a treat in the ER this afternoon. That sexy bird guy I've been hearing about, Mason Kincaid."

"He stopped in?"

"No, silly. EMS brought him in."

"Oh. Oh! He's hurt?" He'd borrowed Jade's Jeep again today.

"I'm kind of limited as to what I can say. You know—along those lines?"

It was after six; dark out. Annie'd heard no sirens.

"But," Gabby continued, "he asked me to contact his partner, Anthony. So I can talk to him. Answer his questions."

"Of course. Just a minute." With her palm pressed

to the phone, Annie cleared her throat, then lowered her voice an octave and adopted a deeper pitch. "Mason? That you, buddy?"

"This is Mercy Hospital calling for Anthony—"

"Yes, yes, what's this about? Is Mason all right?"

"As a matter of fact, he asked me to call. He fell asleep in his car. Must have been there for hours. Got a bit hypothermic. But he's all warmed up now and ready to go."

Annie snickered. "He didn't freeze off anything important, did he?"

"Nope." Gabby cleared her throat. "Anyway, *sir*, he'd like you to come pick him up."

"Will do. Right away."

Annie left the office and rushed down the hall, headed for the conservatory until she saw Weezy exit Mason's room in a very sneaky manner, closing the door quietly behind her and her four-year-old granddaughter.

"Weezy?"

She jumped. "What? Good Lord, don't give a body a fright like that. I'm about to do a load of dishes. Gathering up coffee cups and such."

"Did I say anything?"

They both stared at Weezy's empty hands.

"There wasn't any," she said in a huff.

Annie opened Mason's door and peeked inside. There, on the table, sat a mug.

"Huh. How'd I miss that?" Weezy didn't move.

"I can't believe you're teaching your granddaughter to be sneaky."

"She's helping Granmommy clean, aren't you, punkin? 'Sides, there's a bad bug going 'round her day care, and my daughter has to work."

Annie pushed the door wide. "Better get it, don't you think? Otherwise your cover's blown."

Weezy instantly went off the defensive. "So you think something funny's going on, too, do you?"

"Why? What've you heard?"

Weezy quickly gathered up the mug, and they headed down the back stairs as she shared what she knew. "There's talk in town. Anthony asking all sorts of questions, and not all of them book material, if you know what I mean. Mason listening to talk at the café about what does or doesn't go on up here."

"Have you been cleaning the oven again? You're not supposed to breathe those fumes."

Weezy huffed and defended her point. "Seems to me a man'd be a bit more curious about the place he was sleeping. If you was a stranger in town, and you heard something peculiar about the place you was sleeping, wouldn't you say, 'Hey, wait a minute, I'm staying there, tell me more about this'?"

Put that way, Annie grudgingly agreed. "So, what do they say is going on?"

"Way I heard it, they accused him of staying for kinky sex."

"No," Annie said, stifling a laugh.

"Yep. But speaking of witches, he stopped at the library to ask about books on them."

"So this is why you've been spending more time here. You're keeping an eye on Jade."

Weezy grinned. "Might be looking for the kinky sex."

"Hon, if you'd give Noah half a chance, you could quit looking."

Weezy waved off that thought, and Annie went on to find Jade in the conservatory. There was a woman with her, all dolled up in a dark business suit and conservative two-inch heels.

"Okay. Sounds easy enough," she was saying to Jade. "I put some of this in my bathwater the morning before I go to court. And I carry this bag with me all the time, until the case is done."

"That's right. Also, if you can get the name of the judge beforehand—"

"Sorry to interrupt," Annie said, pausing in the arch. "Hospital called. Mason's in Emergency."

Color drained from Jade's cheeks.

So, Annie thought, *the wind still blows that way.* She wasn't above helping it. "He's asking for you."

"Is he all right?"

"Sorry, all that confidentiality stuff, you know?"

"For me? Well, I . . . But . . . He had my Jeep."

"Take my car. Keys are in my purse by the back door." She turned to the client. "Hi. I'm Annie."

"Cora."

"We'll be fine," Annie said to Jade. "Go."

Jade hugged Annie, not so much as a good-bye, but so she could whisper in her ear, "Not one spell while I'm gone, you hear me?"

Chapter 13

Jade abandoned Annie's fifteen-year-old station wagon in a restricted zone at Mercy Hospital. She might not have closed the door when she got out; she couldn't remember, and she wasn't going back to check.

Was Mason ill? Hurt? Had he and Anthony escalated their previous shouting match, met away from Mystic Manor, and beat the heck out of each other? She couldn't see Mason coming out on the short end of that. He wasn't brawny, but there was a steady force about him, a hint of danger that said he could take care of himself.

The roads had been plowed and appeared safe, but there'd been a drizzle last night. Had he slid on a patch of black ice and landed in a ditch after all?

Seemed more than just her hormones were waking up. On the spur of the moment, she'd opened herself to a relationship, thinking she was ready for a lover. But in light of Mason's pushing her out of his room and staying away all day, then frightening her with whatever this turned out to be, she didn't know if she was ready for all the baggage that came with one.

Mercy Hospital was small, a three-story brick building in a quiet, residential neighborhood. They handled simple things: appendectomies and births, cuts and fractures, common illnesses, various in- and outpatient therapies. Complicated cases went to Hannibal Regional.

Six years ago, she'd waited day and night by the phone for a call from here, waited to hear that they had her husband. At first that's what she'd expected. Days dragged into a week. Then that's what she wanted, because a call from here meant Doug hadn't been rushed to Hannibal, or worse, airlifted to St. Louis.

One week dragged into two, then a month, then several months. No one had to tell her that when the call came, it wouldn't be the hospital.

Jade charged through the automatic door. It led directly into the ER waiting room, where Mason sat doubled over in one of the hard plastic chairs, his body trembling.

"Mason!"

She flew to his side and dropped to her knees, her long cape swirling around their feet, cocooning them together in a dark puddle.

The pain must be terrible to make him shake like that. "They're discharging you when you're like *this*?"

There wasn't another patient in sight, and they hadn't even treated him yet? The nurse sitting next to him was doing nothing about it, either. Jade glanced around, desperate to summon a doctor to help Mason, but no one appeared. She'd take him home, dip into her bag of herbs and spells, and ease his pain herself.

"Tell me where it hurts."

It was important to her to touch him, reassuring even though he couldn't sit up straight. She ran her hands over his body in assessment, starting at his head. No blood there. She skimmed over his shoulders, palpated his arms all the way down to his hands and fingers. No obvious fractures; no yelps of pain. Just one, long, sorrowful moan as he leaned closer to her.

Difficult to hide her frustration with such blatant lack of care, Jade snapped at Gabby. "Why aren't you helping him?"

"Lord, there's no helping—" Gabby dabbed at tears on her cheeks. Her eyes were crinkled with laughter, which vanished when she saw the look on Jade's face. "Why, Jade, what are you doing here? I talked to— Anthony, was it?" she asked in Mason's direction, though he couldn't see her with his head hanging in his hands like that. "He said he was coming."

Jade grabbed Mason's head and lifted it so she could look him in the eye. "You're laughing!"

He tried to speak but couldn't. Finally he caught

a deep breath, and he looked much better once he sat up straight. Jade was relieved, of course. Not a bandage or a cast in sight. If Mason had wrecked her Jeep, he ought to at least have a bandage to show for it.

Why couldn't it have been this simple six years ago?

Why was she so glad it was now?

"I thought you were hurt. You looked as if you were in pain."

Mason's face brightened. Not with laughter again, not over what probably was another anecdote about one of Gabby's grandchildren—she had a passel of them—but with pleasant surprise. "You were worried."

"Don't be silly." Jade shot to her feet. "It's bad for business when the guests end up in the hospital."

"It wasn't as if you had anything to do with it." Mason's eyes narrowed. "Did you?"

"Did you hit your head? Did he hit his head?" she demanded of Gabby, who said nothing, but shook hers to confirm he had not. Jade took the chair on the other side of Mason and asked, "What happened?"

"I went to the lock and dam today." He reached in his pocket and started to hand her the Jeep key, but he fumbled it, and it fell to the floor.

"To photograph the eagles," Gabby tossed in helpfully as she picked it up and gave it to Jade.

"Yeah, like every day."

"Only he fell asleep."

"No-o-o," he denied on a long breath. "I don't

sleep. Not like that anyway. Must've passed out. Next thing I knew, I *came to*"—he emphasized the coming to part, as opposed to waking up—"to flashing lights, a cop leaning over me, and some woman who kept screeching, 'I found him. Oh, Lawd, he's dead, and I foun' him. Musta froze. Oh, Lawd, he's dead, and I foun' him.' I remember it clearly because she kept screeching. Did I mention she was hysterical? Over and over. I began to think she was right, because if I had to hear her much longer, I knew I was in hell."

Jade covered a smile with her hand; best not to encourage him.

Didn't work.

"'Oh, Lawd, he's dead, and I foun' him,'" Mason repeated in a decidedly feminine voice.

Jade leaned around him to ask Gabby, "Is he all right to take home?" and Gabby laughed and said, "Well, I don't know about that, but medically speaking, he's fine."

She was killing him.

Just seeing the frightened look on Jade's face when she'd run in—frightened for him, because she thought he was hurt—was enough to stop Mason's heart. It was as if someone had kicked him in the gut and socked him in the jaw at the same time; he knew he'd been hit, he knew it was supposed to hurt, and damn if it didn't.

It sure as hell got his attention. What a way to go!

But still, she was killing him.

Oh, it wasn't her fault. He was the stupid one who thought he was being smart when he'd opened his mouth and said he never slept. She just happened to be the one he wanted to believe it. She just happened to be awake nearly every friggin' minute of every friggin' day, so how, when, and where was he supposed to sneak in a solid six hours? He would've gotten a hotel room just for napping, but word would get back to her.

Jade walked beside him out to the car. His feet dragged along like concrete blocks. His legs weren't much better. After he bumped into a plastic chair, she held on to his arm the whole way. Not bad; in fact, it turned out to be quite pleasant. She steered him with it snugged against the side of her breast—not on purpose, he was sure—so he could think of little else. He'd have to have died in the Jeep today not to be consumed with carnal thoughts of Jade, him, and little else.

His heavy parka, a sweater beneath, her cape, probably another sweater—way too many clothes between them. He thought about telling her he wouldn't faint if she let go, but hey, if he didn't milk this for all it was worth, he'd have to turn in his guy card.

They didn't have far to walk. Not nearly far enough. He could go for blocks with his arm tucked into her.

"This is it," she said at the yellow curb.

"Restricted zone. Nice if you can get it." He took a second look at the old derelict of a station wagon. With a crooked bumper and dented grill, it looked eager to get a couple suckers on board. "This?"

"What? Big tough guy like you is afraid of a little adventure?"

"Adventure's my middle name." He stepped toward the passenger side, and she let him go when she was sure he'd made the curb. "I'd hold your door for you, but I see it's already open."

"Good. I see you're still conscious."

They settled in.

"You're sure this is safe?"

"At least I won't be falling asleep at the wheel."

"Ooh, low blow. Except I wasn't at the wheel."

She turned her head and stared at him with that look that women owned, the one that said, "Come again?"

"Well, okay, I was, but I was parked at the time. So I was perfectly safe."

"So is this. Annie drives it every day."

Dull interior, worn seats, stained carpet. "Candle business isn't so hot, huh?"

"Some people might take that as an invitation to hit you with their opinion of insurance companies who deny claims for silly reasons."

"Please. I was on death's door already today."

"There was no proof that Annie's husband didn't take her Suburban and go on a long trip, leaving her with the payments. So this is all she could afford."

"Get it? Candles, hot."

"I got it."

"Didn't want you to think I froze any brain cells out there."

"I'm not so sure it's working." She snickered and

said, "'Oh, Lawd, he's dead, and I foun' him. Musta froze—'"

Mason leaned across the seat and angled his head for a perfect landing on Jade's soft, slightly parted lips.

Oh, man. He'd meant the kiss to be quick, to be a fun way to hush her sassy mouth. He wasn't prepared for the slam that hit him dead center in his chest. Felt like a goddamn sledgehammer. How could a man ever be ready for something like that?

While Jade had been working hard to scare him out of her life, she'd crashed past all his self-preservation alarms and swept into his heart.

"Mason?"

She pulled back only inches, her eyes wide and curious. He could feel her breath on his face, warm, soft. Trusting. Intimate. He wanted more. God help him, he did.

"You're thinking too hard." Jade's hand slipped up, tentative at first. Her fingers caressed his cheek. So soft. So trusting. Her tongue darted out and tasted him on her lips.

He knew in his heart she wasn't guilty of anything. And if she wasn't, then he wasn't really stepping over any ethical boundary, right?

Please, God, he wanted to be right. He wanted to sweep her off her feet, take her to bed, make love to her every night for the rest of his life. It would be wonderful, too. Right up to the point where she found out he had a secret of his own, that he'd been lying to her all along.

Sorry, love, I didn't think you'd mind that I've been lying to you since the second we met. Not about everything. Just the basics. Just who I am, what I do for a living, what I'm doing here. You know, simple stuff.

"You stopped breathing again."

He grunted. "Good thing you're driving then." Drawing on all his reserves, which were pretty low at the moment, he pulled back gently and settled himself next to the door. He busied himself with the seat belt, saying, "Might need this."

Jade was slower to recover, he noticed. It seemed like forever before she pulled out of the lot, glancing at him often, studying him, trying to read his intentions, probably. Good luck with that; he wasn't sure what they were himself. He knew what he should be doing, though—steering the conversation, doing his goddamn job.

People were apt to talk freer in closer, more intimate surroundings. Reveal more. Let their guard down some. This front seat was a helluva lot more intimate than that castle-with-revolving-doors she lived in.

"What did you say? Annie's husband left with her car?"

"Abe. He was with Doug. Don't pretend you haven't heard. It won't hurt my feelings any."

Abe. Biblical; odds were, a local. "I admit, I've heard some talk around town."

The residential neighborhood they drove through was quiet, lined with tall trees and brick homes, porches and awnings. A few dusk-to-dawn street-lights. In a nod to the lumber industry, he supposed, most houses were embellished with dentil molding, elaborate gables, even ornamental soffit carvings.

"You want to tell me what happened so I can quit guessing?"

She spared him a glance. "Sure you can handle it?"

"Big tough guy like me?"

"Gabby says you were hypothermic."

"Doc said pre. They warmed me up with coffee." God, he hoped it was decaff. "Try me."

Jade sighed, long and low, girding her loins. "You met Courtney, right?"

"Yeah, in the kitchen. Seemed nice."

"Her husband was with them. He disappeared, too." Jade glanced his way to see if he was going to interrupt. "You're not going to take a flying leap out the door or anything, are you?"

"No, no, that would hurt. I'll pass."

"They were good friends, bought a boat together. We'd had a recent ice storm. They decided to go to the lake and check on it."

"Three full-grown men just up and disappeared?"

He chewed the inside of his lip, deep in thought. Not about the husbands, though; about how he was doing a credible job of being just the right amount of surprised and curious. He stomped down the little birdie that said this was going to come back at a very inopportune time and bite him in the ass.

"That's what they say," Jade continued, not so

hesitant to talk anymore since what she'd said so
far hadn't sent him running. "Depending on who's
talking, they A) ran off to South America to live the
good life; B) got whacked in a drug deal gone bad; or
C) bought a lot of life insurance that was too big a
temptation for three small-town wives, so we stuffed
their bodies into the car and drove it into the river."

"These are your *neighbors*?"

Jade snickered. "For a guy who stops breathing
real easy, I'm surprised you didn't jump after all."

"Door's stuck." He adjusted the vent to blow heat
his way. "Forget about them. What do you think?"

Jade sighed. She slumped a little in her seat, so
little, it was almost undetectable, but Mason noticed.
He noticed lots of things about Jade. Little things,
big things.

Very quietly, she said, "I think something bad happened."

She drove carefully. The main part of West Bluff
was built in a flat pocket along the river, surrounded
by hills that had fed the lumber boom. Unlike up
on the bluff, streets here crisscrossed in a rigid grid,
with terribly imaginative names like Steeple Drive
and Methodist Street routed into vertical markers at
the intersections.

Feeling a little punchy from lack of sleep, he
wondered aloud, "Can a Baptist live on Methodist
Street?"

"Around here it's not so important what church
you belong to as long as you attend. So, yes."

The station wagon creaked and rattled like any old

car, but the heater worked just fine. Warm again, Mason tipped his seat back. His head rolled to a comfortable spot on the headrest, and his eyes drifted shut. No way he could keep up this pace. He might as well just admit it. Get it out in the open.

He might not be thinking clearly. Christ, twice in, what, less than two weeks?

"I'm exhausted. I can't take it anymore."

After a beat, Jade quietly said, "I can put an end to it. I mean, if you want. If you need help."

Hair stood up on the back of Mason's neck, a warning before a deadly strike. "In light of our conversation, that sounds . . . ominous."

They rode another block, crossed Bible Boulevard.

Then Jade got it, and laughed. "No, not like that. Geez, I grow herbs, remember? Some are very relaxing. Lavender. Valerian. Agrimony if you need something stronger, though that might make you sleep like the dead."

Not something he wanted to hear.

"Passion Flower."

Mason lifted his head. "Now that sounds interesting."

"Doesn't work like it sounds. It'll put you to sleep."

"Heard you have poisonous ones, too."

Not a car in sight, but Jade signaled a right turn anyway. "Somebody in the family put those in a couple generations ago. Call me sentimental, but I have trouble killing anything, so I let them be."

Trouble? As in, Trouble, *but I manage?*

"Come on, live dangerously, Kincaid. Your sore throat's gone, isn't it?"

After another cup of whatever she'd brewed for him, he had to admit that it was. He yawned and settled back again. "You could put the big drug companies out of business."

"Doubt it."

He held his hands up like a scale in motion, seeking balance. "I don't know. Natural remedy. Man-made chemical concoctions that cost an arm and a leg, and often as not, don't work. Sounds like a no-brainer to me."

"You think I want the FDA looking my way? Red tape? Lobbyists? Uh-uh. No way. No thanks. If I had to deal with all that, it'd be years before I could give you something to help you sleep tonight. That didn't make sense, I know, but go with it."

What could he say? No? How would he ever explain why he said no?

Oh, sorry, I was going through all your things in your entire house, and I found out you're a witch, and I think it's possible you may have killed your husband, so—

Nah, he didn't think that.

I think it's possible you may have drugged your husband so someone else could kill him—

He couldn't prove it, but there was no way Jade ever killed anybody or arranged to have it done. Just didn't wash.

I think you may have given your husband the wrong thing, or too much of something by accident, and he died, so if you don't mind, I'll pass.

Maybe he could buy that. Accidents happened. A wife could get scared and think it was better to hide the body. Right?

And that explained the other two, how?

Jade drove on autopilot, working things out in her head while Mason got some much-needed sleep.

Six years ago, she'd waited for the hospital to call and say they had her husband. Today, just when she was sure the original spell was weakening, reversing even, they called and said Mason was ready to come home.

Funny, in a cosmic sort of way. If it was a slightly warped, six-year-old spell come to fruition, it had to be the slowest one on record.

She was falling for him; no sense denying it. She'd thought she could be oh-so-modern about this, take it for what it was, for as long as he could stay, then move on.

Ha! Her reaction to seeing him in pain, real or not, had spoken to her loud and clear. For the second time in her life, she was hooked. Clearly, utterly hooked. Just as she'd wanted to be. Just as she'd wished.

Only this time, this relationship came with built-in problems. If the spell that started it all continued to reverse, Mason would leave for good. If it didn't, and he stayed, she'd always wonder if he would've chosen to be here on his own. Especially since he said he never wanted to marry. Where did that leave her?

She wanted a child. Would he have one without marriage? Did she want that? In *this* community?

Poor little thing—might as well stick a pointy black hat on her head and hand her a crystal ball when she sent her off to school.

Other than taking it one day at a time, she didn't know what to do. She couldn't just turn off these feelings she had for him. She had a few choice words for uncooperative spirits, though.

While Mason slept with his head against the window, Jade stopped at her post office box, picked up more mail orders for botanicals, then headed up the hill to Mystic Manor. If it'd been any warmer out, she'd have let him have another hour of sleep, parked in the driveway, but on the heels of a recent flirt with hypothermia, pre or otherwise, she thought better of it.

Turning off the engine didn't wake him. Neither did letting her seat belt retract with a snap against the post, nor closing her door. She walked around Annie's relic and stared at Mason's head, his cheek mushed against the glass.

So peaceful. Experiencing none of her inner turmoil.

That didn't seem fair, so she tapped on his window. "Coming?"

Nothing. She tapped again. Then, grinning, she knew what'd get him up.

"Oh, Lawd, he's dead, and I foun' him. Musta—"

She'd expected his eyes to flutter open, maybe a confused look, at the most a crooked, self-deprecating grin. But Mason woke up growling, she imagined, like a bear who'd just had his hibernation cut short.

By the time he grabbed the door handle, Jade was off and running, shrieking, laughing so hard she couldn't see patches of ice, so she stayed off the walk as she charged through shin-high snow toward the back door.

She didn't have a prayer of outrunning him, and even though it was no surprise when he dropped her in a tackle, the air whooshed out of her, and she fell face-first into the snow and came up sputtering.

For a guy who'd just been carted off to Emergency, Mason had a powerful grip. His arms were around her, so strong. His hands on her, so mobile, though she couldn't feel them as much as she'd like through her cape and sweater and long underwear.

"What are you doing?" she laughed.

"Checking for broken bones."

She elbowed him in the ribs. Between her cape and his parka, it was ineffective, it only made him laugh, so she grabbed a handful of snow and washed his face with it.

"Now you'll pay," he said, pinning her flat on her back with his entire body.

"I'm *sooo* scared." When she looked up into his steel blue eyes and saw the promise of just how she'd pay, she trembled with anticipation.

"Damn, woman—" He made a production of spitting out every flake of snow. "I think you froze my mouth."

"You really have to stop that!" Jade tried to step back, but he wouldn't let her, held her tight.

"Sorry. Sorry. Ah, condom," he repeated, as if the word didn't make sense. "You don't have any?"

"I wouldn't trust anything as old as I'd have around. You?"

"Didn't think they went with a tux. I mean, Christ, what if I reached in my pocket for the ring and one fell out in front of the minister? Condoms were the last thing on my mind."

"So I heard. I believe scuba diving was number one on your list."

"It was a *wreck*."

"It was your *honeymoon*."

His grin was pure light. "If I was honeymooning with you, you'd be on my list from top to bottom."

It was corny; she loved it anyway. Given that she didn't pull away with contempt, he nuzzled her neck, nipped at her ear, palmed her breast until she almost, *almost*, forgot what they were missing.

"I can't believe I was supposed to wish for condoms."

He murmured a distracted, "Hmm?" and conducted damage control. "Would you prefer to make love in front of a roaring fire or next to a tropical waterfall?"

Make love. She didn't know if it was just a line for him, but as surprising as a smack in the head, she realized it hit closer to the mark for her than "hooked on him."

While her momentary silence gave her time to

think and opened her eyes, it had the opposite effect on Mason. He tugged her bra down around her waist and began to lavish attention on her breasts so fast the room started to spin. If they were going to stop, it had to be now.

"Mason?" When she pulled back, he reluctantly let her put some space between them.

Then all of a sudden, he snapped his fingers. "Hey! Anthony. I'll be right back."

Suddenly standing alone, chilled and confused and self-conscious, Jade tugged her bra up. "Ah, Mason, I'm kind of nervous as it is—"

He charged up the back stairs.

Jade threw her hands in the air. "I'm not ready for an audience!"

Chapter 14

Mason barged into Anthony's room, relieved to find him there. He'd been making himself scarce lately, with no explanation. At the moment, who the hell cared?

"Condom. Now."

Anthony slouched on both chairs by the table in front of the window, his ass in one, his sock feet on the other. "Hold on," he said into his cell, laying it on the table as he got up. Already prepared for this from the earlier phone call, he slapped two packages into Mason's open hand. "At least you haven't lost your head completely."

"Two? That all you have?"

"Out." Anthony splayed a hand on Mason's chest, shoved him through the door, and slammed it. Just as quickly, he opened it again. "Your resignation still is *not* accepted."

"Just two?"

"For God's sake, man, make do."

Mason flew to the top of the stairs, then instead of running right down, he went to his room and brushed his teeth. He thought about shaving, too, but decided if he tried that in his condition, he'd show up with more toilet paper on his face than on the roll, so he skipped it. While he was locking his Glock in a camera bag for the night, he heard voices downstairs. More company.

"No. No, no, no," he said, a heartfelt prayer to stop anything from interrupting his plans. His and Jade's; she was as ready for this as he. But as he descended the back stairs, his hopes fell as he heard a woman in the kitchen with Jade. Not Annie.

"Sorry about the short notice, Jade. I kind of got caught short, what with Elisha having twins in the middle of the night. Deborah isn't due for three more weeks, but you know how babies are."

"You want the usual?"

"Better make it extra. Mm, something sure smells good."

"Don't touch it!"

Mason entered the kitchen just as Jade descended on the range with a vengeance. Though they'd barely registered, he'd smelled the soup and seen the two tall candles when they'd first come in. The candles lasted about two more seconds. Jade pinched out the red taper with an angry twist, broke it in half, and threw it into the sink, where it landed with a thunk. The white candle followed, along with a few muttered words he couldn't make out.

"Bad candles?" was all Mason could think to say.

"Bad Annie. I'll explain later." Jade looked up at him with eyes that begged him to understand a sudden change in plans. "Look, I need to get some oils together for Madeline. She's our midwife. A terrific part of our community."

Madeline was about forty, with a huge green bag slung crosswise over her shoulder, red hair and freckles, and a sweet angelic look that probably reassured most mothers-to-be. That didn't last any longer than the candles, though. She was staring at the sink, and from her crestfallen look, she was either going to cry or pass out. Maybe both.

"I'm so sorry. Here I've gone and ruined your dinner . . ."

Jade put her arm around her. "Madeline, no, it's not you."

". . . with *Pierce Brosnan*," she wailed. "If only I'd called first."

"We weren't going to eat this."

"Oh, sure, you're just cooking it for the aroma." Madeline didn't look convinced, but no tears fell. "Smells divine."

"Trust me, you don't want it. Annie's not as good with herbs as she thinks she is, if you know what I mean. And he's not Pierce Brosnan."

Madeline blinked. "He's not?"

"He's Mason Kincaid."

"Oh. *Right*." Madeline winked.

"I'll get those oils."

Jade steered Madeline across the room, and as smoothly as running water, handed her off to Mason. He wasn't sure if it was her idea or his.

"Madeline," he said gently, sliding his arm around her shoulders, "why don't we wait in the study? It's cozy in there."

Jade graced him with a grateful smile, her eyes warm with the promise of an amorous night ahead. Maybe even an adventurous one. They'd need sustenance when they were through.

"And, Mason? Whatever you do, don't touch that soup."

"You sure? Madeline's right—it does smell divine."

"Not even if you're starving."

Mason steered Madeline into the study, all the while wondering what was wrong with the soup. Annie wouldn't slip in some of those bad herbs, would she? Nah, she had no reason to harm him, and she sure wouldn't harm Jade.

Madeline regained her composure. She brushed off Mason's help, pulled the ottoman close, and burrowed her ample hips into the upholstered chair. "What do you think that's all about? The soup, I mean."

"I have no idea. Didn't smell like she ruined it, did it?"

"No, sir, it didn't."

As long as he had a few minutes to kill, Mason lit the logs, stacked and waiting, in the fireplace.

He'd get a nice blaze going. Turn off the lights after Madeline left. He'd even let Jade light candles, which he knew she'd want to do. It'd gotten so that didn't bother him so much anymore. Didn't remind him of his bad day at the church at all.

"So. You're a midwife," he said, once the kindling caught.

"Yessir, fifteen years now."

Two 'sirs' in a row. Mason smiled and tried to look more approachable.

"Hannibal to Clarksville. I've been buying botanicals from Jade for the last ten. Oh, I know what you're thinking. Ten years ago, she was barely legal. Well, in my defense, I came here originally to talk to her mother, and I was a little apprehensive—even a little miffed, if you want to know the truth—when she referred me down the genetic chain. So to speak."

Approachable must have worked; she kept going.

"I mean, really, how could a teenager know enough about birthing and herbs to help me, when I'd been doing it for five years? Let me tell you, though, after ten minutes, I was all ears. Yessir, Jade's one remarkable woman. Say, you'd better sit down. Mason, is it?" She winked again. "You look about ready to drop."

Jade sent Madeline on her way with the herbs and oils she used to help mothers ease new life into this world, thinking that maybe, just maybe, she herself was getting closer. Not that she'd consider having a child if Mason weren't sticking around for the long haul, but maybe just closer.

In the meantime, she'd enjoy the duration without guilt. She wasn't worried about whether he'd respect her in the morning. She already had that. He might not have liked her going off with Noah's nephews, but he'd squared his shoulders and accepted that she was a person who followed her beliefs.

He didn't want to get married. Fine. Knowing what she knew, she wasn't about to talk him into it!

Funny that Courtney's talisman wasn't working. If Jade had seen less of anyone lately, it was Anthony.

She found Mason stretched out in front of the fire, his hair dark against a cream-colored throw pillow, his back to the door. While she felt like leaning against the jamb and watching him sleep for the next, oh, five minutes, she was more concerned about the fire. She didn't leave wood sitting around in fireplaces waiting to be lit, and he certainly hadn't stepped out in his sock feet to get some.

Which left Annie. At the very least, she'd stacked it, maybe even lit it.

She'd also cast a spell in the kitchen—the lit candles were solid evidence—but Jade wasn't worried about Annie's candle-only spells. Generally, those worked well for her. Not that she didn't have the best of intentions with other spells, but she just didn't seem to have the right focus, didn't think things through start to finish, didn't take into account human nature and all the repercussions that came with it. Frequent end result: disaster.

The fire called for countermeasures, no matter who'd lit it.

Jade stepped outside for a handful of cut branches before padding across the carpet. Kneeling on her heels in front of the fire, tossing in a stick with each phrase, she said,

"By the power of one, this spell's begun.
By the power of two,
I clear my home through and through.
By the power of three, I erase any lingering energy.
By the power of four, Annie's workings are out the door.
By the power of five, only my spells survive.
By the power of six, I quickly apply this fix."

There. A nice, romantic fire throwing off some heat, warming the room. The better to remove their clothes by.

Jade stripped off her sweater, deciding with uncharacteristic wild abandon that she didn't care where it landed. There was only one thing she cared about right now.

"Mason?" Kneeling between him and the fire, she laid her hand on his arm and ran it up over his broad shoulder. "Mase?"

He snored and said, "Mm?" in the same breath. He'd gotten to sleep without any herbs after all.

Well, darn.

She splayed her fingers through his hair, in case he was only snoozing lightly and would wake up without a good swift kick in the butt.

He murmured again and tugged her down until she lay in the circle of his arms, protected in the hollow of his body. The fire was hot on her face, hot on her skin. As was Mason behind her.

She wasn't tired. Sleep was a waste of time. But she could lie here with him for a few minutes until he was sound asleep again. She could do that for him. He needed it.

A catnap here, with him, didn't sound so bad. She gave in and burrowed her head into a comfortable spot on his outstretched arm.

Warm tropical water. Neutral buoyancy. Full cylinder of air. Clear mask.

Mason awoke slowly, certain that he was in heaven. He savored something even better: the feel of Jade in his arms, the promise and excitement of making slow, passionate love, the thrill of every sigh he'd elicit from her . . .

He ran his hand along her body, hip to neck, startled to full alert when a phone rang in the distance, and he discovered he wasn't in the Caribbean. He still had Jade in his arms, though, and she wasn't fully dressed.

Silky skin. Silky black bra.

Okay, better than diving—a real eye-opener, that one.

She'd had her sweater on when Madeline was here, hadn't she? He'd remember otherwise. He'd dreamed otherwise, but that's all it had been, a dream. Which was about to come true from the feel of things.

Did Anthony have a camera in here?

Ah, hell, he was covered; he'd tried to resign.

He stuck his nose in Jade's hair, deep in a mass of curls that had gone unruly overnight, and breathed coconut. No wonder he'd been in Aruba-land. He snuggled closer, pressing himself against her.

God, let me wake her like she's never been awakened before.

Jade sighed and hummed. Her whole body rippled as she woke gently, stretching head to toe. Mason pressed closer, wanting to let her take her time, impatient to get naked together.

Should he get up and stir the fire, which had burned down to a mass of coals and half a log? Grab the throw off the sofa? That'd be good, in case Jade was concerned Weezy would pop in and find them going at it.

Going at it. That didn't sound nice. Well, it did, but not the way he usually meant it.

Had she bewitched him? Did he care?

Not the way she was snuggling against him now. There was barely enough room to slip his hand between them and undo his jeans.

Jade hummed again, a little more alert now. She rolled over onto her back, then continued around until they were face-to-face. Crying shame her bra came unhooked while she was turning around. It hadn't required much help on his part at all. Her breasts might be cold all exposed like that, though, so he covered one with his hand.

"Mm," she said, arching her back, filling his palm. "About time you woke up."

"You've been waiting for me?"

"You know it. Oh. My. Gosh."

He leaned back a bit, just enough to see that her eyes were open wide, and she was staring over his shoulder at the window. "Snowing again?" What better reason to stay here all day?

"It's morning."

"Sure is." He put his hand in the small of her back and scooted her closer until she could feel that his body knew it was time to get up, too.

"It's morning," she repeated, as if a wondrous miracle had occurred. That or he didn't understand her idea of disaster. "I slept all night."

"I'll get the throw." He would have, too, if she hadn't clamped a hand on his arm to stop him.

"You don't understand. It's *morning*."

"Happens every day." He leaned in and pressed his lips to hers, kissing her until she was soft and breathless. "Tell me you don't have anything against making love when the sun's up."

She focused on him then, and a slow smile spread across her face. "Why would I have something against that?"

"If you're worried about Weezy coming in, I can carry you up to the bedroom."

"The door's closed."

"You make love in here so often you have a signal?"

"No, goof," she responded to his teasing. "Weezy won't come in when the door's closed because I meet with clients in here."

Leaving lots of good, witchy vibes in the room, he hoped. "Anthony came through for us. Let me throw another log on the fire, and we can wake up real slow."

He was up and had his hand on the lid of the log box before she could say, "It's just for looks. I don't keep wood inside."

He pulled out two logs.

"Annie," she said.

"Yeah, you mentioned her last night. Remind me to thank her."

"Remind me to kill her."

He tossed the logs onto the coals, and when he had the fire crackling and blazing again, he turned to find Jade wrapped in the soft cream-colored throw.

"You look like a burrito."

"You like burritos?"

"I *devour* them. Wanna see?"

"Counting on it, big guy."

This time he wasn't lying to himself. This time that was what she really said. And as he knelt beside her, prepared to go slow and make the morning last, she lifted the edges of the throw and showed him that while he'd been building a fire in the fireplace, she'd been building one here, for him.

Her skin glistened from head to toe, so golden perfect in the light from the flames, which were nothing compared to the flames licking his insides. He ripped off his clothes, sweater to his socks, nothing between them finally except unspoken promises.

Jade pulled him down beside her.

He thought she'd meet his energy with a shy, feminine reserve to remind him that it had been a long time, and he should go slow, but she opened her arms and turned her face to meet him and looked at him as if she'd been waiting for him her whole life. As if he were the only man she could possibly be with. And in that moment, he knew it was the same for him. One door closes; another opens. He'd been saved from a disastrous marriage so he could be here, now, with this woman, who was quickly, inexplicably, becoming his everything.

He thought about telling her that he thought he loved her. Good sense prevailed.

A woman didn't want to hear "I love you" ten days into a relationship that had begun a mere twenty-four hours after his almost-wedding to someone else, even if it hadn't happened. It would be justifiable cause to mistrust the depth of his feelings.

A woman like Jade didn't want to hear "I love you" from a man with secrets, who eventually was going to have to answer for every goddamn thing he said. When the time came, he didn't want that picked apart, picked to death.

A woman would be justifiably skeptical if a man said it for the first time when they were making love for the first time. It would seem false, as if he thought he had to cajole his way into her panties.

He'd keep this to himself for a while.

"I need you," he whispered against her lips, again and again, hoping she wouldn't take it for less than it was, because he'd never needed anyone as much as he did her. Not just today. Not just until the stakeout was over. But forever.

"I'm here," she answered in kind, responding to his words, rippling against him, around him, every time he said it. Nearly purring like a cat.

He could feel Jade's primal urgency, her need for him, as she wrapped her legs around his hips and pulled him closer, until he was nearly too mindless to remember a condom, but he did, and he put just enough space between them to take care of that before Jade tightened her legs around him again and pulled him home.

It was too fast. He wanted better for her, to take care of her, give her what she needed, make it special, and she'd just driven him dangerously close to the limits of his control.

"If we slow down," he murmured against her lips as he kissed her ceaselessly. *God,* would he ever get enough of this woman? "I can last longer for you."

"Next time," she said, arching against him, driving him deep. "I need you *now.*"

He splayed his fingers through her silky curls, letting them trap him as he knew they would, as he held her beneath him and, trusting that she knew what she wanted, what she needed, he thrust hard, sending himself beyond the point of no return.

"Yes, like that. Mason, just like that."

Her words faded away, leaving behind a soft sigh that was his undoing. A soft sigh that at some point transformed into moans of pleasure, cries of pure joy, and her ragged breathing mingled with his until they were both sweaty and sated and limp with release.

Mason rolled them to their sides, and they lay entwined for long minutes, staring into each other's eyes, their fingers floating over the other's skin in a silent language of connection, of unspoken bonds. Bonds that Mason knew would be tested all too soon.

As their breathing slowed, and the air grew chilly, Mason pulled the throw over them again, snuggled Jade against his chest, kissed her temples and her hair and her face until they both fell asleep.

Chapter 15

"Oh, hey. We forgot your Jeep."

"Is this your normal pillow talk?" Jade mumbled against Mason's chest.

In all fairness, the earth had just moved twice, and they'd fallen back to sleep an hour ago, but she still wasn't ready to think. If she started thinking, she had a major dilemma to work through—to keep him or not to keep him?—and there seemed to be no right answer.

She'd probably change her mind about the need to figure out when they'd pick up the Jeep the next time she had to go out, which, if she wanted to make love to this man again, one of them had to do.

And she did. Oh, she very much did.

"You never lay in bed and talked with your husband?"

"I catnapped. Once he closed his eyes, he was dead to the world for a good six hours."

"You never . . . on the floor in front of a fire?"

"Dead fire."

He took the cue and pulled the throw over her bare shoulder.

"We'll pick up the Jeep later," she said, stretching without moving too far from him. She liked the feel of his body alongside hers, his shoulder beneath her head. "Can you drive?"

"Sure."

She smiled, and nibbled toward his nipple. "Not too much exertion on the heels of hypothermia?"

"Did I seem tired to you?" he asked with a sexy rumble that said if they had more condoms, he'd show her just how tired he wasn't.

"Then we can drop Annie's car off for her." And stop by the drugstore.

When she groaned, Mason picked right up on it and said, "What?"

"Everyone in West Bluff will know I'm having sex."

"Because . . . we're going to drop off Annie's car together?"

"No, silly. Because I'm going to stop at a drugstore on the way home."

"Ah. You're going to ravish me again."

"Without a doubt. But . . ."

"Timing's bad?"

"Right on the heels of a presumptive death certificate?—everyone'll think I'm celebrating. Not bad for me, mind you," she hastened to add. Didn't want him to think she had any regrets. "Just looks that way. And then they'll think worse of you, and you might not get the help you need around town . . ."

Mason threw off the throw and sat up. "Hannibal's not that far. Do they know you there?"

Jade bolted upright beside him. "I'll wait in the car."

Mason chuckled. "I feel like a teenager."

"I made love to a teenager once." She'd met Doug in college.

"You dirty old woman."

For that, she took the whole throw to herself when she stood up, wrapping the soft folds around her.

Mason gathered his clothes. "Think I can run upstairs without running into Weezy or Annie?"

"I *was* going to compliment you."

"Really?"

"Something about your stamina."

"Go ahead."

She yawned. "I can't remember."

That afternoon, Annie jumped into her station wagon and slammed the door. She'd left Tricia Sherwood in the slush two blocks back. The woman would *not* give up, following her for the past several days. Needling, needling, needling.

Something had to be done, and Annie didn't mind being the one to do it. This was the last straw. She'd let Tricia bump into her, literally dragged her down into the snow and came away with her black beret. Ha! By the time Tricia'd searched the snow and couldn't find it, Annie was a block away.

But Tricia— Boy, could she run!

Annie gunned the engine and drove down Main Street as fast as she dared. There wasn't time to go home and cast a circle of salt and do a proper spell with candles. She had deliveries to make. Not that she didn't have candles with her; she did. Picturing herself getting pulled over with a lit candle in the car made her laugh. Imagine trying to explain her way out of that one.

She'd make do, though. Jade always said energy was important. Well, her heart was pumping now! She punched a cassette of rhythmic drums into the ancient dash-mounted player and visualized it not eating the tape.

She threw the beret onto the floorboards, ground it under her heel, tapped her hand on the steering wheel in time with the beat, and said, "I want the media to stop hassling all three of us and gathering information on us." Tap, tap, tap. "I want Tricia Sherwood exposed as a real troublemaker." Tap, tap, *grind*. "She should lose her job." Tap, *grind,* tap. "Everyone should see what she's been up to. She should lose her job. If she doesn't let up, I want the cops to get involved. Did I mention she should *lose* her job!"

Grind, grind, *grind*.

"As I will it, so mote it be."

"Are you stalking me?"

Mason whirled around at the sound of Brenda's voice.

"I saw you the other day outside the card store.

And now you're here. Give it up, Mason. It's over."

"Brenda!" He was genuinely happy to see her. "So that *was* you."

She glared at the box of condoms in his hand, then at him. "If you don't leave me alone and go back to Florida, I'll file a complaint. I will. Lyle's family lives here in Hannibal. The authorities will take me seriously. I'll get a restraining order if I have to."

"What? No, wait, I'm here on business."

"I mean it."

"Really. Anthony's uncle sent us to West Bluff."

Her glare softened. "Anthony's here?"

"Well, not *here*. In West Bluff. I just ran over here for the day."

"What, they don't have private eyes in Missouri?"

"Keep it down, will you?" Mason glanced around to see if anyone overheard, then leaned close. "I told you how it is sometimes. A local is too obvious. All it takes is somebody recognizing him and saying, 'Hey, who're you investigating today?' and the whole stakeout is blown."

Brenda folded her arms across breasts that were bigger than normal. She must've been wearing a bra that was too small for weeks, hoping he wouldn't notice, and now it didn't matter.

She narrowed her eyes at him. "West Bluff, huh? Where're you staying?"

"Mystic Manor."

She looked dazed for a moment, then burst out with a laugh. A guffaw, actually. If she didn't pipe down, everyone in the store would know he was an investigator working in West Bluff, and what was news in West Bluff? Three widows, that's what.

Brenda laughed so hard, she had tears running down her cheeks.

"Is that healthy? In your condition?"

She caught her breath. "I'm sorry."

"Whatever."

"I mean it, Mase. For everything. I handled it so badly."

"Yeah, you did."

She started laughing again. "But you are just so stupid."

"Excuse me? It sort of sounded like an apology when you started."

He shouldn't have told her he was working, but in his defense, he'd grown used to telling her everything. He hadn't said whom he was investigating, but that didn't matter. If she mentioned she'd run into her ex, there'd be questions, especially from Lyle's family, who'd think the same thing she had, that he was stalking her. She might reveal his real occupation. All it took was one person hearing something, innocently passing it on . . . It could be in West Bluff in no time.

"I'm working undercover," he reminded Brenda. "You might consider that you owe me one and keep it to yourself."

"I do owe you one, Mase. So here it is, listen up. You're gonna shoot yourself for this." She leaned in to him and lowered her voice. "You're so stupid, you managed to pick the one B&B owned by a witch."

Well, that confirmed it.

"Brenda," Mason said, breaking into a genuine smile. "Why do you think I care?"

"I'm just saying."

"Uh-huh. Well, listen, I'm glad we bumped into each other today, because I wanted to thank you. So thank you. There. I've said it."

He'd taken several steps away when Brenda said, "For what?"

He paused just long enough to face her and say what he had to say. "For being you. For doing exactly what you did. For setting me free."

It was easy to put Brenda out of his mind as he stood in line to pay. He thought about how tough it would be to keep up his ruse of insomnia if he made love to Jade every night and promptly fell asleep until dawn. He'd cover his bases and ask for those herbs she'd mentioned for sleeping. Not that he'd actually take them.

He picked up when Anthony called. If his partner yelled about anything the cameras picked up last night, Mason could always resign again.

"Hey, Anthony. What's up?"

"Where are you?"

"Hannibal."

"Good, I was hoping. Can you pick up three more cameras? Something's wrong with ours. I'm getting nothing."

"At all?"

"Working one minute, then nothing. *Nada.*"

Whew.

"Anywhere else, and I'd think they'd been tampered with."

Mason lowered his voice. "Maybe, ah, someone put a spell on them." He'd fallen asleep reading the witchcraft books, but if he believed 10 percent of what he'd read, it wasn't inconceivable.

"How's your room?" Anthony asked.

"What? Fine, why?"

"I swear mine feels . . . smaller. Like a closet. I can't wait until this job's done. Anyway, the cameras. To put a spell on them, Jade would have to know they were there first. And you saw them, they're minuscule. Weezy's granddaughters dusted right over them yesterday, didn't notice a thing."

"I'll pick them up. Hey, Anthony . . ."

"Yeah?"

"How's it going with you and the bartender?"

There was a long pause. "What brought that up?"

"You know, just asking."

"You getting sappy on me, Mason?"

"Resignation's still on the table."

He heard Anthony sigh. "We've talked a couple times."

"And?"

"We're going out when I get back."

"Good." Mason was nodding to himself as he stepped forward in line.

"Let's get this wrapped up ASAP."

"Is this your I-smell-foul-play radar kicking in?"

"No. Well, it is, kicking in, I mean. But on top of that, I just don't like being here anymore. And before you say it, it's not because of the bartender either."

"I wasn't going to say a word. I'm happy you're

going out when you get back. Hey, gotta go, my turn to pay. Talk to you later."

Get back. Would he return to Pensacola with Anthony?

Yeah, sure, he had to. His blood was too thin to live in the Siberia of the Midwest.

Neither was he so dense that he thought Jade would relocate.

"Did you have a nice night by the fire, dear?"

"Mo-*ther*!" Jade was sitting in the Jeep, waiting for Mason to come out of the drugstore. She tried to squelch the voice of reason that said if he was staying, he deserved to know her secret, but sharing it with him could end whatever relationship they had.

And what was that really? She was supposed to be getting rid of him, but if things were going well, was it wrong to reconsider and think, well, maybe this is how things were supposed to work out? She was torn between accepting the situation and setting it right.

Pure rationalization; he had to go. It's just that her heart wasn't in it.

She had to tell him, then.

"Hello? You still there?"

"Still here, Mom."

"You sound funny."

"I'm on the speakerphone."

"Are you alone?" her mother asked, though she probably already knew the answer.

"What, you can't tell?"

"Don't be sassy. Is he there now?"

"He'll be back any minute."

"You two will make such pretty babies."

"I'm hanging up."

"Oh, don't be so touchy. It's not like I watched."

"Keep it up, and I'm putting a blocking spell on you."

Mona sighed softly. "You slept, didn't you?"

"All night," Jade admitted, aware that she'd broken into a big, silly grin.

"Does he know?"

"That I don't sleep? He says he doesn't either. How perfect is that?"

"Does he *know*?"

Jade blew out a breath, resigned to telling the truth. "I thought he'd be gone by now."

"You're not still sending him away?" Mona shrieked, and Jade was glad the phone wasn't by her ear.

"It's . . . complicated."

"Life's complicated, darling. That's why we're here, to work through things."

"It'd be easier if I could figure out whether to accept the situation at face value or send him back."

"Well, if you want my opinion . . ." Mona proceeded to expound on that.

Jade hadn't expected to fall in love with Mason, not once she knew he was the clone. Telling him she was a witch could scare him off, snuff out any feelings he had for her.

He deserved to know, though. To make up his mind based on the facts. If he hated her for it, if he ran for the hills, that'd take care of the decision for her.

"Gotta go, Mom. My attorney's on the line."

* * *

Mason slid into the passenger seat and leaned across Jade's phone for a kiss that was too short.

"Jade. Elliot here."

On speakerphone, so Mason held back a bunch of sloppy kisses. The guy could be a client. Man, he couldn't wait to find out what Jade did for clients, what kind of people went to a witch for a spell, what they asked for.

"My attorney," Jade whispered, starting the engine while Mason buckled up.

Elliot went through the social niceties briefly before moving on. "Just wanted to catch you up and let you know everything's moving along as planned. The death benefit should be wired to your brokerage account today or tomorrow."

"Thanks, Elliot."

Oh boy, Mason thought, going on high alert. If Stockard wasn't really dead, and the money was here, now was when he'd show up. If he didn't have remote access to Jade's account. *If* he hadn't been here all along. There was still the matter of cigarette smoke lingering in various parts of the house. Faint, it would come and go so vaguely that he couldn't pinpoint it.

"No thanks necessary," Elliot said. "I want those funds at your disposal as soon as possible."

Mason's curiosity was piqued. Jade was in a hurry?

"You've been waiting long enough," Elliot said. "I know you have big plans for them."

Chapter 16

ureka!

Mason made progress late the following afternoon. Damn curious, but there it was, a door in the back of a closet, of all places. Now why would someone hide a door? Multimillionaires didn't have a monopoly on panic rooms, and witches probably had more justifiable reasons to feel persecuted than the very rich did. Maybe Sebastian Delarue had been both.

Mason shined his flashlight in the closet, looking for booby traps.

"God, I love this job." If he couldn't be wreck diving, this was the next best thing.

Well, other than making love to Jade. That went without saying.

Anyone could argue that the door wasn't hidden at

all. Two feet deep, four feet wide, the closet wasn't full of brooms, shelves, or anything else that would, in any way, hide the rear exit. Though it'd be an easy matter to hang a dozen coats in there and duck through them to escape. And maybe it had been used for something like that at one time, but right now, except for the basket of rumpled kitchen towels hanging on the wall, the closet was empty.

Mason prayed the pocket door wouldn't rub, because Jade was in the house, but he was getting desperate, this had to get *done* so he could clear the deck between them. He took a chance and slid it open.

Steps. Going down to the cellar. He closed the door behind him, then tested each tread carefully before putting his full weight on it—no sense being reckless at this stage. At the bottom, he located an overhead chain and pulled it.

Fluorescent fixtures blazed to life. One glance took it all in. No windows. Two commercial-sized washers and dryers sitting on a black-and-white-tiled area, surrounded by a sea of smooth concrete that couldn't have been the original floor. Clotheslines. Hangers. Detergent. Clean towels stacked on a smooth, dust-free table. Everything that accumulates from doing a houseful of laundry. A nice, clean room to do it in. Compared to most Laundromats he'd been in, you could do surgery down here.

Considering he was sneaking around in the house of a woman with a secret life, he was allowed a little catch in his heart at that thought, but further looking turned up no knives, buckets of organs, or restraints.

Not that he seriously thought there would have been. Not Jade.

But a relative?—he wouldn't bet money on a relative.

The walls looked to be plaster, a coating nowhere near a hundred years old. He recalled stories of murderous spouses hacking into the foundation, storing family members, and refinishing the walls.

Keep it together, Mason.

No outdoor access; no surprise there, as he'd searched from the outside. It had been a little tricky poking around in snowdrifts without leaving evidence of having been there. Not something he had a lot of experience with.

Mason caught another whiff of cigarette smoke, but he walked the whole perimeter and still couldn't trace it. The low-ceilinged space ran the length of the house from front to back, but not nearly from side to side. Darn small for such a big house, but still, it was big enough to throw a New Year's Eve party for dozens of your closest friends.

Mason strolled into the conservatory, planning to sit on the bench, peruse the wireless network, and keep an eye on the driveway so he'd know who was coming and going. He'd put off this area because it was the hardest to access without Jade, Weezy, Annie, or that damn dog seeing what he was up to.

The house was bound to be empty sometime, and when it was, he was finishing the whole wing in one swoop. Searching Mystic Manor wasn't something he had to rush, but it was the most logical way to move the job along. One bit of evidence, and he could pack up and go.

All of a sudden, leaving didn't sound so good.

He'd felt something powerful between Jade and him the second he'd walked in the front door, the moment he'd laid eyes on her. At the time he'd been too hungover to recognize it for what it was, but thank God he remembered now. It wasn't because she'd bewitched him; she hadn't had a chance to do so.

As the conservatory door closed behind Mason, warmth and humidity welcomed him, washed over him. Smells intermingled. One green plant looked much the same as a hundred others. He wondered which ones were the herbs Jade had given him for sleep. He'd dumped them down the toilet on the sly and slept like a rock with her in his arms, which is why she needed time to catch up on work and why he was taking chances with her in the house.

He often got a feeling that Jade wanted to talk about something, but either she backed off, or they were interrupted. Like an hour ago, a guy had come to the side door. That blasted door. Why did people need Jade so much, and in such a hurry? Couldn't they handle their own problems?

Sitting down, perusing e-mails on the other computer between Jade and prospective clients, Mason found that Jade was clear on what she would and wouldn't do, how she could help, how much it would cost, how long they could expect it to take. She referred them elsewhere if she felt someone was better qualified. There was also an abundance of thank-you e-mails, detailing how lives had improved after a visit with her, mentioning that they'd recommended her to friends. For the scary people looking for an underhanded way to get a job promotion or to make an uninterested person fall "madly in love" with them, Jade quashed any discussion of malevolent spells and did not follow with a referral.

It appeared she mentored a good number of witches, too, and not just around the state or around the country, even, but worldwide.

Trekking through files finally led Mason to a second website, its file tucked away in an insignificant-looking folder on the hard drive and having nothing to do with Mystic Manor Botanicals. Secretive woman that she was, Jade had labeled the damn thing Stationery and stuck her Craft web files in there. He opened his browser and visited. The site had an active blog, a bulletin board, and a password-protected area—yeah, right, like that worked when he was on her computer—where a small network of witches held their own discussions and consulted with each other.

So that's what she was up to for long stretches of time in her office. There was an increasing number of queries on the witches' loop about where Jade was and what was keeping her so busy these days that she didn't have time to post. Speculation touched on whether it had anything to do with the anniversary of Doug's disappearance or a new man in her life.

Thanks to web surfing and the books he'd bought, Mason followed this easier than he could have a week ago. Jade wasn't just practicing a little witchcraft on the side. She lived it and breathed it. Like oxygen, it sustained her.

Some of the witches were in the closet; some weren't. Discussion showed how Jade had learned the Craft from her mother and grandmother, even her great-grandmother while she'd been alive. How fearful those women had been of discovery and persecution, as each of them remembered generations before, the links in the chain reaching back so far that the legacy of historic witch-hunts had trickled down to the present day. Many understood Jade's insistence that her secrets be protected. Many were of the opposite mind, that the more they were out there, the sooner people would get used to them and not be frightened.

Church bells rang in the distance, as if on cue. Yeah, he could see why Jade was staying in the closet. Although it seemed a good number of people in the area knew, so every day, as far as he could see, her secret was in some degree of danger. But if she'd kept it hush-hush this long, she must know what she was doing. The whole family must. Maybe they did spells about it.

The large, deliciously warm conservatory worked its magic on Mason, set aside the reality of snow and ice, and made him long for Aruba. He wanted to take Jade there. If she wasn't already certified in scuba, he'd talk her into that first. He wanted to show her what he loved most, share his world with her.

Ooh, that hit him right in the gut. Sharing his world meant telling her the truth, didn't it? The whole truth. He couldn't do that yet, but the longer he put it off, the deeper the hole he was digging for himself.

All dreams of diving with Jade flew out of his head when she ripped into the conservatory and threw down the same leather bag she'd carried when she'd gone away with Nathan. Eyes blazing, hair flying— man, she was a sight when she was riled!

She yanked open a cabinet, grabbed a candle. Any tighter and she'd choke it. She paced small, agitated circles, muttering unintelligible words, driven by a powerful need to exorcise some invisible demon while every bird, frog, and insect hiding in this heaven on earth went deadly silent. Moments later, she slapped a mirror into a stone niche, rubbed the candle between her palms, lit it, dripped a few drops of wax onto the mirror, and stuck it there.

Whew, Mason thought. *A spell, live and up close.*

Jade's intensity took his breath away. Even yards from her, Mason felt her power. If he didn't swoop up and grab her, charge back to the waterfall, and make mad, passionate love to her right now, he might go stark, raving mad.

Jade kicked the bag.

Maybe he'd wait to swoop. He cleared his throat to alert her to his presence. Jade glanced his way, then her gaze quickly skittered off, as if embarrassed.

He tamped down his need for her and said, softly, "Can I help?"

"Know a good hit man?"

"Ah . . ."

"Never mind. Forget I asked. That'll work just as well." She tipped her head at the candle, then said, "Mason. You have time to talk?"

In response, he closed the lid on the notebook.

Jade's lips thinned into a disgruntled line as at first she hesitated, then swallowing any misgivings, she perched on the edge of the bench. She didn't cozy up next to him, but spared every inch of the boards as she plastered herself to the other armrest, leaving two lonely feet of space between them. Too far to nonchalantly drape his arm across her shoulders and comfort her, which she looked as if she needed. If he was going to do that, he'd have to scoot over, but her rigid posture warned that she'd take flight if he tried.

"I . . . don't know where to start really." She hung her head, stretching tight muscles in her neck. "But two people . . . us . . . who are becoming friends, or, ah, more . . ."

"More's good."

She flashed him a grateful smile, which just as quickly faltered. "Yeah. We shouldn't, ah, keep secrets from each other."

"Is this about the spell you just did?"

Jade's head snapped up. Her eyes bore into his, searching, as if in doing so she could divine the answer. Softly, warily, she said, "You know?"

His response was a sort of lopsided shrug, an arch of the eyebrows that he used to convey more clearly than words, "How could I not?" because he was afraid if he said it, it'd come off cocky. His gaze slid from the large pentagram inlaid in the floor, to the candle burning in the niche, to the archway that led to the drying room and all its bottles of herbs and oils. And probably potions.

It was too soon for Jade to breathe a sigh of relief, Mason could tell, but she did look less wary. Eyes could be windows; wheels behind hers were turning a mile a minute. He read them clearly.

Should she flat out admit it, spell it out, tell it like it was?

Should she mince words, make light of it, talk around it?

What if, what if, what if?

Buying time, Jade picked wayward specks of herbs off her sweater where they'd caught in the rolled cuff at her wrist. Then, tossing her hair over her shoulder, she came to a decision.

"He was pretty mad when he left," she said, referring to her visitor. Her voice was tight, but not shaky. "No telling what evil thoughts he's having. The mirror will reflect them back to him."

Times three, Mason recalled from the reading he'd done.

"The candle sends the energy on its way," Jade explained.

"Simple enough."

"Much of witchcraft is."

The corner of her mouth twitched then, and Mason knew she was letting down her guard. For him. He was touched by her trust. He'd never betray it. She wouldn't think so, of course, when she learned he was deceiving her every minute of every day.

"Nowadays, people are used to more-vivid imaginations drawing pictures for them about witchcraft," she said. "Gone are the days of a nose twitch and *whoosh,* there's a brand-new car in the driveway. Now it's pixies that pick up children, plants with deadly cries, snakes born from chicken eggs . . ."

"Owls carrying messages," he added helpfully.

"What's so odd about that?" she asked, matter-of-factly. A moment later, she burst into laughter. "That does it, I'm signing up for CPR class next week. No telling when I'll need it." She took a deep breath, perhaps for fortification. "So you're not going to freak out about sleeping with a witch?"

"Not if you agree never to use witchcraft on me."

Without hesitation, she nodded.

"You know how important this is to you?"

She nodded again.

"It's just as important to me that I hear you say it."

Jade looked him right in the eye and said, "From now until your dying day, I'll never use witchcraft on you." Her gaze was steady, honest.

"Good enough."

"Mason, this is a big secret for me. Most people here won't tolerate a witch in their midst."

"Yeah, I met the librarian."

Jade winced. "And she's not the worst of the lot. Organized religion is rampant in West Bluff, if you haven't noticed."

"Kind of hard to miss that. And yet," he said lightly, "you lob Tupperware containers into the river."

She shrugged prettily.

"So what'd the guy who's getting the mirror treatment want?"

"He lied. He said he wanted help finding something, but it was obvious he'd never lost it. He just wanted something that didn't belong to him."

"How could you tell?" *Can you tell that I've been lying to you, too?*

"He dropped a name."

"Well, off with his head, then."

"Don't think I wasn't tempted. The man he mentioned isn't local. He lives outside Paris, and the only place his name exists in West Bluff is in my computer. So I have a hacker on my hands. My tech guy, the one I trusted—I can't let just anybody on my computer with what's on there—moved away two years ago. I guess I've fallen behind the times."

"Can't you just do a spell to hide your files or something? Lock up anyone's computer who hacks in? Look, I don't pretend to know how witchcraft works, but what good is it if you can't protect what you have?"

"Spells are like any other energy. They wane. They have to be repeated. I do my best to protect my secrets from people who mean me harm, but it's time-consuming to keep after it. I'll have to find someone."

He'd offer to help, but really, it'd be like hiring a well driller to dig his grave; it was getting deep fast enough, thanks anyway.

"You know anything about computer security?"

He grimaced. "I can take a look at it. But why trust me?"

She smiled. "You haven't ratted me out to anyone yet."

"I could tell you were keeping it under wraps."

"You didn't tell Anthony?"

"He's just as observant as I am. But not to worry; he won't tell anyone. Though it seems you have a lot of local traffic through here for not wanting anyone to know."

"They all have reasons to keep it to themselves."

"But, Jade, they don't. Noah told Nathan. Nathan brought someone with him."

"Well, I do sacrifice a rooster at the end of each spell and tell them that's what'll happen to them if they ever talk."

Mason felt hair stand up on the back of his neck.

Jade's laugh revived him like sparkling chimes.

"Oh, I get it. CPR again."

She grinned with unsuppressed amusement, literally bouncing on the bench like Lily did when she was proud of putting one over on Uncle Mason. Only with Lily, it wasn't for real. With Jade, he was constantly caught off guard.

Damn, he had more reading to do.

"I'm sorry," she said, though she didn't look it. "That wasn't very nice."

"I can tell you won't try not to do it again."

"True."

Jade scooted across the bench and nudged him

with her shoulder until she'd burrowed in beneath his arm. Right where he liked her. He felt complete when he held her. Even Aruba was a distant thought; scary as that should have been, it wasn't.

"Dare I ask what Annie did to the soup?"

"With Annie, you never know."

"Does it have anything to do with, say . . . poisonous herbs?"

"Oh my gosh, no! Is that what you thought? Annie's a kind and gentle creature who wouldn't hurt a fly."

"But I wasn't supposed to touch her soup."

"Okay, she wouldn't hurt a fly *intentionally*."

Calmer now that Jade had quit ranting, the tiny birds dared to take flight again, flittering around overhead, going about their business. One flew close by the niche, its slipstream causing the candle's flame to flutter and dance.

"Now that you've told me your big secret, may I ask questions?"

Jade cuddled close. "You're comfortable with this?"

"So far."

"Then I'll tell you anything, if you agree to tell me when I'm getting out of your comfort zone."

"I'm a pretty open-minded guy. We may never get there."

"We'll see. Ask away."

"Let's see. Oh, I know. Can't believe I almost forgot. *What* was with all the candles the night I arrived?"

"Imbolc."

He tilted his head and stared at her. "God bless you."

She laughed at that. "Imbolc's a celebration, a fire festival really, marking the midpoint between the winter solstice and spring equinox. We light candles to celebrate light and new life."

"Ah. Let's see. Do you ever eat without candles?"

"They frown on it at McDonald's."

"Uppity bastards. No class."

"So you're getting used to them?"

"They're growing on me. It's not one here or there so much as the dozens you had going that night. The last thing I remembered was hundreds of candles in the church and then all of a sudden I sort of woke up here, and it looked like a repeat." He fell silent.

"Of the worst day in your life?"

"I thought so at the time."

"You recover quickly."

"It's complicated." That was putting it mildly. "So complicated, in fact, that I meant every word when I thanked my ex."

"For dumping you."

He poked her in the ribs and made her wiggle, which had its own rewards. "You like saying that, don't you? I prefer 'letting me off the hook.' We weren't right for each other. Granted, she might have chosen a better way to do it. A better time. Still, I can't help feeling grateful." He set the notebook on the floor, leaning it against the bench. "I'm thirsty. What say we open a bottle of wine?"

"A drink to truth and honesty—yes!"

"I was thinking of cozy dinners, crackling fires, and new friends."

"You're trying to get me drunk again," she said with a bubble of laughter.

"I never got you drunk."

"You tried."

"Sweetheart, I have plans for tonight." He nuzzled her neck, zeroing in on the sensitive spot behind her ear. "And I want you sober for every last one of them."

Chapter 17

B&B Owner Dies Second Time

Jade shrieked when she read Friday's headline in *West Bluff News*.

Across the master suite, Mason dropped a log short of its mark and crouched in a protective stance, looking like Bond about to whip out a gun. "Christ! Don't *do* that."

"Sorry. But— But—"

He straightened quickly and set about righting the log with tongs before the room filled with smoke.

"Wow," Jade said. There was a lot there to admire.

He looked at her over his shoulder. "What?"

"Rambo and Bond rolled into one. Where'd you learn that who-do-I-shoot-first crouch?"

"Movies."

Life should be so easy. She'd made a promise that, on the surface, was all fine and good, and she'd never break that promise. Truth was, though, she'd already used witchcraft on Mason, but if she confessed that the only reason he was there was due to a spell she'd cast, he'd be hopping mad that she'd done so already, or that she hadn't told him up front yesterday. While he seemed to be an upstanding guy, she hadn't known him even two weeks, so how did she know he wouldn't retaliate by giving away her secret?

Wouldn't that make a great front-page headline?

Witch's Husband Dies Twice

Couldn't be much worse than the trash she was skimming. "Who *are* these people they're quoting? Listen to this. 'We played poker every week.' News to me. 'We weren't allowed to play at Mystic Manor, though.' Bullshit. Anonymous, of course. Now I ask you, is this responsible reporting?"

Mason puffed up. "You want Rambo and Bond to deal with them?"

He made her laugh. "You kind of lost it without the scowl and the crouch. I half expected you to whip out a gun."

"The dog stole it."

"Do you see imaginary dogs often?"

"If I did, they'd be little ankle biters."

A beat passed when neither said anything. Jade decided there was no time like the present. "Seriously, Mason. You know a lot about me, but I hardly know anything about you."

"I shoot pictures, love, not people. Totally boring. What else is there to know?"

"Exactly." She waited expectantly, knowing there was a lot more to this man than met the eye, yet he was very tight-lipped about it.

He'd taken ten minutes this morning to prepare a tray and bring it upstairs, piled high with Weezy's flaky, homemade cherry turnovers, juice, and even the damn newspaper. He pushed it aside and proceeded to crawl on top of Jade and show her he wasn't boring at all.

He nipped at her neck, pushing the narrow strap of her nightgown off her shoulder. "Guess your mirror trick didn't work on the reporter."

"It's not a trick. Call it a spell or call it magic, but not a trick. And I told you, the energy wanes." As was her focus at the moment. "I forgot to renew it. I've been *busy*."

She glared at him, because really, if he weren't so sexy and persistent and *here,* she would've remembered that the reporters would feed off last week's death certificate and this week's wire transfer, the fact that there'd been a memorial service on the first anniversary of Doug's disappearance and now, according to the article, maybe there'd be another.

Could she have prevented this attention-grabbing headline by talking to Tricia Sherwood?

Not likely, if experience was any judge.

But because Mason was so sexy and persistent, along with funny and just downright likeable, she couldn't maintain the glare longer than five seconds, which is exactly how long it took him to nibble his way to her breast. Heat arrowed right to her core, and she unashamedly stretched and purred beneath him.

She'd never had a Bond/Rambo spy fantasy before, but she was working up to it.

Mason awoke to a ringing cell phone later that morning. He scratched his chest and blinked, trying to orient himself.

Oh, right. Jade's room. No wonder he was so warm on the right side. Jade was snuggled in to him, using his shoulder as a pillow, her nude body soft and pliant and plastered to his, just as he liked. She might have insomnia, but it seemed if he kept her satisfied and worn-out, she was his for the whole night.

A double reward.

The phone started up again, insistent.

"Mine or yours?" he asked through a yawn.

"Are you kidding me? I have a cheery little ring, not a foghorn." Jade rolled away, her touch replaced by a cold draft as she pulled the covers with her.

Damn. Mason answered with a brusque, "H'lo?"

"I'm looking at our friend," Anthony barked.

Instantly on high alert, Mason bolted to the edge of the bed. "I'm listening."

"Right at him."

Jade couldn't overhear, but all the same, he hurried into the adjoining bathroom and closed the door. For good measure, he turned on the water.

"Better get down here, Mase."

"Get a picture." He stepped into his jeans, sniffed yesterday's shirt to see if it would do.

"Camera's not working. Get on it, buddy. He's the right height, gone a little pudgy around the middle and in the face, but the bone structure's dead on. Pun intended. I'm sitting outside the café at Main and Chapel."

"I don't know. You think it's Stockard?" Mason snapped off a dozen long-range photos with Anthony hovering behind him.

"Could be."

"Not positive, though. Hungry?"

"Couldn't keep me out."

Ordinarily, Mason would leave the big camera and lens in the car when approaching a subject, but since he was supposed to be out photographing eagles anyway, he kept it with him as part of his cover. He had a palm-size camera in his pocket and the Glock in its holster.

Like everyone else, he and Anthony were wearing ball caps today. Anthony's said "Pete's Garage, Love 'em & Leave 'em."

"Friend gave it to me," Anthony said, when Mason stared at it.

"Accepting gifts from strangers." Mason tutted. "The bartender will be devastated."

"Leave it to you to wear a fish."

"Couldn't find one with a sunken boat."

"I guess not."

They settled at a four-top by the window. Mason

didn't have to ask Anthony to point out the target; it was like looking at a bad "after" photo.

Mason ordered coffee, eggs, hash browns, bacon, the works. Anthony ordered coffee and a corned beef sandwich, and commented that the only thing he still liked about West Bluff was Weezy's cooking.

"You're not getting bad vibes?" Anthony asked. "In general, I mean?"

"Nope."

Anthony studied Mason intently. "Yeah, guess not."

"That why you're making yourself scarce?"

"I keep moving around, hoping something will catch my attention and make sense." Anthony shrugged. "Nothing so far."

They both watched Pudgy's beer glass and flatware like hawks; photos would be good, fingerprints conclusive.

"I thought that was you I saw come in here."

Lyle stopped by their table, blocking the view. Mason sat back in his chair and sighed with deceptive calmness.

"Brenda told me she talked to you. I can't *believe* you're here."

Mason kicked out a third chair. "Take a load off, Lyle."

Looking surprised at the invitation, Lyle sat. Eyebrows raised, Anthony tossed Mason a silent query.

"The florist."

"Ah." Anthony sat up straighter.

"Don't go reaching for any hardware, boys," Lyle said, and Mason and Anthony both chuckled at the ridiculous line, so much so that Lyle frowned and said, "What?"

"Nothing," Mason said. "Want a beer? It's on me."

"His thirty days aren't up yet," Anthony said, meaning Mason's.

"What? Oh. Hey, I don't expect you to pay that. That was Brenda's doing. She went crazy with the red marker."

"Being a little hormonal, was she?"

Lyle flashed a proud poppa-to-be grin, then remembered who he was flashing it at, and his expression sobered.

"I'm not stalking her," Mason said. "I explained—"

"She told me what you said. I know what you do."

Mason threw up a hand. "So much for confidentiality. Look, Lyle, you can't be telling anybody why I'm here."

"He knows why we're here?" Anthony whispered harshly across the table.

"Not *exactly*," Mason said, trying to save the job he'd resigned days ago. Pure reflex.

"It was easy enough to figure out," Lyle said. "I can't believe someone thinks Jade is capable of murder"—he had the decency to lower his voice, further attesting to the fact that he knew and liked her—"and I think it's despicable that you're staying in her house, accepting her hospitality, while you try to prove she did it."

Anthony leaned toward Lyle. "That's not *exactly* why we're here."

Lyle surged to his feet, sending his chair scraping backward. He forgot to keep his voice lowered. "If you don't agree to leave town right now, I'm going up to Mystic Manor and tell Jade what you're up to."

Heads swiveled their way. Anthony mumbled a curse, then tried to smile their way out of the unwanted attention.

"Sit down before I shoot you in the foot," Mason said lightly, banking on Lyle thinking he wasn't joking.

Color draining from his face, Lyle sat. If Mason hadn't snaked his foot out and pulled the guy's chair under him, his tailbone would've kissed the floor.

Jade had helped Lyle. Somehow. Mason knew that without question. And now Lyle was feeling protective.

The threat of having his cover blown before he had a chance to reveal his own secret had been worrying Mason long enough to make him do more thinking about relationships than he'd ever wanted to do. Jade was the most confident, comfortable-in-her-own-skin, selfless woman he'd ever met. Being with her, part of her life, was like nothing he'd ever been prepared to feel.

In fact, it didn't seem right. People didn't go around every day feeling like this. They couldn't; wasn't possible. If they did, everybody'd know it. No, what he had with Jade was something special. Something indescribable. Something worth fighting for. And that meant protecting his secret at all costs.

"The way I figure it, you owe me one," Mason said.

"I— *What?*"

"You stole my bride, Lyle." Since the guys at the neighboring table were openly staring, Mason turned his head and included them in the conversation. "There I was, all dressed up in my tux at the church. And where was my bride? Running off with this lightweight. Now I ask you, doesn't he owe me one?"

Nods all around. Hopefully they were forgetting Jade's name had even been mentioned.

"See, Lyle. They think you owe me." For Lyle's ears only, he added, "I just a need another day or so. Then I'll tell Jade everything."

"I don't think—"

"I know where you live, Lyle."

Lyle rose to his feet again, with a whole lot less surge this time. He sputtered and headed for the door, but, last thing before he left, he turned back to Mason and nodded. "One day."

"Might need a couple."

He didn't linger. Pudgy was behind him, in a hurry to leave, urging him through the door.

"Hey, Stockard," the gruff short-order cook behind the counter barked. "Forgot t'pay again, asshole."

Anthony's head twisted toward their target. Mason quickly checked the counter, only to see Pudgy's spot already cleared. Fingerprints, gone.

"Don't have my money yet, Caleb. I'll pay when I get it."

"Aw, go crawl back in your hole," the grizzled cook

sneered to Stockard's departing back. To those remaining at the counter, but no one in particular, he said, "That widda's no friend a'mine, but seems to me somebody oughta do 'er a favor and tell 'er the truth 'bout that lowlife."

Chapter 18

Pink hearts, as agreed. Cupids with arrows.

Jade was wrapping dozens of West-Bluff-correct homemade treats for Jazzy's party. Valentine's Day was the next day, but with no school on Saturday, the class was celebrating early.

She was just about to leave when Buzz stomped snow off his boots and came in with the mail. It was already ten o'clock. If she didn't deliver these in the next fifteen minutes, the teacher was going to have heart failure.

"Did they change your route again?" she asked. Buzz normally timed his arrival to chat with Weezy and Noah, who both started at the crack of dawn.

Buzz sighed loudly, alerting Jade.

"What?"

"Supervisor says I have to give you this." He handed her a slip of paper. "I'm sorry as all get out."

Jade read the notice that her mailbox was not regulation and must be replaced, as well as relocated to the other side of the road. "*What?*"

"It isn't right."

"I'll say it's not!"

"No, I mean I looked at it. It *is* regulation. You're just being hassled."

Jade slapped the notice onto the breakfast bar. "Well, thank you, Tricia Sherwood."

"Shoulda let Noah give her a noogie."

"Yeah."

"I'm real sorry I had to be the one to give it to you."

"How do I appeal it? No, wait, I have to deliver these to Jazzy's classroom. Tell me tomorrow, okay?"

"I'll bring the forms. You bring the power."

He looked at the treats hungrily. Jade pulled back the red-heart-covered clear plastic and put two on a napkin for him. If she hadn't been flustered by the time and the notice, she would've done it sooner.

"Thanks. Oh, one more thing." Buzz reached inside his coat and pulled out a brown box. Long and narrow, it had specks of raw earth stuck beneath the clear packaging tape holding it together. "Expecting this?"

"Mother."

He immediately held it at arm's length, gingerly. "Great. I was keeping it warm. My innards aren't going to suddenly shrivel up or anything, are they?"

She squinted at him. "Hmm. How do you feel?"

"Funny. I know you gotta go. I'll set it in the drying room."

After the party, Jade found a ticket on her windshield. Malfunctioning taillight. How the heck could someone know it malfunctioned when the car was parked?

Small pieces of red plastic on the asphalt were a clue. Thanks to Tricia Sherwood, Jade's low profile was blown. People were suspicious of her. Generally she stayed beneath their radar, and they left her alone.

She promptly conferenced Annie and Courtney, and warned them to be on the lookout for trouble.

"She snuck up on me in the tampon aisle," Annie griped. "I hate that."

"You know what you can do with that?" Jade began to suggest a simple spell.

"Oh-h-h-h trust me," Annie said with a drawn-out laugh. "Already did it."

"Well," Courtney said. "I got pulled over *with* Jazzy in the car and questioned by that *shit-ass* sergeant who's lived here for—"

"The cops," Annie gasped. She sounded distressed, but Jade thought now wasn't a good time to go into it.

"Thank you for interrupting. Now I can say it again. That *shit-ass* sergeant who's lived here for ten years because he thought *I* fit the description of someone suspected of childnapping."

From Courtney's language, Jade surmised Jazzy presently was not within earshot.

"Shit-ass?" Annie giggled.

"He *questioned* my *child*."

"Ooh. He's lucky it was you," Annie said. "Jade'd make sure he was too busy to do that again."

Out of curiosity over the whole witch thing and with more information under his belt, Mason revisited the locked bedroom.

One altar sat on top of an old, dark, heavily carved dresser. Mason opened the top drawer. He'd checked them all previously, but hadn't found anything to point toward finding Stockard or his body, and he'd moved on. He lingered now.

Candles in every color of the rainbow. Red for sex, love, lust, and *right now*; he had no trouble remembering that one. Orange and yellow, he didn't remember what they were for. All colors related to more than one intention, but he wasn't going for a degree in this stuff.

Hey, not bad for a few hours of reading, though. Maybe Anthony's discomfort had to do with a spell in the house. Maybe not; he hadn't felt it the first week.

The second drawer held a large flat box with dividers, a rock or crystal in each cubby. There was incense, not one or two, but many. Little jars of oils: rosemary, patchouli, jasmine. Like candle colors, every item had multiple intentions. Now he knew what the charcoal discs were for, how a witch would light one and sprinkle a crumbled herb or a mixture of herbs on it as it burned, scenting the air.

Energy, Jade had said. Witchcraft was all about energy.

Mason got the feeling this altar belonged to Jade's mother, the other to her father.

The marble-topped table had only a center drawer with a few white candles, two oils, and a dozen cones of incense divided into two bags. Seemed the crystal bowling ball sitting on a heavy three-legged silver stand was the main tool here. He hadn't read enough yet to know what that was about. All he had was a picture in his mind of a gnarled old crone bent over it, holding a young woman's smooth hand, telling her how many children she'd have and what tragedies would befall them if she didn't heed the signs.

Maybe he'd seen too many movies.

His phone vibrated on his belt, and he answered.

"It's probably not him," Anthony said wearily. "I turned up a photo of Stockard's lazy-ass brother. Unless Dougie killed the guy and took his place, which isn't totally inconceivable coming from someone who stands to make a million bucks doing it, it was Davy Stockard we saw today."

Mason started pacing. "Which would explain the other two, how?"

"Exactly. And I think his parents would've noticed."

"Anybody talk to the guy who sold them the insurance?"

"Courtney's husband brokered the deal. Looks aboveboard."

"Damn."

Mason signed off, thinking about look-alike brothers while he stared at the crooked collage of building photos, which fell off the wall when he straightened it. Catching it was fortuitous. Besides saving it, he discovered papers stuffed inside the back.

He unfolded old, faded, cracked paper, heavily marked with minuscule notations and hard-to-decipher glyphs.

Hallelujah, a set of building plans.

The cellar was there, all right, and just as large as the house, not the little laundry section he'd found. If he was reading it right, there should be a full cellar, divided roughly into thirds. He'd been in the middle one. He traced what appeared to be a passageway with his index finger. If it was, then access to the southern section was right . . . about . . .

He turned his head and stared at the closet. Now that he'd seen what was behind door number one downstairs, he had every reason to get to the back of this one.

Like the other, this closet had a pocket door in back leading to a set of stairs. This time they dropped two stories into a completely separate cellar. One with cigarette smoke, men's clothing and freshly laundered sheets, metalworking tools and silver table knives. No one was there, but the shower was still wet.

Eureka!

The best way to learn anything was to let people talk.

Well, except Lyle. If Lyle talked, Mason was in deep

shit. While the mild-mannered florist had appeared intimidated by Mason's warning that he knew where he lived, that he might even shoot him in the foot, it also seemed he liked and respected Jade. Probably enough to overcome his fear and blab.

Mason made a quick call. "Hey, Anthony."

"Hey yourself."

"Have you found out how Jade and Lyle know each other?"

"Not even his checkbook is talking."

Something had to give. The camera in the locked bedroom hadn't picked up anyone going in or out, though it was obvious someone was. In fact, the replacement cameras seemed to have bugs in them, too, so he was just writing it off as one heck of a protective spell on Mystic Manor in general and staying more alert.

Even if Jade didn't know she knew anything, a simple fact, even a pseudofact, could flip a switch and turn this whole case around. Now that she knew he knew her secret, Mason could prompt her. Hopefully she'd keep talking, filling in holes as she went.

Timing was perfect when Jade asked if he had time to join her for dinner on Saturday evening. It was obvious she was expecting him to say yes; she already had a tray of appetizers out, along with place settings for two.

"It's a B&B," he said, careful not to appear too eager. "By definition, you don't have to feed me dinner."

"I'm a good cook, though."

"Darlin', you could burn it to coal, and I'd eat it."

"Why, you charmer, you." She batted her eyes and made him laugh.

He eased up behind her and looked over her shoulder to see what she was rinsing in the sink.

"It's salmon—you like salmon, right?"

"Just checking to make sure you didn't filet that reporter," he kidded, opening the topic.

"If I did, she'd be in the river, not my sink."

"I read the article."

"So did a lot of others. I had to wash egg off my Jeep. Courtney's ready to kill; Jazzy went out to ride her sled, but she was teased so much, she ran home."

"Crying?" Mason guessed, his heart going out to a little girl he'd never met.

"According to Courtney, Jazzy was so mad, she went online looking for a 'fix those mean ol' kids' spell."

"I'm sure I couldn't spell 'spell' when I was— Wait, I don't know why, but I thought she was little."

Jade snickered. "Five."

"I hope you're going to do something about that."

"Oh yeah."

Mason was filled with new insight, which around Jade usually amounted to a whole lot of new questions. Like how you kept kid witches from hurting others with spells before they were old enough to cast responsibly.

Listen to him! Maybe the Black Weekend booze had fried a few brain cells after all.

As he watched her work, he found himself longing for babies with dark, curly hair, and he didn't care if they wiggled their noses and made donkeys fly.

"Somebody stole Annie's purse in the grocery store, and the management didn't even want to call the police for her."

"But if they don't know you're witches—"

"People don't like people who are different, who don't fit in. And when something bad happens to outsiders, our so-called Christian residents are quick to think the worst. Doug didn't believe it either, at first."

"He didn't belong to a church?"

"Oh no, he and Annie and Courtney's husbands all belonged. Three different ones. They were all very personable men, very social, Courtney's husband in particular. Their plan was to charm people from the inside out."

"Was it working?"

She bobbed her head in a yes-and-no kind of way. "The trouble with that was eventually, when they went missing, there were three very vocal congregations pushing the police to charge us with a crime."

If he let her go on like this, he'd lose control of the mood. "Can I help with something?"

"You can pick out a bottle of wine."

"Chardonnay?"

"Sounds good."

He found the opener and did the honors. "You'd think the paper would've mentioned a few facts, like what your husband did."

"You mean other than boating and fishing with his buddies?"

"Yeah, you know, for a living. Was he an herbalist, too? Did you run the B&B together? Just curious. You don't have to answer if you don't want."

"I don't mind." Jade pulled Brussels sprouts out of the refrigerator.

"Ah . . ." Mason said.

She grinned. "No Brussels sprouts?"

"Feel free to cook some for yourself."

"That's okay, they would've just been a small side. I have a veggie casserole ready to come out."

Mason poured two glasses and handed one to Jade after she pulled stoneware out of the oven and set it, steaming, on a pair of side-by-side trivets.

"Mm, smells wonderful." He leaned over the dish and savored the aroma. "Keep this up, and I'll be a fresh-herb convert before you know it. Are those the trivets that disappeared from the dining room wall?"

"My, you're very observant. I know, I know, photographer. But still, I think it's weird how much you notice. You probably know how many freckles I have on my face."

"None."

She smiled at him, because he was right. Because he'd noticed. "What color my eyes are?" She closed them so he couldn't cheat.

"Green."

"Too easy."

"Mid-to-dark, more than one shade, like mature

tree leaves in late summer when there's been plenty of rain."

Jade blinked and stared at him. "Wow."

He grinned triumphantly and popped a cherry tomato into his mouth. "Now that we've established my *incredible* powers of observation, what are the hieroglyphic-looking symbols on the trivets?"

"Runes."

"As in fortune-telling stones?"

"Yes and no. There's much more to runes than that. Sometimes I carry them with me—"

"You'd need a big purse."

She smacked him with a pot holder.

"Hey, not nice."

"You're lucky I didn't have the wet fish in my hand."

He tried a cube of white cheese, decided he liked it, and ate the whole thing. "Go on. You carry them with you. What else?"

"I carve runes on candles, draw them in the earth, and on slips of paper I put in charm bags. You look a little confused. Maybe it'll be easier if you think of them as shorthand for specific kinds of energy." Using pot holders, she lifted the pan aside just long enough to show and tell. "For instance, Jera, on the left, symbolizes rewards, like a harvest; a time of celebration. The other one, Algiz, is a defense rune, for protection."

"Are we celebrating something?"

Jade picked two red napkins sprinkled with tiny white hearts out of a drawer and waggled them in the air, tipping her head to the side in that come-kiss-me way Mason found utterly irresistible. "Is it too soon?"

"For . . . ?" Funny she didn't mention the huge death benefit and whatever "big plans" she had for it. "Oh, Valentine's Day! Fine by me."

"Good. Thought you'd gone off the deep end there for a second."

"I was going to warn you about fortune hunters."

"At least I know you're not one."

"How's that?"

"When you walked through my front door, you didn't know me from Eve."

"When I walked in your front door, I didn't know my hand from my foot."

Jade laughed. He loved it when he made her laugh.

"Fear not. I have remedies against men with ulterior motives," she said with a wink, as she rolled the napkins into brass heart-shaped rings and set them on the tray.

"Boy, you're prepared."

"B&B, service industry . . . remember?"

"Yeah, but I thought you provided a different kind of service. One that doesn't pay too much attention to traditional holidays."

"You catch on quick."

"So the second one, Algiz—are we protecting something?"

"Me. From further backlashes from that blasted news article."

"In Chicago, nobody'd think anything of a widow

inheriting a death benefit. It just seems bad because you live in a small town."

"That's how I like it—below everyone's radar."

"Will this protect Annie and Courtney, too?"

"They'll do their own spells. Oh." She looked as if she'd made a terrible mistake. "Maybe you didn't know they're witches, too?"

"No. No, I didn't." Damn, he hated lying to her. But how could he know, except to admit he'd been snooping? Great opportunity, though. "So, what about your husband? Doug, was it?"

"That's right, you asked about him. Let's see." Carrying the tray, she led the way into the dining room, where Mason quickly helped her set up. "He helped with the bed-and-breakfast side when he wasn't teaching, but when it came to plants, unless it was a rose or a dandelion, Doug didn't know one from another."

"What'd he teach?"

"English."

"Excuse me. I will start e-nun-ci-at-ing every syl-la-ble now."

"Only if you want to sound like a robot."

"Good. Where's the candles? I know you want candles. Or is it, where *are* the candles?"

"In the drawer behind you."

He pulled it open. An assortment, of course. "Red?"

"White's fine."

"Candleholders?"

"Pick a pair."

He glanced into the china cabinet, then back at Jade. "Is this a test? I pick the right pair and win the heart of the maiden in the tower?"

She tipped her head again. He wished she'd never stop doing that.

"Not a test. The heart's still up for grabs."

At her words, his heart soared with hope, and he tucked incredible joy away until he could safely show it the light of day.

He selected a silver pair of candlesticks, heavy, elaborately carved. "What would you call this? Gothic?"

"I may have to get out my pointy hat."

"I'd like to see that sometime." He couldn't stop grinning as he pushed the pair together. "So, are you doing a spell every time you eat?"

She stared at him.

"What?" He examined the candles; nope, not crooked.

"I'm waiting to see if you stop breathing."

"Ah. I'm over that."

"Not breaking out in a sweat either."

"I'm telling you, I'm all man."

She laughed again, which was just as he'd intended. He didn't spew out corny lines like that for any other reason.

"I guess you need to light them then."

"No, go ahead," she said.

"Want to carve runes on them first?"

"Mason. They're not for spells. Light them."

"So, time won't come to a standstill . . . your mother won't suddenly float in . . . your dog won't start speaking in English . . . Actually, that'd be a good thing. Then I'd know what he's thinking."

"What's with you and a dog?"

"Love. He's a little scary."

"What's scary is that you think I have a dog."

Mason waited for a punch line that didn't come. "No dog?"

Jade shook her head slowly, which did nothing for the hair standing up on the back of his neck.

"Bear, then. It could be a bear."

She laughed at him. "I promise. No animal will appear and speak English before you."

"The fish won't walk in here by itself?"

"The fish!" Jade rushed from the room.

Chapter 19

ason was having a perfectly good wreck-diving dream when the sound of flutes edged its way in. As dreams so often do, it made perfect sense to turn his back on the wreck, to swim over to a mermaid playing beautiful, haunting music underwater.

It was Jade's smooth porcelain face, her long raven-colored curls floating within the aura of light surrounding her, her sexy green eyes beckoning him ever closer, her naked breasts playing peekaboo behind a school of colorful, darting fish. He shooed them away, pulled her into his arms, and began to make love to her.

The tail got in the way, though. *Damn.*

Mason woke with a pillow squashed in the circle of his arms. The soft notes of the flutes, though, were for real, and he rolled through the darkness to find Jade gone. The clock read midnight. Last he remembered, she'd said she was going to soak in a bath and come back.

Had her insomnia returned? He hoped not. For the first time in his life, he discovered there were many pleasures in sleeping with someone, other than sex. Warmth, comfort, companionship. Trust.

Nope, don't go there. No need to ruin a perfectly good hard-on.

He went in search of Jade, fully prepared to spread her out on the nearest furniture and make love to her right there. He walked through the house, trading one fantasy for another as he went from room to room without a glimpse of her.

The conservatory! The *waterfall*. He might get the ultimate fantasy yet.

As it turned out, he didn't find her there, either, but the flutes sounded closer. Lyrical notes drew him to the window looking out on the backyard.

A full moon rode high in the sky, bathing the snow-covered yard in so much reflected light, it was almost as bright as day. The windowpanes were flawed and wavy, so Mason stole into the kitchen for a better view.

Jade wore a white cape tonight. When she raised her arms to the sky, palm up, he caught a glimpse of bare thigh that made him wonder if she was nude underneath. Looked like some kind of ritual. Hopefully he hadn't arrived too late to watch her work naked beneath the stars. He couldn't tell if he was witnessing the beginning, middle, or end.

No, not the beginning. There was a circle drawn in the snow, a mound piled in the center, four small snowmen built around the perimeter, evenly spaced every ninety degrees. East, south, west, and north. He'd read a little about this. She'd marked the four quadrants with snowmen. The one to the east, nearest the river bluff—

He ran up to his room, grabbed his binoculars, and resumed watch through his window. Damn, it was cold. He dragged the quilt off the bed and wrapped it around himself. He could see her breath on the air now, the short, furry boots beneath her cape. Her body moved rhythmically to the tune of flutes, and drums now, too.

The snowmen were clearer from here, each one holding something different: a striped windsock; a red candle, lit; a snowflake ornament, shimmering in the moonlight; and a potted plant. The mound must be a temporary altar, as she struck a wooden match and lit a white candle resting in the center and incense off to the side. There was a plate of cookies, a mug of steaming liquid. Small blobs scattered around looked like flower petals, but from this angle, with white on white, it was impossible to tell.

Jade faced each direction in turn, speaking to the night. He was just about to open his window to see if he could hear what she was saying, but she turned toward him then, and he thought better of it.

If she got naked soon, he wanted to join her. Not nude, of course. Not even if it were summer. If there was a camera out there somewhere, he didn't want someone else recording it.

He wanted to be closer. Gathering the quilt tighter around him, he raced down the back stairs to the kitchen window.

Jade was eating a cookie, tipping the mug to her lips. When she set the plate and mug on the ground, Mason figured that must be about it. She took a remote out of her pocket; the music stopped.

She held out one hand, palm up again. She stood silent for a long moment, then turned and waved for him to join her.

"How does she *do* that?" he murmured. No fool he, he shoved his feet into the hiking boots he always left by the back door. Snow kicked up over the tops and trickled inside, but he kept going.

"Love your cloak," she teased.

"I hope you don't mind—"

"Take it off."

"Huh?" He came to a standstill three feet away.

She tossed her cape aside, white velvet pooling on white snow. A silky white gown clung to her body, hugging every curve, delineating every valley, making no attempt to hide winter-chilled nipples.

Hell, if Eskimos lived through colder nights than this, maybe he could handle it.

Jade glanced skyward. "Wiccans call this a Chaste Moon."

"I hope that doesn't mean the nightie's not coming off."

She smiled slyly. "We'll see."

"Are you Wiccan?"

"I'm eclectic, but this is one of their traditions I like. It's why I made snowmen to mark the directions. They believe a Chaste Moon is time to do something fun, to let your inner child play."

She flopped on her back. After she shrieked against the chill, she made big arcs in the snow with her arms and legs, laughing as if she didn't have a care in the world. Mason hugged his quilt tighter.

"Come on!" she said.

"I think I should tell you what *I* believe."

"We can make a whole party of snow angels." Jade jumped up, moved six feet, and flopped down to make another.

"I *fervently* believe it's *way* too damn cold for a Florida boy to try a stunt like that."

Jade shrugged one shoulder. "Okay." Then she got a wicked gleam in her eyes. "But I'm starting a new tradition. After you indulge your inner child, you get to have grown-up fun."

"If I lie in that snow, I won't have anything to have grown-up fun with."

Jade's laugh floated on the breeze that kicked the windchill down another ten degrees.

"How's playing by the waterfall sound to you?" she asked.

Mason dropped the quilt.

The conservatory felt warmer than usual after a half hour in the cold night air. Earthy, in a basic, sexual sort of way. Moonlight reflected off the snow, softly lighting the perimeter plants, and candles flickered and glowed along the flagstone path that led Jade and Mason through the interior, to the waterfall.

They'd left their boots and the CD player by the back door. Jade couldn't remember where she'd dropped the cape, but she'd find it tomorrow. She had better things in mind right now. Mason had witnessed a ritual. Not only had he not run away, he'd stepped forward to join her. She'd never felt so close to a man. So in tune. So accepted. So in love.

"It's quiet," Mason whispered as the glass doors swung closed behind them.

"The birds are asleep." She often worked here through the night, and one phase of the day seemed as normal as any other.

She could have seduced Mason outdoors, but each time they'd been in here together, when he'd looked at her, she'd seen the heat in his eyes and known that while he wanted to make love to her anywhere, it would be more powerful for him in here.

He was always watching her. Studying her. As if without a camera in his hand, he needed to memorize every curl of her hair, the arch of her eyebrows, and having seen the heat in his gaze, probably every curve of her body. It gave her a heady feeling, powerful even, to know he found so much about her so . . . interesting.

"Wait for me by the waterfall," she said softly, letting his hand slide out of hers.

He tightened his grip. "Not a chance."

"I have a hot drink simmering in the cauldron. There's enough for two."

"I want you first."

Ripples of excitement zinged through her as he led her deeper along the path, heating her to the point where she might have to go back out in the snow or self-combust. At the waterfall, Mason pulled her to him slowly, reeling her in, tempting her with his need for her, a need that shouted *right now,* when she'd intended to make love to him slowly, to show him how deep her feelings ran.

His gaze, as soft as a caress, slid over her body. Her pulse skittered, racing out of control, with nothing more than their fingers touching. If he turned the seduction up a notch, she'd be a puddle of desire within seconds.

She stepped into his space, so close she could feel his breath on her hair. The toga-wrapped quilt was chilly under her hands, and she began to ease him out of it.

Mason reached for the thin strap on her shoulder.

"You first," she said.

"I want to see you." His voice was rough with desire, which spurred Jade to make quick work of the quilt until Mason stood naked before her.

He was beautiful. Sparks of appreciation and lust and desire flared in her core, and she moved closer, breathing him in, shivering as every nerve she had came alive and cried out that this was right, *he* was right, and nothing about loving this man could ever be wrong.

He'd offered no commitment. She didn't care. People disappeared from commitment.

Not her, though. She'd been holding on to her heart for six long years, waiting for the right man. She'd spent her entire life waiting for someone who would make her feel desired, cherished, the way Mason made her feel as he gazed into her eyes and lowered her to the quilt.

"This one's for you," she whispered, releasing his mouth, working her way south.

He dragged her back up, breast to chest.

"But . . ." Her gaze wandered to the waterfall and back to his eyes, which had darkened with a desire so intense, she wished he'd let her do something special for him. "I thought this would be your fantasy."

His grin was so hot, she nearly had an orgasm.

"My fantasy, love, is to hear your screams of pleasure over the waterfall."

"My, aren't we confident?"

He laughed and rolled her onto her back, and she let him have his way, let him tease and lick every inch of her, and when she couldn't help herself, when she got so noisy that she was grateful the cascading water drowned out some of her cries, Mason took her even higher, letting her top the mountain and crash over the edge, landing safely in his arms.

Mason felt the change in Jade. He recognized deep passion when it was directed straight at him. For the first time in his life, it didn't scare the crap out of him.

It didn't, but knowing that she could take it all

away when he finally told her the truth did. It was a dilemma over which he had little control.

It took days for everyone to be gone at the same time, but finally Jade was out, Weezy was gone, and there was no sign of Annie or the dog Jade said didn't exist.

Well, hell, he knew it existed. The real question was who it belonged to—nothing with that much meat on its bones was lost and starving—and how it kept getting into Mystic Manor.

Mason had returned to the conservatory, at last, when Brenda called.

"Lyle told me what you said."

"Brenda. Hi." Mason wedged his cell phone between his ear and shoulder and moved on to the next cabinet, progressing steadily deeper into the wing.

"Lyle doesn't believe he owes you anything," Brenda continued. "I didn't handle things at all well, so I've been stalling him, maybe even talked him out of telling Jade, because if anybody owes you, I guess it's me."

Mason was silent.

"Mase? You still there?"

"My mother taught me not to argue with a pregnant woman."

Brenda chuckled. "I always liked your mother. Listen, don't say I told you, but Lyle's furious."

"He doesn't seem the type."

"I know," she said with a great deal of surprise. "I think impending fatherhood has brought out his protective instincts. Really weird."

"Changing your mind?"

"Uh, no-o-o."

"Just curious."

"Look, Mase, if you're really on a job, well, I just didn't want Lyle to blow your cover, that's all. Are we even?"

"Sure, Bren. Appreciate it. I hope the baby looks like you."

She just laughed and hung up.

Mason closed the last cabinet. Not a darn thing the insurance company would want to hear about. It had been a waste of snoop time, and somewhat of an eye-opener, but nothing compared to the drying room, which he got to next.

Yes, he knew Jade was a witch.

Yes, he'd read half a dozen books cover to cover.

Still, when he straightened up on the far side of the low, deep arch, which was like a tunnel to another world, he was in the midst of a hanging garden of herbs. Old shelves, some warped with age, held hundreds of dark glass bottles with cork stoppers, all sizes, shapes, and colors. And a cauldron—my God, a *cauldron*!—hung over glowing embers.

The books covered cauldrons, of course. But reading was one thing, and seeing a working one up close and personal quite another.

He peered over the rim. The simmering liquid didn't smell bad; it also didn't smell like anything he'd want to taste. And even if it did, he wasn't stupid enough to consume an unknown concoction put together by a woman who grew toxic plants. It'd be a helluva note to die by accident and have Jade finally charged with a crime. He wasn't going to touch the plant in the sink either. He wasn't even going to *smell* the plant in the sink.

Jade's life certainly was very different from any he'd ever known. If nothing else spelled it out, everything in here did. And not just on the surface. Standing here, seeing a cauldron, an athame, a crystal-tipped wand, the altar set up on the mantel, it hit him. An in-your-face reminder that witchcraft was very real.

To an outsider, Jade seemed perfectly normal.

Scratch that. That implied she was abnormal, which she wasn't. Just different. But the differences, all piled on top of one another as he'd been turning over rocks, turned out to be no less than cultural differences.

"Whoa, what's this?" he murmured.

Mason opened a secret drawer holding eighteen soft pouches, more or less. Lumpy pouches.

Damn. For the first time, instead of excitement at a find, all he felt was dread. If he opened those, he'd be nothing more than a trespassing, lowlife snoop.

He'd searched a lot of places over the years. Houses, apartments, gyms, pool houses, sheds, garages, offices, warehouses, secret retreats, motel rooms, vehicles, storage lockers, even a toll booth once, and on and on. All sanctioned by someone with a need to know and the money to pay for it.

But he couldn't do this. He couldn't open these, not even one of them. It was simple enough to feel them, know they held wands, and move on. Nothing in there needed to be disclosed to a third party. Not even to Anthony.

He might not be able to tell Jade the truth, but she deserved his respect.

"I saw it!" Anthony said when Mason topped the stairs the following afternoon. "Sounded like a damn buffalo running down the hall. I lost him when he turned the corner."

Mason caught Anthony's air of excitement. "Just now?"

"Yes! He was coming from back there, and I know you said he just kind of stares at you, but his tail was tucked between his legs."

Mason studied the empty hallway where the dog had come from, then snapped his fingers. The locked bedroom! He jogged toward it, calling, "You coming?" over his shoulder.

He needn't have bothered. Anthony was on his heels.

Mason had the lock down pat, and he was in the room so fast, he thought he saw the closet door swing shut. He *knew* he heard footsteps on the stairs.

He drew his Glock; Anthony followed suit. They took precautions as they opened first one door, then the other, and hurried down the steps.

"I've been down here," Mason said. "Foundation's solid. No way out. He's trapped."

"Let's be very careful then."

"Hey!" Mason called out. "I know you're down here. You know you're down here. My partner's going to cover the only way out. Why don't you just make it easy on both of us and show yourself?"

Nothing.

"Maybe you should tell him why we're here," Anthony suggested. "So he doesn't think we're crazed witch-hunters."

"Good idea. See why I teamed up with you?"

"You teamed up with me because you were out of work and needed to pay off the diving shop."

"Of course, if he's Stockard, he'll be madder at two PIs who want to turn him in than two, what'd you call them, crazed witch-hunters?"

Anthony waved his gun. "Go on. I'll cover you."

"Hey!" Mason called out.

"You really after Stockard?" a quiet voice asked.

Mason and Anthony zeroed in on his location behind a tall antique armoire, then glanced at each other, thinking *definitely male* and *probably too old*.

But you couldn't be too careful.

"We're here to make sure he's dead," Anthony said.

"Uh, partner, if you're going to speak up, you should think it through first."

"Huh?"

"That sounds like we're here to kill him."

"Oh."

"If he's alive, he deserves killing, I'd say." A gray-haired man poked his head around the corner of the armoire, testing their forthrightness.

"Too old," Anthony said. "Too short."

Hands up, the elderly man stepped out and sort of waved in the direction of their drawn guns. "Too damn old to shoot."

"Oh. Sorry," Anthony said, holstering his weapon.

"Not so fast," Mason said. "Who are you?"

"Henry Delarue."

"Uncle Henry," Anthony said, his tone laced with respect. "You are one hard man to find. I've been looking all over for you."

"I like my privacy."

"You couldn't find *him*?" Mason asked.

"Lost his trail twenty years back."

"He's in the goddamn *cellar*."

"Hell, you haven't even found the whole cellar."

"True." Mason addressed Henry. "How do we know you're not in cahoots with Stockard?"

"He was okay. He was good to Jade, I guess." Henry put his hands down. "But if he's alive, and I'm the one finds him, you can bet the law won't be catching up with me."

Mason holstered his gun. No way that answered his question, but if the guy liked his privacy that much, he'd have nothing to gain from helping Stockard disappear.

"You the one sleeping with my niece?" Henry asked Mason.

"You the one screwing with our cameras?"

Henry cackled. "Not bad for an old fart, eh?"

"What?" Anthony said, affronted. "That was you? You know what those things cost?"

"Can't say as I care."

"We're looking for any evidence that Stockard's alive and defrauding the insurance company," Mason explained. "There's only one place I haven't searched yet. You going to show me where it is?"

Henry shook his head. "There's things there not fit to see. If Stockard's there, it must be what he deserves."

Chapter 20

he money's a dead end," Anthony said, sprawled in a chair by the window while he and Mason compared notes. They'd begun meeting in Anthony's room each evening so there'd be no possibility of Jade's slipping in to see Mason while they were talking business.

It wasn't that he was opposed to their relationship. How could he be, when he liked Jade, and when he himself was caught up in the excitement of twice-daily phone calls with that cute bartender? Neither of them really liked the club scene. Turned out they knew some of the same people, so they all planned to catch a play in Old Town when he returned, then grill a late dinner and hang out on the beach. So he understood how Mason was feeling.

Still, the timing was all wrong. Mason's sleeping with Jade while he was passing himself off as a freelance photographer was unethical, no matter what the reasoning. If discovered, it'd reflect poorly on Mason and the agency, and that in turn would effect Anthony's ability to earn a living and keep his siblings in school.

Mason was looking good these days, working overtime to find the last cellar, back to himself—maybe better—fully recovered from the wedding that almost was. Lucky guy; getting hitched to Brenda eventually would have broken his spirit.

Mason had the other chair. "Dead end? You sure?"

"Jade put the money in trust for Stockard's parents and his brother."

"All of it?"

"Every last dime. The parents are disabled, haven't worked since long before he disappeared. Guy I talked to said Jade was following her husband's wishes."

Mason smacked his palm on the armrest, a display of triumph and determination as he sat up straighter. "That does it then. Giving it all away is proof that if her husband is alive, she knows nothing about it. So it's time I—"

"No! I beg you."

"What? You didn't even let me finish."

"Stockard could've cooked this up with his parents."

Mason scowled at him.

"I know, I know, I don't believe it either." Only

because the other two didn't fit into the equation at all. Unless Stockard had killed them to muddy the waters. "Nevertheless, you can't tell Jade anything."

"Anthony, please, I *need* to tell her."

Anthony pulled a two-column newspaper clipping out of his wallet and unfolded it.

"No, no, not that again." Mason groaned. His head dropped back on the doily-covered cushion, his eyes rolled, and his tongue hung out like a dying dog, and Anthony ignored those theatrics because he had something to say and he damn well was going to make his point.

"Remember when Priscilla was written up in the newspaper for reviving that kid at the beach? Got a nice award—did you know that? She wants to be a doctor. You have any idea what it costs to send a kid through medical school these days?"

"Just shoot me now. No, don't," Mason said, getting up suddenly. "Not until Priscilla can save my life. Hell, I'm going to bed."

"Alone?"

"Not effing likely."

"Mase—"

"Turn on the TV. Loud."

A movement on the monitor caught Anthony's attention. He jumped to his feet as one of the few cameras still working caught someone sneaking into the house. "Shit. Mason, wait."

"Yeah, yeah." He kept walking, reached for the doorknob.

"*Wait!*"

Mason wasn't listening, so Anthony fired a rolled-up pair of socks at his back.

"Hey!" Mason spun around, hands up to ward off more ammunition.

"Where's Jade? Davy Stockard just came in the side door."

"Maybe he wants her to do a spell for him."

"He's got a gun."

Anthony had never seen blood drain from anyone's face as fast as it did Mason's.

"Your husband's in the conservatory!"

"Mom. Hi. How are you?" Jade propped the cordless phone between her ear and shoulder while she continued sorting through a dozen cardboard boxes. Uncle Henry had packaged her botanical shipments as usual, but he'd left a note apologizing for being "distracted by recent events"—what, he didn't say—and suggesting she do a double check, so she was matching contents with invoices when her mother called.

"Now you listen to me, Jade," Mona said imperiously, and with a sense of urgency that wasn't unlike her. "This is serious. I see your husband."

"Sure you do. Buried under the yew, I suppose? Seems appropriate, don't you think, since it's used to raise the spirits of the dead."

"He has a gun."

"You know, that plant's been growing like a weed the past couple years. I wonder if that's why."

"You are such a sassy brat."

"Mason likes it." Jade smiled to herself. "It's good to see you're still practicing. What're you using today? Water? Crystal ball?"

"You know, if you hadn't spent so much time on your mail-order business, Doug might've been happier."

"Good going, Mom. You've been dying to say that for six years."

"Well, it's true! Why else would he drive off in the dead of winter with two other men?"

"Ah, to check his boat?"

"Who goes to check a boat in the winter?"

"Anyone who's concerned about it after an ice storm."

"He should've stayed at home," Mona said angrily.

Hindsight, Jade thought, but she said, "So who are you mad at? Me, or him?"

"I wanted grandchildren," Mona said with a huff.

"Yeah, well, I'm working on that."

"You are?" Mona's surprised sigh clearly said Jade was forgiven.

Jade thought it a good note on which to end the call.

"Your father's getting married."

Okay, not a good time. So this is what had her mother a little peevish, making up some preposterous story about Doug being in the conservatory just to justify an attention-getting phone call.

"That's why he's not there this month." Mona misinterpreted Jade's silence and took up the slack. "Poor baby, you want me to come home?"

"No! No," Jade said, softening her tone. "Dad might want to bring her by and introduce her. It is his month, you know. We all agreed."

Davy Stockard stepped through the arch, entering the drying room on the tail end of a revolver.

"Oh. Mom, you know what you were seeing a few minutes ago?"

"Of course, dear."

"Can you see him now?" Personally, Jade couldn't take her eyes off of him.

"Well, no, I'm not concentrating now."

"Let me congratulate you, then—you're getting pretty darn good."

"Am I?" Mona sounded proud of herself. "Hey, whaddya mean? He *is* buried there? He was shot? What?"

"Hang up," Davy said.

"Mom? Gotta go."

"Is that him I heard?"

"It's Davy."

"Hang up!" Davy shouted.

Jade set the phone down without pushing the OFF button, hoping it wasn't asking too much for Mona to listen in, wise up, and send help. Soon.

"Davy. Hi."

"I want my money."

"Davy, we talked about this. Remember?" Jade spoke slowly, holding his attention, buying time. The moon wasn't high yet, but it was full; anything could happen. "We all got together. Your mom and dad, and you, and me."

Marigold, yarrow; she carefully assessed her supply of herbs in case Davy's finger slipped and she ended up with a new orifice.

She continued a dialogue with Davy, feigning calmness and serenity. "Doug's lawyer was there, too, remember?"

"Doug promised he'd take care of us."

"He did, Davy."

"He said if anything happened to him, there'd be money."

"There is. It's in a trust to help take care of your parents. And you."

"It's not fair!"

"Your brother worked for his money."

"I owe money. The café. The gun store. The taxidermist, 'cause I got a ten-point buck. The gas station. New tires. Sears, 'cause I bought Mom something nice for Christmas, 'cause I'm supposed to get money."

"Doug paid for that policy. It'll take care of necessities, like an apartment, your food, your medical bills—"

"All my friends. I been telling 'em I'd pay 'em back when I got my share."

"—but if you want extra cash, you have to get a job."

Jade had set it up the way Doug had wanted, in spite of knowing her in-laws would gripe about this and that, why they couldn't have more. It was their nature. The revolver was unexpected, though.

A rap at the window drew Jade's and Davy's attention toward the backyard.

Anthony? Without a coat and hat?

Davy was as distracted as Jade, which was the whole point, she realized, as Mason flew through the arch and tackled him to the floor. Honestly, she'd barely had time to get scared, and there he was, doing his Bond-Rambo thing again.

"Ow! Hey, get off!" Davy shouted. He quickly ceased struggling.

Mason rose to his feet, Davy's weapon in his possession. As he dumped the bullets, he seemed to be wrestling with a decision. He looked at Jade. "I should call the police."

Mason pocketed the bullets and tucked the revolver into the waist of his jeans as if he'd done it a thousand times. Very sexy. Watching him was far more interesting than trying to figure out what to do about Davy.

Without taking his eyes off Davy, Mason added, "Or you could just let me finish him off."

"Hey, no, man. Jade knows I wouldn't really hurt her." Davy scrambled to his feet, watching Mason warily.

"He'd be easy to kill," Anthony said, strolling in as casually as if they rubbed people out every day. He punctuated with a little twisting motion of his hands, like wringing a chicken's neck.

Davy grabbed his throat and swallowed hard. "No,

no, hey, man. Keep the gun. Honest. I'm too chicken to hurt anybody. Tell 'em, Jade."

Mason pinned him with a long glare before turning to Jade. "What do you think?"

"You shouldn't have brought a gun in here, Davy," Jade said. "You went too far."

"I know. I'm sorry." Davy hung his head.

"The police?" Mason's brow lifted in question, as if he already knew the answer.

"Well . . ." Jade thought of what Doug would want her to do. Shook her head.

"Right. Then it's only fair, Davy, that you know I'll be watching you. That if I so much as *think* you might scare Jade again, I'm going to take action." Mason stepped into Davy's space and looked him in the eye when he growled, "And I don't mean calling the cops. You get my drift?"

Davy nodded like a dashboard chihuahua.

Anthony zeroed in on the source of a thin, reedy voice and picked up the cordless phone. He listened a moment, then handed it to Jade. "Your mother?"

Snow still covered the landscape, but the walks, streets, and most driveways were clear when Mason stepped outside on Monday morning. He had no camera, no destination in mind, just . . . outside.

"Conscience botherin' you?" Henry appeared out of nowhere, as he had several times in the last few days. Now that he knew why Mason was snooping through the house, he didn't keep to himself so much anymore. It wasn't that he was more sociable so much as he was being more obvious about keeping an eye on him and his partner. Kind of a warning: *I'm everywhere. So behave yourselves or you can disappear, too.*

"You have anything to do with those guys disappearing?" Mason asked.

"Nah, I liked Doug. He was good to Jade. Never lied to her or anything."

Ouch. "I'm not doing it on purpose."

"Sure you are."

"Okay, but I'm not doing it to be mean. It's temporary. She'll forgive me."

No comment.

"Won't she?"

Henry didn't say anything for a minute, then tipped his head to the sky. "See that moon?"

"Pretty hard to miss." It rode overhead, the eastern side lit by the early-morning sun.

"Moon in the fourth quarter," Henry said, "is the best time to end things. Not just anything, mind you. Things you want to go away for good. Permanent-like."

"That so?"

"Like keeping your purpose here a secret," Henry suggested.

"This is a witch thing, right?"

Henry shook his head. "Oh, witches use it, all right. Astrologers use it. Lots of people. Farmers."

"Farmers?"

"Sure. Best time to treat weeds . . . and other pests. Gets rid of 'em for good."

Mason stared down at the old man. "Wouldn't be trying to tell me something, would you?"

Henry shrugged. "I'm just saying."

"Who knew professional photographers were so tough?" Jade said, teasing Mason as her friends congratulated him effusively on saving her from Davy.

"Ah, it was nothing," Mason said, grinning because it felt good that Jade wasn't hiding how she felt about him from her friends.

She'd just relayed the days-old story to the Monday morning rendezvous around the plank table. Not once had she said, "But don't tell anyone," or pulled her hand from his grasp. She was so trusting, he felt like a heel. Getting things out in the open couldn't happen soon enough to suit him.

"You were so brave," Jade said, kissing his cheek.

"Stockard's a loon," Noah said.

"I'll say," Buzz agreed. "Lucky he didn't 'mistake' you for 007, when we all know it's just a part you play."

Mason loved watching the easy way Buzz teased Jade, mussing her hair, sorting through her mail.

"Ooh," Noah said, "next time we see him, we should tell him you really are a secret agent."

"Jade, too," Buzz agreed eagerly. "What'll her number be?"

"I need a number?"

"Yeah, you know," Mason joined in. "If I'm 007, you get to have a number, too. Otherwise it's not official."

"I see. What would you suggest?"

"I wouldn't give you anything less than a ten," Mason said, earning him instant adoration from all the women and knowing smirks from the men. Not that he gave a flying fig what anyone except Jade thought. Personally, he'd give her a twelve, but he'd tell her that in private.

Two-year-old Hannah started to scramble to her feet in the child seat, and Mason smoothly scooped her onto his lap.

"She's messy," Weezy said, hustling to his side. She'd been watching Mason with open skepticism, as usual. She didn't seem to buy his story that he was in the "writing" phase of the project, where he could spend more time around Mystic Manor and less out photographing eagles.

Mason cuddled the toddler the same as he had all his sister's children. "She's fine. You ready for more 'nana, Hannah?" he asked, then teased her with the rhyme in a singsong voice until she giggled. Seconds later, he realized everyone else had fallen silent. "What?"

"Nothing," the guys said, shrugging it off.

Weezy had a new look in her eyes, friendly, like the first time they'd met, before she'd figured out he'd wedged his way into Mystic Manor without an invitation.

It was nothing, though, compared to the way Jade was looking at him. If there was any question this woman wanted to have babies, it was gone now. *His* babies. Christ, that sounded good.

That did it. He was telling Anthony today to find someone else to finish this job. He was coming clean. There's be no more talking him out of it.

Buzz and Noah began tossing around ideas on how Courtney and Annie could spend their new money. Anthony called. When Mason's phone vibrated on his belt, he snapped it up, passed the toddler to Weezy, and politely withdrew to the dining room.

"We have to talk," Mason said right off.

"My uncle called. We're done. I'm *outta* here."

"They pulled the plug?"

"Packing as we speak."

Finished!

"Think this'll work out the way you want?" Anthony asked.

"I'd be a whole lot happier if someone had taken one look at us and confessed."

"People disappear every day; fact of life. Jade accepted it a long time ago. There never was a chance you were going to be her knight in shining armor, but you, my friend, have to look on the bright side."

"There's a bright side?"

"Stockard's disappearance eventually brought you to Jade's door."

"Yeah, that's worked out so well. I hate that I'm going to hurt her."

"I know. Listen, I booked the first flight out for me. Figured you'd want to stay a while. You know yet how you're going to tell her?"

"I'm open to ideas."

"Lyle flew out last night, so you don't have to rush. Ease into it gently."

"Right."

"And keep your gun handy."

Meanwhile, back in the kitchen, Noah said, "Hey, we haven't hashed over any Dear Alice letters lately."

"Alanna!" Annie and Jade corrected.

"Oh, yeah, yeah, that's right. Never can remember that name. Always enjoy them though."

"I printed some off the e-mail account," Annie said, pulling folded pages out of her purse. "I was going to work on them while I wait at the dentist's office, but sharing with you men is always so, ah, enlightening," she said tongue-in-cheek.

"Hear that, Noah? We're enlightened."

"I heard that."

"Not exactly what I said." Annie passed the letters around the table.

Jade looked forward to this as eagerly as the men. They all had a different take on things, which Annie often found useful, and they often had spirited debates over what advice was right.

The first two were no-brainers.

"Tell him to talk to his basketball coach at school," Buzz said, referring to the one Weezy read aloud from a high-school athlete. Noah was all nods next to him.

Weezy jumped all over the letter Annie read from a young grandmother. "It takes more than just the parents to make sure kids turn out right. She has to correct those babies now or they'll just be a handful later. Don't mean she can't love 'em and hug 'em just the same."

"Who's next?"

"I got one," Noah said.

Dear Alanna,

There's a man living in a woman's house pretending to be something he's not. Since this woman helped reunite me, my fiancé, and our unborn child, we feel we owe her a favor and maybe should tell her about this man. Trouble is, he is my ex-fiancé, a private investigator working undercover, and since I recently dragged him to the altar and then jilted him (through no fault of his own), I feel I owe him too, sort of, and should not let my fiancé blow his cover.

Three sentences. That's all it took to ruin Jade's life. She marveled at this, stunned into a block of icy calm because it was the only way she could keep breathing, keep her heart beating.

How could no one around notice that her world had just ended?

"Hey, wasn't Mason just jilted?" Buzz asked, oblivious. "We should get his take on this."

When Jade's world stopped spinning, she glanced at Annie. She appeared equally startled, though Jade would bet she didn't feel as if a semi had run over her.

Annie said, "Wow, look at the time," and jumped to her feet, but Noah held the letter out of her reach and said, "There's more."

Could it get worse? Jade wondered, sick to her stomach as Noah continued.

Do I sit back and do nothing? Sort of let one favor cancel out the other? Do we tell her and jeopardize my ex, or not tell her, knowing she'll probably get hurt?

Jade stared nowhere in particular. The wall maybe. Another dimension. She was afraid if she connected with this, she'd break in two.

"I can poison his coffee," Weezy said, touching Jade's shoulder, drawing her back, surprisingly still upright in her chair.

"I can cut his brake lines," Noah offered.

Jade scooted her chair back and stood up. She didn't remember her knees ever shaking like this before. It made her mad.

"Jade . . . ?" someone said. She didn't know who.

To no one in particular, she said, "I'm going upstairs. When he comes back, stall him."

Chapter 21

It hurt that Mason hadn't confided in her. Jade wondered why for all of three seconds.

Of course he hadn't confided in her. *She* was the damn case.

Or the death benefit was, or her husband. It was all the same deceitful thing.

She tore through Mason's room, on a tear to find whatever there was to find. She could've stormed into the dining room and asked him to his face, but if he was the liar she thought he was, he'd just deny it. His steel blue eyes wouldn't even blink.

She knew it was true. She knew it, knew it, *knew it*, and like a fool, tears welled up and blurred her vision.

Stupid not to trust her instincts.

Stupid to let him stay when she had a policy not to.

She rummaged through the top drawers of the high-boy before it dawned on her that if Mason was hiding something, it'd be secure under the disgusting clothes he'd arrived in, so she knelt and yanked open the bottom drawer.

Empty. Too bad. The smell alone could've knocked her out and put her out of her misery.

Anthony, she remembered, had asked that she skip the daily cleanup in his room because he hated having his stuff moved. While it wasn't that odd a request at the time, and he'd let the girls change his linens, it now raised Jade's suspicions. She stormed into his room without bothering to knock.

"Oh! Jade. Hi." Anthony body-blocked the open suitcase on his bed. The look on her face must have said it all, because he started gushing. "Honest, he wanted to tell you days ago, but I wouldn't let him. We had to stay undercover. See, we already had a couple weeks' time in . . ."

"Really." It was all she needed to hear.

"There was a lot at stake . . ."

"Now you're just making me madder."

"Oh-kay," he said, closing the lid behind him.

The socks in the river and the Banishing Oil and every other spell to get rid of Mason hadn't worked, so Jade knew the Universe had a different plan in mind. Knowing it didn't make her any less angry. This was just plain unacceptable. She wanted him out of her life *now*.

She ignored the stabbing pain in her heart that accompanied that thought. Mason was *not* a part of her. She ran to her parents' room, found it unlocked, threw her arms up in the air at the realization that she'd had no privacy for three weeks and hadn't even known it. She helped herself to a red pillar out of Mona's dresser, took it back to Mason's *former* room, and lit it with enough energy to chase out the hardiest of men. She didn't even have to call it up; it was just there, pulsing through her body, scratching to get out.

Then she threw open the window and really set to work.

It was cathartic, throwing Mason's belongings out into the snow. By the time he picked them up, they'd be frozen. Considering how much he hated the cold, she toyed with the idea of turning the hose on everything.

And yet, none of her efforts made her happy. Far from it. She had a knife in her heart, tears running down her cheeks. If she had to go through any more relationships like this to find the right man, she might as well not even try.

Because Mason had been the one. She knew it, the same as her heart knew how to beat.

He'd been the one.

And for her, losing him had more far-reaching consequences than she could have imagined. Without Mason, there'd be no babies. No children to raise in the house where she'd grown up, to tutor in the ways of the Craft, the lore of the plants.

Because worst of all, having found Mason, then lost him, she knew she had no heart left to share.

Luggage in hand, Anthony ran down the back stairs, saying a quick prayer of thanks to have escaped unharmed. He had less than an hour to make it through airport security and safely on to the gate. After that, he could forget about a very angry Jade and concentrate on his hot date in Pensacola.

He found Mason in the kitchen, backed against the wallpaper by one small grandmother with a butcher knife. The kid was nowhere in sight. You had to admire a mob that had its priorities straight.

"What'd you do, tell everybody at once?" he asked, frantically searching angry faces for any signs of a second assault, not breaking stride on his way to the door.

"Anthony, wait! Get her off me!"

"You have a gun. Use it." Anthony paused at the door for one last word of advice. "Oh, changed my mind. Lose the gun before you talk to Jade. She's really pissed."

Time to come clean.

Mason felt some measure of relief in the knowledge that he would no longer have to work out the logistics of how and when to tell Jade. Of course now he had to work out how not to get a pissed-off witch to fight back by casting an angry spell on him.

Though she'd promised.

Yeah, as if she'd feel honor-bound to keep her word to a man who'd been lying to her.

She couldn't be as scary, though, as Weezy pressing him up against the kitchen wall with a butcher knife beneath his chin.

"Shoe!" Hannah shouted, looking out the window.

"Courtney," Weezy pleaded, hiding the knife reluctantly.

"Sorry. She just got away from me for a second." Courtney picked up Hannah to take her back to the dining room, where she'd retreated as soon as everyone had turned on Mason.

"Cam'ra!" Hannah pointed out the window. "Cam'ra fall down in snow."

Everyone watched as another Nikon flew by, sans parachute, and landed in the snow next to Mason's shoes.

"Does she know how much that camera cost?" Mason grumbled.

Weezy, Buzz, and Noah glared at him. Annie whispered words, a chant maybe, and he wished she'd glare at him, too, instead of whatever she was up to.

Jeans, new sweaters, and dark briefs got hung up in the bare redbud trees between the house and walk, but the cameras plunged right through the branches and hit the ground.

"Oh, quit looking like that," Jade snapped at him as she stormed into the kitchen seconds later.

"My cameras," he said weakly. Inside, he was relieved that she was still talking to him.

"My *dignity*," she spat back with a hostile look that held him against the wall better than the knife had.

"You want us to tie 'im up?" Buzz offered.

"Take 'im down to the dungeon?" Noah suggested eagerly.

Dungeon? The third cellar he hadn't found was a dungeon? *Good God!*

Jade scoffed. "I don't want to be cleaning up after him. I want him to leave."

Hearing her say it hurt more than Mason had thought possible. More than a knife and dungeon combined.

Jade slapped his notebook computer onto the breakfast bar. Mason bit his lip, keeping his objections to himself lest it go out the window, too.

She opened a drawer and pulled out a hammer.

"Oh no," he said. He wasn't given to a lot of introspection, but even he knew the computer's fate was symbolic of their relationship.

Jade spun it around so Annie could see the screen. "Check it out. Everything that's on your computer? Right there."

"What?" Annie said in disbelief.

"No," Mason said. "It's just networked."

Jade tucked her chin and glared at him as Annie tapped keys and scrolled through files.

"Really," he said. "I can see what's on your computers, but I didn't copy anything to the hard drive."

"Computers?" she emphasized the plural.

He nodded weakly. "But in my defense, it was my job, and I didn't share what I saw with anyone."

There, *whew*, he'd gotten it out, though as Jade's glare grew colder, he didn't think his defense stood a chance in hell.

As Jade spoke to her friends, her smile was calm. It *dripped* calm. "I'd like to have a few words with Mason in private. Would you all mind?"

"Hell no," Annie said, her relief palpable. As she brushed past Mason, she whispered, "Should've let me do a spell. At least then you'd have a chance."

Shit, this wasn't how he'd imagined it. Would telling Jade now help, or hurt? In the commotion of everyone's leaving, Mason narrowed the gap between himself and the woman he loved.

"Worried?" Jade asked, misinterpreting what must be a look of utter confusion on his face.

Earlier, he'd known it was too soon. If the words left his lips now, she'd—

Jade slammed the hammer into the keyboard.

Mason winced at the crunch. "Really," he said. "It's a perfectly innocent computer."

"Unlike you."

He kept his mouth shut; wisely, he thought.

"Three weeks. You've been paid to live under my roof and lie to me for three *weeks*?"

She gave the computer two more whacks, turning her head to the side when shards of housing and bits of keys flew into the air. Slivers of gray skittered across the counter. Some lodged in her yellow sweater.

"I don't imagine you come cheap. Who has that much money?"

Mason still didn't answer, until she turned toward

him and waited expectantly. "The, ah, insurance company that issued your husband's life policy."

"What, they were willing to pay you thousands of dollars to find something they could use against me?"

"No! They just didn't want to pay if your husband turned out to be alive. People do that, you know. Scam insurance companies. To the tune of thirty billion dollars every year."

"Yes. People can be *very sneaky*." The monitor went next. When the whole mess was mangled, Jade threw the hammer aside and brushed her hands clean. "There. Now there's nothing left in my house for you. You can go."

"Jade . . ."

Her hand shot up. "Do not waste . . . your . . . breath."

Mason stepped closer to Jade. He wanted to reach out, to pull her into his arms and hold her, tell her it would all be right again, it'd just take time.

"You're right. I'm a heel. But I was doing my job—"

Her hand shot up again. "Don't. Talk."

"Jade, please, this is what I do. You have secrets. I was undercover. What's the difference?"

The anger that boiled in her eyes told him that of all the questions he could have asked, of all the arguments he could have presented, that was the wrong one. When she spoke to him again, it was with quiet venom.

"I wanted an honest, trustworthy man I could count on to keep my secret, not a lying, sneaky slug who'd

keep secrets from me. I let you stay in my *home*."
Her eyes burned into him. "I shared my sanctuary
with you. My conservatory. My friends, who mean
the world to me."

Every word was true. He knew it, and he felt like a
heel. She'd let him close, and what had he done?

"I let you into my *bed,*" she said without breaking
stride. "I fell in love with you, you big slug, and *you,*"
she enunciated very clearly, so there'd be no misunderstanding how angry she was, "*disrespected* that."

Jade stormed into the conservatory, instinctively
seeking comfort, a safe womb in which to curl up
and hide. The thought of living without Mason hurt
just as much as knowing he'd lied to her.

She stood stock-still among her plants. Never
before had she been too upset to draw succor from
them, too distraught to draw in healing energy, too
angry to see straight. She didn't even hear her cell
phone at first. When it registered, she collapsed on
the bench under a tree and curled into a fetal position. It was useless to try to hide her sniffle when she
said, "Hi, Mom."

"Talk to me, honey. Tell Mommy why the redbud
trees have men's briefs in them."

Mona's regressive maternal tone should have made
Jade smile, but instead, she felt more tears well up.
She rubbed her eyes, trying to stop them.

Starting at the beginning, she told Mona her feelings about moving on with her life, finding love,
having children, the works. As she talked, as she re-

lived the last three weeks, the highs and lows of being in love and having her heart ripped in two, tears ran freely down her cheeks.

"I screwed up, Mom," she said finally, plucking at her shirt, dabbing it to her face until it was soaked. "But I tried to fix it. I tried to send him back, honest."

"I know, sweetheart. I know you, and that's what you would do. But, Jade, sweetheart, now I want you to listen to me. You're very hurt and angry, and you have every right to be, I'm not saying you don't. So you won't like this, but if you think about it, you'll know it's true."

Jade was blubbering too much to argue.

"The spirits know what you need and what you don't, sweetheart. Sometimes, in spite of all we do, they step in and give us what's best for us. You're very good at what you do, and I don't want you to lose confidence over this. It happens. Accept it. Then go kiss and make up."

"Are you *nuts*?" Jade stared at Mason, jumping up and down, snagging clothes off bare branches. "You *want* a lying, sneaking, slug for a son-in-law?"

"You didn't call him that to his face, did you?"

"I most certainly did. I want him out of here. Uncle Henry's out in the yard with him."

"Yes, de-briefing the tree. That's a good one, isn't it? De-briefing . . . Never mind. I see him."

"Okay, Mom, I think you should stop scrying now. You're starting to scare me."

"What're you going to do?" Mona asked.

What else could she do? "I already did it. Soon as he's done out there, Uncle Henry'll make sure he leaves."

Mason stood in the snow, his coat unbuttoned, his hat somewhere, in his pocket maybe, his gloves gone who the hell knew where. Who the hell cared?

Jade felt used. He got that. She was too mad to listen to anything he said in his defense. He got that, too.

It looked as if his bags had been jettisoned from an airplane and exploded on impact, splotches of dark clothing dotting white snow. Henry Delarue milled around the detritus of Mason's belongings.

"You gonna take me on next, old man?" Mason asked.

Henry laughed. "No, I reckon you don't need me heaping hurt on top of guilt. Oh, don't look so surprised. You forget, I've been watching you for weeks now. You and that other fella. What kind of partner runs off with the car and leaves a man stranded, anyway?"

"The kind who understands that I'm not leaving here until Jade realizes I love her and we belong together."

Henry's lips pursed. He nodded his head. "I've seen how you look at her. Finish picking up your things."

"I'm not leaving."

"You can stay with me."

With that unexpected but very welcome invitation, Mason swept everything into his suitcases. "Ready."

"This way then."

He followed the old man away from the house. "Ah, Henry?"

Jade's uncle shuffled through the snow as if he hadn't heard him. Across the driveway, into the yard, angling north and slightly toward the street. Snow crunched beneath their boots.

"Henry?"

Into a grove of pine trees, whose boughs dipped under the weight of the snow.

"Henry!"

"Almost there."

Deep in the grove, the land dropped off a bit. Henry's steps slowed, finally stopped. Mason halted beside him, staring into a ravine cut by surface runoff. He would've been embarrassed if anyone knew that he felt reassured by the weight of his Glock.

"You planning on leaving my body down there?"

Henry tipped his head toward the ravine. "Remember the third cellar you were looking for? Entrance is down there."

"That right?" Yeah, the Glock was feeling pretty good.

"I can't take you in through the house."

"Well, that's true enough."

Henry grinned up at him. "I can see you're kind of nervous about this, so I'll go first."

Mason dogged Henry's heels down a sloping path. By all rights, the surveillance job was finished. He was off the clock. Satisfaction in locating the remaining cellar couldn't be justified by anything other than curiosity. Besides, it'd keep him on Jade's property.

Their heads were well below street level when Henry peeled frozen vines away from the hill, saying, "They'll grow back next spring." He reached inside and patted the wall until he found what he was looking for.

"A *torch*?" Mason said. He didn't know why anything surprised him anymore.

"You don't expect me to go in there in the dark, do you?"

"Afraid of spiders?"

"I'm not too fond of that big black dog's been hanging around."

Torch lit, Mason followed Henry into a narrow tunnel that looked like a natural crack in the rock. There was no snow in here, and without the wind, it felt warmer. "Jade says there is no dog."

"Maybe Jade's not supposed to see him." Henry's voice sounded uneven as it bounced off rough edges.

"Why not?"

"Might not be real."

"Felt real to me."

Henry glanced over his shoulder. "You touched it?"

"Damn thing hit me in the nuts and left me to die."

"It attacked you? So . . ." Henry resumed his march toward the house, not sharing his thoughts.

"So, it's just a dog, right?"

"Don't know, son."

"What else could it be?"

"Shapeshifter. Watcher."

Mason had heard of the first and didn't buy that for a minute. "What's a watcher?"

"Witch sends an animal out to do its watching. When it returns, the witch absorbs everything it saw and heard while it was out and about."

"Okay, I'm not buying that one either."

"Yeah. Prob'ly just a dog." Henry left the narrow passageway and stepped into a larger space. He flipped on a series of very dim wall sconces. "Ah, good, they still work. Not much call for electricity down here."

"Holy shit," Mason said when he stepped into the third cellar. He set down his suitcases, eager to look around.

"No, no, no," Henry said. "Pick those up. We're not staying here."

Mason did as bid, but he didn't follow Henry in a straight line across the floor either. Not when the walls were ringed with candleholders, and there was a flat-topped four-by-six boulder in the center of the floor to stare at.

"That's an altar, isn't it?"

"It's ancient history," Henry said with disdain, moving through the area without pause.

"Jade doesn't cast spells down here?"

"The early Delarues were coven members. That's when this was used. The outside entrance allowed local witches to come and go unobserved. Man could go hunting, walk in the woods, disappear for a few hours, no one thought anything of it. Used to be an old path up from the river, too, but it's too treacherous these days. I reckon nobody would've noticed a canoe or two on the river at night. Sure easy to hide them down below, climb up here, melt into the darkness again when they were done. Or go fishing. Come on, son. Speed it up."

"You don't like it in here."

"Not so much."

"There bones and stuff in here?"

"You're creepin' me out."

Mason couldn't stop staring at the dark splotches on the altar as he strolled by it. "Not feeling too great myself."

Staring at that, he'd missed the fireplace on the far wall. Hanging inside was a black iron cauldron, big enough to boil a body.

Henry said, "Gimme a hand," and when they swung the cauldron out, the floor of the fireplace rose.

"Gives new meaning to ash dump," Mason muttered, only marginally relieved that when he poked his head into the hole, he could see that the electric wiring extended into the subcellar.

"You first," Henry said.

"Me? I don't know where I'm going."

"I'm too old. What if the ladder breaks? I need you to cushion my fall."

"I don't know . . ."

"Look at it this way. You know I won't be waiting down there to bash you over the head."

"Yeah."

"You know the dog didn't climb down there, so he won't be ripping out your throat."

"Not feeling too positive knowing you've been thinking of my demise."

"Oh, for cripe's sakes." Henry elbowed him out of the way.

Mason pulled him back. "Never mind, I'll go first. You hand my bags down when I get to the bottom, okay?"

To say he tested every rung on the ladder was an understatement. The lone bulb at the bottom didn't do much to show him exactly how deep he was going, and he was relieved when he felt the floor only seven or eight feet down.

Was Jade wondering where he was? If he called her later, *when* he called her later, would she pick up?

"Hey, Mason," Henry said, tossing both suitcases into the hole at once.

"Ow. What?"

"Nice knowing ya."

Chapter 22

Sleep began to elude Jade again. So did common sense, as she found herself wandering through Mason's room in the middle of the night, sniffing his scent on the pillow, the open bar of Luck Soap on the sink, the towel he'd used.

She'd grown used to sleeping through the night, waking up in Mason's arms. She'd never stop missing that. She'd never stop missing him.

He'd lied to her. All along. What was true? What wasn't? How would she ever know?

Obviously she needed a spell to get her life back on track. With a fourth-quarter moon, though, it was appropriate to cast an ending spell, not one for starting over.

She played with different phrases, all revolving

around ending her feelings for Mason, ending her relationship with him, ending his ability to walk upright without dragging his knuckles.

She didn't address issues of a new love or a child; no one could replace the connection she'd had with Mason, and the thought of growing old without children hurt too much.

Mason was convinced he'd gone absolutely, positively, friggin' nuts. Staying in snowy, icy, frigid West Bluff. Hiking through a crack in the bluff to move in with a practical joker—that bit at the ladder was *so* not funny. Henry snored like a grizzly bear curled up deep inside its winter den. Every night, Mason lay on his back on a blow-up mattress, staring up at the dark, thinking overtime how to get it all: Jade, marriage, kids, the whole nine yards.

Was she able to sleep without him?

Oh, man, he had to come clean about the insomnia, too. Their whole relationship was a redo.

Henry snorted awake and said, "I can hear you thinking."

"Think she's cooled off yet?"

"You should buy her a trinket."

"I don't think Jade's the trinket type."

"Shows what you know about women." Henry snored for a minute, then snorted again and said, "She collects snowmen. You know, statues, ornaments. Trinkets."

So much at stake. Now that Mason was free to tell Jade he loved her, he had to be sure he got it right, so she'd believe in him and have no doubts. No way he was relying on Henry's advice. *Buy her a trinket,* Mason scoffed. Advice from a crusty old bachelor, of course.

Still, he wasn't sure where to begin to win over Jade's heart, so he started with thumbing a ride into Hannibal the following morning for necessities, like a car.

Along the way, an idea started to take shape. Females had been trying to force commitment on him since before he knew what they were good for, and here he was on the opposite end, needing advice.

"How's it going?" Anthony asked when Mason called.

"I've rented a car."

"Staying for a while then. Thought you might. Made any progress?"

"Bought a heavier coat." Fire-engine red and fire-engine yellow, it was designed for someone horrendously color-challenged. Also very "lofty," according to the salesclerk. He didn't mention that he was now wearing insulated overalls that came only in a camouflage pattern intended to fool deer and turkeys destined for the food chain. "You know how to make a snowman?"

Anthony chuckled. When the out-of-the-blue question wasn't followed by a punch line, he sobered up and said, "You serious?"

"Yeah."

"Geez, nothing to it. Start with a snowball and roll it around the yard until it's really big. Then stack one on top of another, stick some rocks in the head for eyes, maybe put a hat on top. While you're doing that, I'll start filling out a medical claim. What'll it be—frostbite or mental health benefits?"

"Both."

Mason set to rolling a ball of snow around the front yard until it got bigger and bigger and started to look like, hm, a blob. His first attempt was pathetic. Frosty didn't look like anything to sing about with his raggedy coat of dead leaves and gumballs. In fact, he required heavy grooming.

He drove through West Bluff again, a good way to warm up and take stock of the competition at the same time. Seemed snowmen generally were constructed in three tiers, but it wasn't a hard-and-fast rule. Most were short. All were stout. Several were impaled with dead branches. He rather enjoyed that.

By afternoon, he was standing back, admiring his third snowman. Better; decent, even, but too generic and not nearly good enough to impress Jade. Henry had told him the story behind the collection she'd adored since she was five. Mason might not understand women as much as would be good for him, but he did understand that Jade was traditional and romantic, and he'd better figure out how to relate to that. He retreated inside via the tunnel to think while he thawed his insides with hot coffee.

He had five snowmen taking shape on Thursday when Jade stepped out onto her front porch. She was wearing her long cape, so it gave Mason hope that she'd stay and talk, though her arms were crossed over her chest tight enough to ward off anything he had to say.

"Most people do that in their own yards," she said.

Mason patted a more-artistic snowman, one with sculptured shoulders and arms. "You weren't supposed to see them yet."

"Pretty damn hard to miss in my own front yard."
Oh, yeah, still pissed.

"I started yesterday." His boots crunched through the snow until he stopped at the bottom of the steps, cautious to keep his distance lest she shut down completely, because he so desperately wanted her to hear him out instead of storming into the house. "I want you to know that I haven't told anyone your secret. I never will."

No comment.

Okay, make conversation. "You look tired. Is your insomnia back?"

Jade's brow puckered ever so slightly, warning him that maybe he could've worded that better, and damn, he wanted to, she deserved his best, she deserved the truth, so he tried again.

"I guess I should tell you, I don't have trouble sleeping. Well, I do *now*, of course. Now I'm brokenhearted, and who can sleep like that? But I mean other than that."

"It was a lie?"

"It was."

"You have no idea how badly I want to do a truth spell on you."

"I know I hurt you very, very deeply. You have every right to be angry."

"*Pfff.* You think I need permission from *you?*"

"I will *never* lie to you again."

Jade looked away, angry, not listening. She blinked back tears and paid more attention to a squirrel scampering in the oak tree overhead than on what he had to say.

"I mean it, Jade. Not so much as a half-truth. Not even by omission. Ask me anything. I'll tell you."

"You used me."

"I don't suppose I can change your mind about that. But I want you to know I love you."

She didn't take the bait. "Where've you been staying?"

"With Henry."

"In *my* basement?"

Mason tried one of his trademark cute smiles and shrugs, then discarded those and went with pure honesty. "I think it's better I stay close. That way I can be here when you're ready to hear me out."

He dug at the snow with the toe of his boot. He thought about asking to go inside where it was warm. He knew he had to just get it done.

"For the last year or two, Brenda just kept at me. Kept saying we should move our relationship to the next level, and the next level was marriage, and before I knew it, we had a church reserved."

Jade sighed and glanced at her watch. He took the hint.

"I'm over thirty, and I've never asked a woman to marry me."

She startled, like a doe in the road. "You're not—"

"Jade, I love you."

Her eyebrows arched as she called him on it. "And we both know your track record with the truth."

He would not be dissuaded. "I never knew what falling in love was until I met you. I can't imagine the rest of my life without you."

There, she almost smiled.

"You're delusional," she said. She stormed into the house, closing the door with a resounding bang.

Mason grinned broadly, happier than a man had a right to be. After all, the love of his life was still talking to him.

Damn Mason Kincaid.

Jade had thought he'd gone back to Pensacola. She'd thought she'd never see him again. But when she'd stepped out onto the front porch and laid eyes on him, her stupid, traitorous heart had thumped in excitement before settling down to an uneven skipping beat that made her oh-so-aware of every word he said, every breath he took, every look of hope and sign of regret.

And then the jerk had proposed! Almost.

Mystic Manor had never been so lonely before. Not even after Doug had gone missing. As much as she'd loved her husband, she didn't remember him being as much a part of her heart as Mason had become in three weeks. Maybe that said something about marrying too young, or maybe the feelings had waned in his long absence. It didn't matter which. It only mattered that she'd risked her heart and had it battered and broken.

Jade worked through the night on an order of ritual inks for an occult shop in Denver. After that, she had a long list to keep her occupied. Changing clothes, grocery shopping, going by Annie's because now that she had capital, she wanted input on enlarging her cabin and workshop in the woods. After that, she'd find other errands. Anything to keep busy. Tomorrow morning, she had clients flying in.

When she turned onto her street late that afternoon, traffic was backed up all the way down the bluff. The typically five-minute drive took twenty, and all the way up the hill, bumper to bumper, she murmured charms to assist victims of whatever terrible emergency was blocking the road, whether it be an accident or a fire.

At the top, she found the source of the problem. Mason's five snowmen had tripled. You could tell he was from Florida and didn't have a clue, as they all faced the front porch. They were pretty neat, though. Not just round balls stacked on each other, but sculpted with some thought put into making each one unique.

But still!

No wonder people were lined up, staring. And not just locals. Tourists came to West Bluff to see the eagles, why not make it a two-fer?

Mason was waiting for her by the garage. He opened her door, all smiles, even when she hit him with her most scathing frown.

"What about low profile is so hard for you to understand?"

"Relax. They're not here to see you."

"They're *staring* at my *house*."

"Trust me, if they're talking about anyone, it's me, not you."

She grinned a little, and though she tried to cover it by getting out of the Jeep, Mason noticed anyway. He noticed too much. Now she knew why—a trained investigator.

"What?" he asked.

"I overheard something in the grocery store about an abominable snowman. I just figured it out."

Without asking, he grabbed half a dozen bags of groceries and waited for her to lead the way.

"What? All of a sudden you want permission to enter my house?"

"Seems right, since Henry isn't here to invite me in."

Oh, he was so slick, getting that in. "It doesn't bother you at all that I don't want you here?"

"Will you marry me?"

The look she gave him should have indicated clearly that she thought he had two heads, but since he didn't look the least put out by her opinion, she said, "No," to make it perfectly clear.

"Then I can't leave."

"So. If I agree to marry you, you'll leave?"

He grinned at her. "Now that'd be silly, wouldn't it?"

* * *

"What in Sam Hill are you doing out in the front yard?" Henry asked. He'd made dinner: a paper plate of grilled cheese sandwiches and canned spaghetti.

"Making snowmen." Mason was so hungry, he tucked into his food as if it were Jade's herb-enhanced stew.

"They're gonna melt, you know."

Mason shivered. "When does it warm up around here?"

"Could be next month. Could be next week."

"Guess I'd better hurry then."

"What d'you have in mind, son?"

"You'll see. Is there a resale shop in town?"

"Yeah, down on Baptism Road."

"Let me guess. That'd run along the river."

"If you don't find what you're looking for, there's always Clarksville and Hannibal. Cripes, son, you eat like a growing boy. You want some more?"

"Thanks. You have an internet connection down here?"

"You see one?"

"Hell, I didn't see a hidden entrance under your bed from the third cellar either, but that doesn't mean it's not there." He sat back while Henry dumped the pan of spaghetti onto his plate. "I haven't had this stuff since I was a kid. It's pretty good."

"What do you want on the internet?"

"Honeymoon reservations. Think Jade'd like Aruba?" If she didn't take to diving, he'd be content wherever she wanted to spend time. All he wanted was to be with her. "Do you know if she's certified?"

Henry stopped abruptly, stared at Mason, then shook his head. "Speaking of certified . . . Son, she's not gonna say yes. Especially with you spending all your free time outside in the snow, when you could be buying her something she'd treasure, like, oh, I don't know, *a diamond ring*."

"But that's just the point, don't you see? I'm doing something I hate in order to give her something she loves."

"She's right. You're delusional."

"Persistent."

"Like I said."

Mason had never worked so hard to win a woman. He'd certainly never envisioned working at getting one to accept his proposal, certain that the rest of his life hinged on the outcome.

Without Jade, he'd be . . . nothing. Without purpose. Wandering lost and alone. God, it sounded so lame. He didn't dare say any of that out loud. The sad part, though, is that it was true. Now that he'd fallen in love, *truly* in love, second-best would never do. If Jade didn't want him, if she couldn't love him back—

No, he couldn't think that way. He'd pull out all the stops. He'd give it his best shot.

Chapter 23

Annie jumped into the passenger seat of Mason's car. "Drive. I don't want Jade to see us together."

Sitting in the driveway, Mason looked at her quizzically and started the engine.

"You're not giving up, are you?" If anyone asked her opinion, Jade and Mason were meant to be together, but it was Saturday already, and Jade wasn't giving in.

"If you're here to give me advice," he drawled, "I hope it's better than Henry's."

As they eased toward the street, Annie gazed at the growing army of snowmen gathering under the towering oak trees, and said, "I'm really good at giving advice. Maybe if I knew what you were up to."

Everyone in West Bluff and all of the tourists wondered what he was up to. You couldn't walk into a store, café, or gas station without getting drawn into speculation.

"If you spray snowmen with a hose, do they get all shiny like icicles?"

Annie laughed. "I have no idea."

"What's so funny?"

"There's a pool going on you. When you'll turn hypothermic."

"What's the deciding factor? When I walk off the bluff?"

"That's one of the criteria. Turn left here. I'll be able to hike back through the woods." Annie settled back against the door. "It's a shame they assigned you guys to watch Jade, when, of the three of us, she has the most to lose."

"Her low profile, and all?"

"It's more than that. I mean, come on, the city's run by the same people who run the churches, and West Bluff has ordinances against people like us conducting business within the city limits. One breath of her spellwork gets out, and Jade's in for a fight."

"Good grief, Annie, there must be dozens of people around here who know she's a witch."

"Yes, and they haven't said a word," she said pointedly.

"Neither have I. And I won't. That's a promise. Anthony and I didn't share any of that with the insurance company or the other teams."

Annie was silent for a moment. "Other teams?"

Mason grinned. "Didn't want you to feel left out."

"Ahh, the black van." She'd seen it a few times. Mostly she'd noticed because she'd been driving her old wreck and thought how nice it would be to have the van for deliveries.

"So who's betting in this pool? Noah and Buzz?"

"Everyone who ever talked to you or saw you since you came to town. Pot's up to eight hundred dollars."

"Really? You betting?"

"Sunday, 11:00 P.M."

"Now see, that's no good. I'm in bed every night long before then."

Annie shrugged. "It's a witch thing. Fourth-quarter moon. Hard aspects to Mars and Pluto—that could be accidents and death. Speaking of witch things, I didn't just jump in your car to see if you were still lucid. We all like you, Mason."

His brow rose in silent question.

"Well, you're right, not *every*body. Someday you can tell me why Miss Lisabet has it in for you. She's the librarian. But I mean those of us who got to know you. Weezy and Noah and Buzz. We all like you, and we think you're good for Jade. So I'm here to offer to do a spell for you."

"No!"

"What?—oh, quit looking as if you'd rather hit a tree. It's a good offer. My candle spells always work."

"Ah, wouldn't that be unfair to Jade? Unethical, even?"

Annie was put out at his reaction. "Do you want her or not?"

"Oh, I want her."

"Well, then?"

Mason pulled off to the side of the road, thinking it over carefully before he turned to her with his answer. "You know what, Annie? I appreciate it. I do. But I love Jade, a lot, and I don't want to do anything that she might consider not on the up-and-up when she finally comes around and says yes."

She saw nothing in his eyes but intense honesty, and pain. "You're that sure of yourself?"

He shook his head. "Between you, me, and the fence post, I'm scared shitless. I think I'm only going to get one chance. I'm sure this is it. And I have no"—he winced in place of an expletive, which just made it that much more heartfelt—"clue how it's going to turn out."

Jade spent the day with her guests from Montana, who'd laughed at the weather report and said nothing less than a blizzard could have stopped them from coming to Mystic Manor. They had a spring wedding planned and wanted spellwork to cut all ties to former spouses. She'd scheduled them for this weekend in particular, due to the Balsamic Moon.

Clients came with emotional baggage; they couldn't help it. When the Abernats retired for the night, Jade stepped out into the backyard, closed her eyes, lifted her chin to the breeze, and let it wash over her. She needed this time to remove negativity, to cleanse herself for the following day.

"No moonlight tonight," Mason said behind her, his voice deep and seductively quiet.

For a huge body that rode the sky in a predictable pattern, people sure could be clueless. She could have explained that a fourth-quarter moon sets before the sun; she didn't bother. She was afraid if she talked to him, she'd be opening the door where she'd locked up all her feelings for him.

"You doing a spell?"

Jade sighed. She didn't open her eyes; better not to encourage him. "I'm trying to relax."

"Good." He waited a beat. "Is it working?"

She couldn't help smiling. That wasn't too big a betrayal, not like a laugh. What was it about this man that made her want to push him off the bluff but hold him tight at the same time?

"I just have one question," he said.

"If I were doing a spell, it would be to send you home."

"Yeah, I figured. But," he said pointedly, stepping close, blocking the wind, "I'm still here."

She opened her eyes. "Need a ride to the airport?" She flashed him a look that she hoped showed irritation, but instinctively knew she'd failed horribly when he smiled and said, "Can't go yet."

He reached out slowly. Jade steeled herself for his touch, thinking that now that she knew the truth, it should feel cold and deceitful, but her traitorous body thrilled at the sensation of his warm hand grazing her cheek, tracing the line of her jaw. When he wrapped his fingers behind her neck and drew her close, she breathed him in, not finding the cleansing she'd sought from the wind but something deeper and far more satisfying.

Mason leaned into her, and their lips met. She was powerless to stop it, to break it off, not because of his hold, but because of that intangible property that pulls soul mates together.

He teased her at first, touching and releasing, brushing over the corner of her eye, the curve of her ear, the length of her neck, turning foreplay into an art so hot, she thought they'd melt a crater in the snow.

"Mase—" she whispered on a long sigh. It was too late to ground herself. Too late to pull away.

"I love you," he said, his lips brushing hers.

"No."

"I do. I will never hurt you."

"You already have."

"But you'll forgive me."

She didn't want to. If she opened her mouth, she was afraid she'd agree.

"Marry me, Jade?"

She shook her head slowly. Summoning all her strength, she took a step back, feeling lonelier than ever as Mason's hand fell away.

"When hell freezes over."

He grinned—the last thing she'd expected.

"Haven't you heard?" he said. "Last night, it did."

Jade's insomnia was back with a vengeance. It wasn't the peaceful, good use of time she remembered, but eight more hours each day to regret the moment Mason had blown in her front door.

The next afternoon, he was charming her Montana guests in the study. He might as well wear a shirt that said, *Able to deal with needy people, as requested.* Karl and Diana Abernat sat side by side on the sofa, laughing as if they found him highly amusing. Mason stood close to the roaring fire, one arm propped on the mantel as casually as if he owned the place, marveling aloud that the Abernats had tons more snow in Montana and came here instead of the Caribbean.

"Oh, Jade, have you seen Mason's snowmen?" Diana asked, bubbling with excitement. "They're just lovely!"

"I haven't looked today."

"Oh, but you must! Quick, before we leave for the airport." Diana slipped her arm through Jade's and led her out the front door, onto the wide porch. "Goodness, there's a lot of traffic. Karl! We should leave soon."

Jade gritted her teeth. "They're taking pictures." People were abandoning their cars on the narrow shoulder, walking through her yard, taking pictures of the snowmen. And more. "Of my *house,* Mason."

Mason bent down and whispered in her ear. "Don't worry, I covered all the pentacles with pine branches. I hope it's not bad luck."

She relaxed a little, solely due to his foresight and absolutely *not* because she liked how his warm breath tickled her ear.

"What a wonderful idea!" Diana said. "Karl, honey, get the camera out of my bag, will you? My goodness, I don't know which one is my favorite!"

There were plenty to chose from, Jade noticed. Since yesterday, they'd transformed into unmistakable icy replicas of people she knew. Courtney's likeness had its arm around a pint-size Jazzy. Annie's was topped with a blond wig and a pink scarf.

"A wig?" Jade gave Mason what she hoped he interpreted as the evil eye. "You put wigs on them?"

He smiled and shrugged. "Wigs, hats, what's the difference?"

Weezy's model wore a flowered apron, brandishing a skillet in one hand and a spatula in the other.

Buzz was easy to pick out, and Jade said, "I'm pretty sure it's a felony to put a federal uniform on a snowman."

"If they arrest me, you can destroy the evidence."

"If they lock you up, I'll destroy the key," she said, trying so, so hard not to smile. The trouble he'd gone to wasn't lost on her.

The reporter had a black beret, a notepad and pen. The milkman carried bottles, and she supposed the dopey-looking ones with thick overalls and earflaps were supposed to be Noah's nephews. Miss Lisabet wore wire-rimmed spectacles and carried books. Gabby had a stethoscope draped around her neck; the extinct nurse's cap must have come from an antiques store. Madeline bundled two blue receiving blankets in her arms.

"Oh, I love the twin snowbabies!" Diana gurgled,

snapping pictures. "I can't wait to show these back home. Nobody there does anything like this. Mason, you must really love the snow."

Jade held her tongue, because she knew how much he truly hated it. Yet it was obvious he'd done this for her.

"Notice how the looky-loos hang back behind the wall instead of intruding?" Diana said. "It's cozy, like an enclosed garden. They can tell there's something private about it."

"Used to be," Jade said in a dry tone. "Ah, Mason, can I get your opinion on something inside?"

"Sure, love."

She'd no sooner gotten Mason alone in the foyer than he shoved the door closed and pressed her up against it in a kiss so hot, the fire in the study paled by comparison.

"Will you marry me?"

When Jade could speak again, she said, "I'll call the police and have you removed first."

"I met the chief. Sherman, right? Nice guy. He stopped by to do traffic control and visit with Henry. Tell me, is there anyone in town who *doesn't* know your secret?"

"Only a few thousand you haven't met. Mason, you have to stop this. You have to leave. You know you want to go back where it's warm, where there's no snow. Remember? Eighty degrees? Surf pounding?"

"Go back? I'm not leaving."

"Your job's in Pensacola."

"You're here. There are companies that'll refer work to me. Sometimes I'll travel. You know, I'm glad we're having this little talk."

"It's warm in Pensacola."

"But *you're here*."

Jade growled low in her throat and shoved him to arm's length. "That does it. I've tried to be nice, but if you don't leave today, I'm locking you out."

"I saw a hose in the garage. Would you mind if I borrowed it?"

"Yes! I would!"

Mason grinned. "Didn't think so."

She growled and pushed past him, unable to think straight when he locked those steel blue eyes on her. When he teased her as if she still loved him.

After the guests departed, Jade spent the night catching up on the witch network, interrupted only by an e-mail from Anthony. She leaned back in her chair, wondering how he'd gotten her private address.

"Oh, of course," she muttered with a du-uh attitude. They were detectives; she probably didn't have a single secret left.

Anthony was brief and to the point.

Dear Jade,

No one would hire us to do the more critical stuff if we blew cover whenever it suited. See attachments. Then if you're not going to get

*over it and give a great guy like Mason a break,
will you please send him back to Florida where
he can be of some use?*

*Also, a small wood-inlaid box got into my
luggage by mistake. Sorry. I'm returning it by
FedEx.*

Jade started to hit the DELETE button, then thought,
Why not? The attachments were carefully chosen and
included news articles on how Mason had successfully protected a senator's twelve-year-old daughter
from a crazed stalker (now serving time), retrieved an
elderly woman's life savings following a scam (thank-
you note included, inviting him to Thanksgiving for
the rest of her life), and caught a temp agency using
unsuspecting employees as drug mules.

So he was good at what he did, so what? So his
work was sometimes important. Big deal.

Too antsy to stay at the keyboard, she stepped out
back to let the breeze work its magic.

The sky was pitch-black, the stars brilliant pinpoints
of light. Somewhere below the horizon, the moon eased
into the next new cycle. The time of endings had come
and gone. Yet Mason was still here. Was her mother
right? Jade breathed deeply and tried to accept that the
Universe must have special plans this time around. It
wasn't easy. She wasn't convinced.

There were ways to learn more. In the conservatory, she lit a candle, sat on the stones with it behind
her, and gazed into the pool at the base of the waterfall where she and Mason had made love.

As she grounded and centered herself, she reviewed the little things that hadn't made sense before: Mason's familiarity with a handgun, the Bond-Rambo crouch she'd teased him about. And she supposed the three death benefits hadn't been small potatoes to the insurance company, so she could see why they'd surveilled the house even though she didn't like it.

As Jade quickly transitioned to an altered state, the surface of the water changed from fluid, to misty, to dark velvet, then ceased to register on her consciousness at all, mirroring the changes in her perspective. In the void, she saw two lit tapers running together, but instead of melting into a common pool of wax, they merged and formed one perfect candle.

She closed her eyes and bathed herself in white light. When she gazed into the water again, she saw herself lying in Mason's arms, sound asleep.

The divination was as clear as day. No visions of life alone. No getting tarred and feathered and run out of town. But still . . .

She tried once more. When she saw bridesmaids with straw hats, silk shawls, and bouquets of roses, she gave up.

The front doorbell of Mystic Manor rarely rang, so when it did, it drew Jade's attention.

"Hi, I'm Tricia Sherwood." The redhead on the porch looked so proud of herself, as if she'd single-handedly turned the front yard into the most popular tourist attraction in two states. This morning's logjam had snagged the school bus. The children were noisy, hanging out the windows, pointing toward the house.

Jade's smile was saccharin. "Welcome to my nightmare."

"Oh." Tricia grimaced. "You don't like being popular?"

Jade's acerbic laugh clearly said, *Oh, my dear, you are sooo naive.* "Sorry, I don't give interviews."

"Oh, no, that's not why I'm here. I just got a promotion— Well, I guess you don't care about my silly ol' promotion. Anyway, I thought I'd stop by and see if that sexy eagle photographer is here?" Tricia's giggle was replaced by a concerned frown and a glance over her shoulder. "But now that I've seen the bridesmaids, I'm thinking I'm too late."

"What bridesmaids?"

"You haven't seen them?" Tricia stepped aside, giving Jade full view of her front yard. She faded into the background when Jade saw the transformation that had brought traffic to a standstill.

"Oh, my," she said with a long sigh.

Mason clearly had gotten inventive with the garden hose, misting the branches until the vapor froze in hoarfrost. Trees, bushes, vines; all were layered. The sun hit it, setting ice crystals aglitter like millions of sparkling diamonds, turning it into a winter fairyland that eclipsed her namesake's morning after.

"Tricia?"

"Yes?"

"Traffic's moving again. Go away."

"Oh. Okay."

In contrast, the snow sculptures had a smooth, glossy coat of ice and bore an amazing resemblance to a wedding party. Annie and Courtney's likenesses currently were decked out in straw hats and silk shawls, baskets of flowers, and rhinestone buttons up the front. Jazzy held a basket of rose petals, Uncle Henry wore a top hat. Weezy was draped with a mink stole.

"I hope the fur's not politically incorrect," Mason said. He stopped at the foot of the steps. "But the antique mall was overrun with them, and I sort of thought Weezy'd like it."

He had iron stakes under one arm and a plastic bucket in the other.

"For a guy who hates the cold, you sure outdid yourself." Jade heard awe in her own voice, too late to squelch it, knowing Mason wouldn't miss it. He never missed anything.

"Came out kind of pretty, didn't it? I'll be honest with you." He didn't say it as if making a point, but all the same, it did. "I was going for a smooth ice effect, but the crystals are pretty nice."

"It's called hoarfrost. We don't see it very often. As soon as the sun gets hot, it'll disappear."

"I'm guessing that's before July."

Jade laughed. "Probably before noon."

"I have a few other things to be honest about."

"You want to . . . come inside?"

"In a minute. Hold on. Oh, wait. Here." He set everything down and stripped out of his heavy coat.

"You'll freeze," she said with demurral.

He jogged up the steps, holding it out. "I've worked up a sweat. Go ahead, take it. This sweater's warm enough." When she didn't, he stepped close and draped it around her shoulders. "There you go."

His voice carried a ragged edge, Jade noted, the kind that had nothing to do with the state of his health and everything to do with what lay between them, holding them apart. He stood in front of her, tugging the edges of the coat together. She stared at his bold-patterned sweater and thought how soft it would feel if she just put·her head on it. How strong and hard his chest would be beneath her cheek.

Mason backed away, holding her gaze until he tumbled backward down the steps and landed in the snow.

"I could lie here and pretend I'm hurt," he said. "But I'm not."

"Being truthful doesn't mean you can't ever tease me again."

The stakes turned out to be a dozen garden candleholders, which he stuck in the snow around the sculptures and topped with pillars out of the bucket.

"I got the candles from Annie. She swore they were charmed with good intentions and nothing more."

"She knows about this?" Jade indicated the bridesmaids.

"You mean did I explain?—no. I just plug away; people just watch. I started the perimeter wall around the snowmen with the idea of a church wedding in mind. Then it dawned on me that you wouldn't get married in a church, but with the whole town driving by every day to see what changes I've made, I couldn't very well outfit them with capes and wands."

Living in the basement couldn't be fun. Spending hours in the snow. Getting rejected every day.

Loyal and true.

Mason lit the wicks, one by one.

"I see you've overcome your hatred of candles."

"I've overcome a lot of things. You're the most important thing in the world to me. I know, what with our history and all, that you're having some doubts about believing that, but it doesn't make it untrue."

"I'm not sure what to believe anymore."

"I know," he said, and when he gazed up at her, she believed him. "You just have to jump in with both feet. Like me. Hell, if I'd met a witch six months ago, I would've, I don't know, bought a wooden cross and worn garlic, or something."

"That's for—"

"But look at me now. You promised not to cast spells on me. I believed you." He lit the remainder of the candles in silence.

"Your lips are moving."

"Candle magic. I'm making wishes."

Jade felt her brow arch. "You're using witchcraft on me?"

"Not exactly. One of them is: Don't let anything I did here endanger your secret. The others are: Give me strength to tell you everything; keep me safe when I tell you how I snooped through your house, looking for evidence that your husband was still alive."

"How snooped?"

"Top to bottom."

"Everywhere?"

He walked up the steps. "You have no secrets. Unless they're hidden in your box of tampons. I left that alone."

Jade grinned. "Sounds like a good place to hide my valuables."

He came to a standstill before her, trying to stop a teasing grin that would not be controlled. "And most important: If at all possible, please let you forgive me before I freeze my nuts off."

Jade bit the inside of her cheek, refusing to grin at his humor. "You should know, one of the first rules of witchcraft is not to tell others what you're wishing for."

"Spellcasting 101, I'll make a note of it," he said, his head bobbing in acceptance. "And why is that?"

"Because if people know what you're wishing for, they can work against you."

"There's one more. If you're ever going to agree to marry me, please make it today."

"I can't."

It wasn't the answer he wanted. She could see disappointment register in his eyes, in his very soul.

"It's not that simple," she said, knowing she had confessions of her own to make.

"They say love never is, but you know what? Life never seemed so clear to me or so purposeful before I fell in love with you." Mason focused on nothing briefly as he chose his words, then looked at her with such longing, it nearly broke her heart. "It is simple,

Jade. Just take it one day at a time. I'll never give you cause to regret it. And every day you'll know that. And someday, a week or a month or a year from now, you'll look back and realize it's true."

"Here's the deal. I used witchcraft on you. It was before I said I wouldn't, but I think you should know that I cast the spell that brought you here. Actually, as long as I'm telling you everything, it started before that. I cast the spell that helped Brenda make up her mind and take a stand, which is when you got dumped—"

"*Jilted* is starting to sound so much better."

"And *then* I cast a spell for the perfect man, and they kind of got . . . mingled." There, she'd said it, got it all out between them. Because with secrets like that between them, there was no hope.

Mason's disappointment disappeared, replaced with a broad grin. "You think I'm perfect?"

"Focus, Mason. If you can't focus, few of your wishes will come true."

"But they might?"

"Hush, I'm not done. Then I cast a lot more spells to send you back."

"How many?"

"I don't know," she said, exasperated.

"Cotton ball in my pocket?"

She nodded.

"Tupperware in the river?"

She had trouble looking him in the eye, but she did it anyway. She owed him that much. "Throwing a used article of clothing into the current signifies the owner getting swept away. I used your dirty sock."

"Oh, right, the one you stuck in your pocket."

"How could you know that?"

Mason winced, clearly uncomfortable with this. "I haven't confessed everything yet. There were wireless cameras in the house, too."

She would've shrieked, but she was too stunned. "Is there anything else?"

"God, I hope not. You?"

"I did maybe a dozen spells. But I stopped after I said I wouldn't do any."

"Hm." He glanced at the dozen candles he'd just lit. "I don't want to brag or anything, but it seems your success rate's not as good as mine. I was going to ask for a good witch recommendation, but, hm, now I don't know. See, there's a certain woman I want to charm into marrying me, but she keeps telling me no when I want her to say yes."

"Have you asked her lately?"

Hope flared in his eyes. He stuck out his hand. "Mason Kincaid, private eye."

"What?"

"I thought, now that all our secrets are out, we should start over."

Jade slipped her hand into his, and didn't resist when he pulled her close, folding both her hands inside his. "Will you marry me, love?"

She *loved* when he called her love.

"Because, honest to God, I need you so bad, it's hard to breathe without you. It's hard to wake up in the morning without you, and go to sleep, and eat, and—"

"Yes, Mason. I will."

He released her hands and swallowed her in the circle of his arms, hugging her one moment, kissing her the next, lifting her off her feet and swinging her around until they fell off the porch together, and Jade didn't remember wishing for *persistent,* but was grateful nonetheless.

"Damn, I'm freezing," Mason said, pushing snow aside, brushing more off Jade.

She graced him with a seductive smile and said, "I know a warm spot by a waterfall."

Author's Note

Dear Reader,

I hope you enjoyed Jade and Mason's love story. They turned out to be two of my favorite characters! Next up in the Witches of West Bluff series is Annie's story, then Courtney's. Join me, won't you, to see what's in their future.

Fondly,

Jenna McKnight

Avon Romances

the best in
exceptional authors and unforgettable novels!